Previously published Worldwide Suspense title by
SLOANE STEELE

IT TAKES A THIEF

BETWEEN TWO THIEVES

SLOANE STEELE

WORLDWIDE

TORONTO • NEW YORK • LONDON
AMSTERDAM • PARIS • SYDNEY • HAMBURG
STOCKHOLM • ATHENS • TOKYO • MILAN
MADRID • WARSAW • BUDAPEST • AUCKLAND

W⦿RLDWIDE™

Recycling programs
for this product may
not exist in your area.

ISBN-13: 978-1-335-52307-5

Between Two Thieves

First published in 2021 by Carina Press.
This edition published in 2022 with revised text.

Copyright © 2021 by Shannyn Schroeder
Copyright © 2022 by Shannyn Schroeder, revised text edition

This edition published by arrangement with Harlequin Books S.A.

For questions and comments about the quality of this book,
please contact us at CustomerService@Harlequin.com.

Harlequin Enterprises ULC
22 Adelaide St. West, 41st Floor
Toronto, Ontario M5H 4E3, Canada
www.ReaderService.com

Printed in U.S.A.

BETWEEN TWO THIEVES

This book is dedicated to my Panera supper club pals, who brainstormed so many ways for me to create these capers.

ONE

Nikki skulked in the shadow of yet another rich douche-bag's house in a posh north Chicago suburb. "Cameras down yet?" she whispered into her comm.

In her ear, Audrey said, "Gimme a sec. There's a glitch."

"What? I thought we had all the glitches worked out." She leaned against a tree and waited for Audrey to do her tech magic.

"You're a go," Audrey said.

"Wait." A whisper came across the comms.

"What is it, Mia?"

"I don't see Bethany Rivers. She was here, but now she's not."

"So?"

"She may already be on her way home."

Nikki scoffed. "The party is a good thirty minutes away. By the time she gets here, I'll be long gone."

"I don't know when she left," Mia said sharply.

Nikki rolled her eyes even though no one was there to see it. She did some quick calculations for how long she actually needed to be in the house. Unless the woman pulled up right now, Nikki would have plenty of time. She'd been in much worse situations than this. And she'd done it alone. "It's fine. Audrey, keep a look-out once I'm in."

Nikki had no idea what bug crawled up Mia's butt. *She* had picked the date for the heist based on when the happy couple would be out of the house at a social function where both Mia and Jared could keep an eye on them. Nikki snickered as she picked the lock on the back door. Perfect Mia had screwed up the one job she had.

As soon as the door swung open, the alarm began its repetitive beep. Inside the kitchen, Nikki hooked up the special decoder Audrey had given her and it began cycling through numbers as the beeping continued. "You sure this thing will be fast enough?"

"Yeah, it's an old-school model—"

The beeping stopped.

"Wow. Sometimes I forget how good a hacker you are." Nikki tucked the scanner back in her bag, reassembled the faceplate of the alarm keypad, then made her way to the living room. The small sculpture was sitting on an antique table in the corner, just as Mia had described.

"I put the cameras back on while you're in there so I have eyes outside," Audrey said.

Nikki got close and flashed her light on the sculpture. It wasn't hideous, like some of the pieces she'd stolen for Mia and Jared. The metal formed two intricate Celtic knots. Pretty enough. But what made it valuable was the material used. It was copper dipped in gold. Actual, real, 24-karat gold, in multiple layers. It was said to have a solid half inch of gold, but since gold tended to be a soft metal, the thing was fragile.

Nikki unpacked the box carrying a forged replica and set it on the antique table. She had no idea what materials London had used to make the counterfeit sculpture, but it certainly wasn't real gold. Then she picked up the original and nestled it in the prefabbed box.

"Better get out. A car is pulling into the drive," Audrey said in her ear.

"I guess Mia was right. I didn't have a half hour." She switched off her penlight and shoved the box back into her bag.

"The car is dropping her off out front, so you should head to the back. I'm cutting the cameras again so you're not seen."

"I have to walk past the front door to get back to the kitchen." Nikki's heart picked up its pace. She closed her eyes and took a deep breath. In her mind, she pictured the layout she'd studied for the past week. The closet was her best bet. She edged around the room and snuck into the coat closet at the end of the hall.

"Where are you?" Audrey asked as the front door opened.

Light peeked in from under the closet door. Nikki squatted down and waited to see if Mrs. Rivers needed to stow a wrap or shawl. If she curled into a tight ball, she'd blend in with the shadows. Touching her forehead to her knees, she regretted the chili dog she'd eaten on the way here.

Taking slow, shallow breaths, she considered her breakout plan if Mrs. Rivers did catch her. Nikki had seen pictures of the woman. She wasn't all that big. If Nikki rushed at her and knocked her over, she'd get out. Of course, the police would be called, but they wouldn't find anything missing. As far as contingencies went, it wasn't bad.

"The stupid alarm isn't set again. Men," the woman

muttered on the other side of the door. Two clicks of her heels and Nikki heard her tapping on her phone.

Move it along, lady.

Mrs. Rivers set keys on the table near the closet. Nikki held her breath. Then heels clicked down the hall.

Nikki cracked open the door and watched Mrs. Rivers climb the stairs to the bedrooms. Once she turned the corner, Nikki released her breath in a slow stream, then slipped from the closet and out the front door.

"I'm out," she said, a little more breathlessly than she liked. Maybe it was time to add swimming to her conditioning if holding her breath for a couple minutes was too much. "Give me thirty seconds to clear the cameras and then you can put them back on."

She sped through the trees and out to the quiet street. "All clear."

"Cutting it a little close, weren't you?" Audrey admonished.

Surprisingly, Mia hadn't said anything the entire time Nikki had been making the switch.

Nikki tightened the straps on her bag and removed her cap and gloves. Then she jogged to the next block, where London was waiting in the team's van.

London appeared unbothered by the entire scenario as she bopped along to the music on the radio. Her long light brown hair swayed as she danced to the beat in her seat.

"No such thing as too close, unless you get caught, which I didn't," Nikki said to Audrey as she climbed into the van.

London turned off the radio and pulled away from the curb. "How was my counterfeit?"

"Near perfect as always," Nikki responded.

"Yeah, it was."

"If you were so sure, why ask?"

"Everyone needs their ego pumped on occasion."

"The champagne is chilled and ready when you get here," Audrey chimed in.

"I think we should go out to celebrate. I'm in a party mood."

"I'm in," London said.

"I'm out," Audrey added. "I have a date. My boyfriend promised to take me home and ravage me. That beats getting drunk with you. Sorry. Not."

"Fine. Whatever. London and I will have our own fun. Party pooper."

She wouldn't begrudge her friend the happiness she'd found with Jared, who was technically one of their bosses. He and his cousin Mia had assembled a team to avenge the crimes of their fathers and make reparations to the victims. At this point they were more than a team of coworkers. They'd become friends.

It had been so long since Nikki considered anyone a true friend, the feeling was weird. Good, but weird.

They went back to the River North apartment that acted as their headquarters. While everyone except her had their own personal residences, they met and planned here. Nikki also pretty much lived here as part of her agreement with Jared to stay out of trouble.

The women shared a quick drink of champagne, a ritual Nikki had been doing for many years—a ritual she used to do alone. Then she got ready for a night out. While she normally leaned toward dive bars, London insisted on going to a club, which meant dressing up and wearing heels, which London was already doing. The artist never dressed like a thief.

"Oooh, look at you!" London squealed. Reaching out to touch Nikki's hair, she added, "You should leave it down more often."

"It gets in the way if I leave it down." In truth, she only kept it down when she was running a con. Men preferred their women to be soft and harmless. She could look the part when she wanted to.

"Pretty easy job tonight," London said as they climbed into her car.

"Yeah." Except she was on edge. It wasn't good or bad, just restless. Which led to recklessness. She reached over to the radio and turned the volume up, pumping the beat through the car, and dancing in her seat.

While stuck in traffic, both she and London rolled down their windows and sang. London had a parking spot reserved in a nearby lot and they walked to the nightclub. London wore a white gauzy dress more suited for the beach than a downtown nightclub. Nikki preferred her jeans—easier to run in if needed.

People were lined up down the block to get in. Nikki groaned. "I know you want to dance, but how about we go to my kind of bar and I'll pay for the jukebox all night?"

London tugged her arm. "Trust me." She led them around the corner to the back door, where there was another doorman, but no line. "When you go out enough, you learn some tricks."

At the door, London smiled.

"Just the two of you?" the doorman asked.

"Sure thing," London answered, handing him a twenty.

Without another question, he opened the door and let them in.

"I should travel with you more often," Nikki said.

"I think if you wanted to get in on your own, you wouldn't have any problem."

They walked down a dark hallway and turned a corner, which put them near the bathrooms. The music was thumping here and Nikki felt the press of a crowd, one big enough that she could get gloriously lost in.

On the main floor, she looked around. An upper level showed people leaning on the railing watching everyone on the dance floor.

"Dance or drink first?" London yelled.

Nikki snorted. "Drink, of course."

London took her hand and pulled her away from the bar. Did the woman not understand? A moment later, they stood in front of a slot machine that dispensed shots. *Of alcohol.*

"A shot machine? Where has this been my whole life? I need one in the living room." Nikki ran a hand lovingly across the top.

She slammed two shots and then let London pull her to the dance floor. She didn't know what London's goal for the night was, but Nikki was looking for a guy. Most any guy would do. It didn't take long before a couple of men joined them. The press of bodies and the thumping beat let Nikki relax.

Her brain emptied of all thought. She closed her eyes and leaned back against one of the men. His hands gripped her hips as she wrapped her arms around his neck behind her. Hips grinding, back to chest, they swayed to the rhythm.

Two songs later, Nikki turned in his arms. "How 'bout a drink?"

"Sounds good," he said close to her ear, his deep voice sending a thrill through her.

Man, she loved a guy with a deep voice. His face was pleasant enough—dark brown eyes and full lips, a nose that held hints of being broken—but nothing overly remarkable. Which made him perfect. Easily used and forgotten.

WADE PALMER STARED at Dodger, the gray hair wild on his head, blood staining his white button-down shirt, face swollen. *Silly old man. When will he learn?*

"Watch it."

The raspy voice snapped Wade's attention and he refocused on wrapping the man's bloodied hand. *Damn. Did I say that out loud?*

"It's written on your face. The look of disgust, like you think you're better'n me. Don't forget who pulled you off the streets and taught you a skill." Dodger pointed at him with his good hand before settling back on the faded paisley print of an armchair that was older than Wade.

Wade hadn't forgotten, which was why he was here in Dodger's crappy South Side apartment in the middle of the night as soon as Dodger had called. Even though he'd sworn he was done. He wasn't going to keep coming back to rescue the old man from his own self-destructive behavior.

"A skill you threw away instead of honing. What a waste."

Wade didn't respond to Dodger's poking as he moved to clean a cut over Dodger's left eye. Dodger would never understand why he'd done his best to leave the life of crime behind him. He had been a good con man. Dodger had, in fact, taught him quite a bit. It had been Nikki, though, who'd made him the man he was. And if he couldn't be with Nikki, he had no desire to be a thief.

"Are you going to explain what all this was about?" Wade applied peroxide to the cut.

Dodger hissed. "Your bedside manner sucks."

"I'm not here to make you feel good, just keep you alive. Who did this?"

"Doesn't matter."

"Really? So this settles the score, then? I can leave tonight and not worry about this happening again?" Wade knew better.

"You don't need to worry about me. I can take care of myself."

Wade pressed the bandage to the cut, using a little more force than necessary. "Oh yeah, this looks like you're doing a great job of taking care of yourself."

"Screw you."

"Look, Dodger. You know you're going to tell me sooner or later. Why not cut the crap and tell me now so we can figure out a plan? How much do you owe?"

"A lot."

Again, not surprising. Dodger had always been a gambler, ever since Wade had met him and Nikki when he was eighteen, fresh out of the foster care system with few skills and fewer prospects. Back then, Dodger had bet on horses and baseball games. But they'd brought in plenty, so his habits hadn't taken much of a toll on them. Gambling had always been Dodger's vice, but to a young Wade, it didn't seem like a big deal. They always had a place to live and food to eat, which was better than where he'd come from.

But Nikki had known. She'd seen the writing on the wall long before Wade had.

Thirteen years later, and Dodger would bet on anything. It didn't matter if he had money to back the bet or not. Everything was a sure thing. It had only gotten worse since Nikki left. Every sporting event was a chance to gamble. If a bookie wouldn't take a bet, he'd create his own with a random stranger on the street. He'd wager on how many times a dog would stop to piss on a walk or how many people would cram into one train car on the El during rush hour.

"How much is a lot?"

"Doesn't matter now. He doesn't want money."

That didn't sound good. Who didn't want money? It wasn't like the guy wanted Dodger dead. He'd had his chance while beating him. But dead men don't pay.

Dodger remained silent, which meant whatever the guy wanted was pretty bad.

Wade stared at him and waited.

"Think you can stare me down? I taught you that trick, too."

Wade rolled his eyes. "Just say it. What does he want?"

"A thief."

"What?"

Dodger paused before explaining, as if to measure

what he planned to say. "He wants a painting and expects me to get it for him."

Wade laughed in earnest. While Dodger had been something in his prime, he hadn't been in his prime for a long time. He'd made sure to pass on his knowledge to Wade and Nikki so they could do the heavy lifting on a job. Wade couldn't even remember the last time Dodger had pulled a job. Thought of one? Sure. Executed? Years.

He definitely wasn't in shape to do one now. Wade knew where this was going. "I've been out of that life for a long time. I'm out of practice."

Dodger snarled. "You think I want you to steal it? I'd be better off gettin' a kid off the street. I couldn't trust you with this."

Wade tried not to let the comment sting, but it did. He was out of practice, but he was still Dodger's best bet. Too bad the old man didn't see it. Then again, Dodger had always sucked at knowing when he had a good thing.

"What's wrong with you? You need to wake up. I'm all you've got. Whether you trust me or not." Wade didn't know why he bothered. The old man just constantly pissed him off and pushed him away.

He stood and cleaned up the first-aid supplies, closing the lid on the ancient metal box. During the first con he'd done for Dodger he'd gotten his butt kicked, and Nikki had used this same box to fix him up.

At what point did it stop? If Dodger wanted to handle things himself, so be it. Wade had his own life. He'd spent years taking care of this man who wasn't even his father.

He threw away the wrappers and bloody gauze and went to the front door, the battered wood so flimsy it would hardly keep anyone out. "Make sure you keep those cuts clean. And lock up behind me."

Wade had tried to get Dodger to move someplace safer many years ago, when they were still working together. But Dodger refused because being in a seedy neighborhood made it easier to blend in.

Dodger would call within a few days, once he realized that he couldn't pull a job without Wade. So instead of worrying about what Dodger had gotten himself into, Wade went home to his life. He pulled into his driveway and looked at his dark house.

The stark contrast of where he lived now compared to where he'd come from or where Dodger currently lived wasn't lost on him. Wade's neighborhood was single-family residential homes with mowed lawns and block parties. People walked their dogs and waved as they passed. No drunks to step over to get to your door. No cop cars with sirens and lights pulling up every other night.

He'd worked for years to give himself a normal life. A regular house with a yard. A dog to come home to. He'd thought at some point he'd find a woman, have a family, but that hadn't happened yet, so he was trying to reevaluate what that normal life was supposed to be. He'd never had normal growing up, so everything he thought he wanted came from what he'd seen in friends' lives and on TV.

But none of it fit quite right. Except his bulldog, Flynn.

He stepped from the car and went to the house. Before he reached the top step, Flynn barked and rammed into the door. "Relax, buddy. I'll be in in a minute."

He unlocked the door and had to give it a shove because Flynn's massive body was lying against it. Wade barely got the door closed before Flynn was snorting and slobbering on him.

"I wasn't gone that long, man." He gave the dog a pat and belly rub. "Come on. Time for bed."

He stripped on his way through the bedroom with the hope that Flynn wouldn't eat his clothes in the middle of the night, but he was too tired to care.

Moments after Wade climbed into bed, Flynn jumped up and curled into a ball on Wade's feet. Normally, Wade would nudge him off and tell him to go to his bed in the corner of the room, but tonight, he wanted the comfort of his friend.

Dodger's attitude shouldn't still affect him. He didn't know why he wanted the man's respect, but it mattered. Everything he'd accomplished in life had been to make Dodger proud of him. Maybe it was time to give up on that desire.

I should've listened to Nikki years ago.

Thoughts of Nikki filled his head, so he reached for his phone and searched for evidence of her online. Over the years, he'd tried to track her down, but if she didn't want to be found, she wouldn't be. He Googled her usual aliases and came up empty. Then he searched for high-end burglaries. Although to his knowledge, she'd never been caught, he had an idea of what jobs she was behind. Mostly he enjoyed the idea that she was out there living her best life—even if he was no longer in it.

TWO

NIKKI SNAGGED ANOTHER glass of champagne and sipped as she walked through the living room of Max Ingram's house. Tailored suits, designer gowns, and plenty of flashy jewels caught her eye as she walked the perimeter, distracting her from her mission. *Focus.* She turned her attention to taking in the extraordinary security measures. *Damn. Mia wasn't kidding about this.* A burly guy stood at the foot of the stairs with a dog sitting at his feet. The dog looked like a military sentry on duty. Her heart thumped in response.

No worries. The stupid dog won't attack a random guest.

In her ear, Jared's voice said quietly, "You're on duty. That's your third glass of champagne."

She turned and saw him standing near the patio. Then she pointedly scratched an itch with her middle finger, making sure he took note. Although the champagne was quality, she still preferred to blend in as the help. Unfortunately, Ingram had his own waitstaff, so she couldn't jump in for a shift and disappear.

Even worse, between the alarm system and the dog, she didn't see an easy way to breach the house undetected. And the painting Mia wanted was too big to take tonight. Of all the jobs they'd planned so far, this one was proving to be most difficult.

A woman in a gold dress sidled up to Nikki and said, "Hi. I'm Maria Darpos. I don't think we've met."

"Hi."

The woman waited patiently, and when Nikki didn't answer, she prompted, "And you are?"

Mia was suddenly at her other side, presumably to rescue her. *She should know better.* Nikki despised being underestimated.

Before Mia could open her mouth, Nikki lowered her voice and said, "Do you know Baxter Padgett?"

"Of course. Everyone here knows Baxter."

Leaning even closer, Nikki said, "I'm his mistress."

Maria sputtered and stared at Nikki, who only offered a sly smile and a lift of her shoulder. Then the woman scurried away.

Through gritted teeth, Mia said, "What happened to keeping a low profile tonight?"

"What was I supposed to do? She made a point of talking to me and expected me to interact. It would've been more suspicious for me to dodge her."

"Do *you* know who Baxter Padgett is?"

"Yeah. Dude's like ninety. If she asks, he won't deny it. I make him look good." She finished her champagne and set the glass on the table beside them. "Now, if you'll excuse me, as Jared has pointed out, I'm on the clock."

Nikki wandered down the hall and toward the kitchen. No one stopped her, although she did get a few odd looks. She'd hoped to find another way upstairs to at least get eyes on the painting. There seemed to be a staircase for the servants to use, but the kitchen was bustling with activity, and she couldn't see if it would be a clear path.

By her count the hallway had a motion detector, and every window on the first floor was wired. Mia had a right to be concerned. Ingram didn't leave much to chance.

As she neared the foyer again, she heard a voice that made her stop in her tracks. It couldn't be. She knew that voice—it was scored on her soul—but she thought she'd never run into Wade again. Last she'd heard, he was out of the game.

She tucked herself next to a tall potted plant, hoping to stay clear of the dog and the host. She peered through the leaves to get a glimpse. *Damn it all to hell.* There he was. His blond hair a little shorter, slicked back in an odd way, and he wore glasses that hid his eyes. He was still in shape and wore a suit well. She'd recognize him anywhere.

"Mr. Ingram. It's so good to finally meet face-to-face."

"Walter, it's about time. I've heard so much about you from Brad."

Walter, my ass. Wade Palmer was running a con on her mark. Having Wade around would mess with everything they were trying to do. Too much exposure. Part of her wanted to run, but she wanted to figure out Wade's scam. If she knew what he was after, she could avoid him.

The men exchanged bogus pleasantries and Nikki rolled her eyes. Stupid crap like that was why she hated a con. It was so much simpler to just take what she wanted. Wade shifted, and Nikki moved to get out of the way. She didn't want him to see her, so she ducked into the bathroom down the hall.

As she flipped on the light, her heart bumped again at her reflection. The blond wig didn't suit her coloring and any idiot could probably tell it wasn't natural, but at the same time, they wouldn't really remember her either. She tucked the chin-length hair behind her ears and leaned against the sink.

A knock on the door jolted her.

"Occupied," she called. "I'll be out in a minute." She ran the water for effect and let it run over her wrist, the motion and temperature calming.

It had been a trick Wade taught her when she panicked on a job. Panic struck when she was caught off guard.

She didn't panic anymore. She did the planning, so there were no surprises. She twisted the taps with more force than necessary to stop the flow of water. After patting her hands dry, she turned the doorknob with a friendly smile on her face and a prepared apology on her lips. But as soon as the lock unlatched, the door pushed in, and she stood toe-to-toe with Wade.

Whatever calm she'd thought she felt before opening the door fled, as did the air in her lungs. Wade was here, in her space, staring into her eyes as if years had not passed. As if he had every right to have his hands on her.

"Nikki." Her name came from his lips in a puff of air. He stared at her like she was a mirage and might fade in a moment.

She stepped back out of his grasp. "What the hell?" she asked with forced bluster.

"It really is you." He tucked his hands in his pockets and rocked back on his heels. "I thought for sure I was following some other woman until you called out. What are you doing here?"

Pointing at the gown she wore, she said, "Working." She picked up the crystal dish from the counter and shoved it into her purse. "I assume you're doing the same, *Walter*."

His eyes flashed at the sound of his phony name.

"Times must be tough if you're stooping to snatch small trinkets."

She smirked. "Every little bit helps. Isn't that what Dodger taught us? Heard you were out of the game."

"I am. Mostly."

She wanted to ask. Wanted to know what he'd been doing. But she couldn't afford to care. She pushed past him to get to the door.

He touched her arm, sending a jolt of awareness through her body. "Secret's safe?" he said quietly.

"I've *never* been a snitch." For a second, they both stood in silence, and she was pretty sure he was remembering when they first met and she let him steal from her. She'd felt sorry for him and let him get away with it. Then she'd had to hear from Dodger forever about how some dumb boy got the better of her.

"I know," he finally mumbled.

She opened the door and as she stepped back into the hall, she heard, "Good to see you."

How was she going to convince Mia to walk away from this job?

WADE STOOD IN the bathroom for a full five minutes after Nikki left. The scent of her perfume trailing in her wake woke parts of him that he'd tried to ignore.

At least he hadn't acted like a total fool in front of her. Younger Wade would have fallen at her feet and begged her to come home. How many times over the years had he envisioned doing that?

Of all the things Dodger had taught him, remaining cool under any circumstance had proven to be the most beneficial, especially when it came to Nikki. She looked good, even in the blond wig. Blond never had been her best disguise. It was unnatural against her bronze skin. Not that it mattered. Her mouth was always what drew him in: the physical aspects of it—the plump lips, the sneer when she was agitated—as well as the sharp tongue it held.

He didn't buy for a minute that she was in this mansion, surrounded by the filthy rich, just to swipe a soap dish. She had something bigger planned. This was a case job, which could cause all kinds of problems for him and Dodger. He stepped from the bathroom and strolled back to the living room.

His gaze immediately landed on Nikki, no different than if she had a homing device attached. He stood near the bar and kept a watchful eye on her. She giggled appropriately with guests, but her eyes were always on something other than the person to whom she was speaking. Her engagement was seemingly high, so no one noticed, but he was looking for it. He needed to know what her target was.

She sucked down two glasses of champagne as she wandered the room. When she landed on a tall, bulky guy, Wade had to force his feet to stay put. The man twisted as he righted her. She'd literally fallen on Brad Ingram—a trip through the air on her heels. The only indication he saw of it being completely phony was the fact that she managed to force the man to catch her, but she didn't spill a drop of alcohol.

As she apologized profusely and sloppily, Wade's hackles rose. It didn't matter that he knew it was all a game, he couldn't stomach her flirting with another man in front of him.

You're being ridiculous. She hasn't been yours for years. You no longer have a claim on her. Let her play her games.

He turned his attention back to the crowd. He needed to figure out how to get Max to show him the Devereaux painting. Nikki's obnoxiously loud laugh stabbed his ears.

"So embarrassing, don't you think?" a quiet voice came beside him.

He shifted to face the woman at his side. "Quite." Then he extended his hand. "Walter."

"Kira. Nice to meet you."

"Can I get you a drink?" he asked, as if she weren't capable of waving down the bartender for a free drink.

She held up her champagne flute, and he smiled sheepishly. Best to look harmless.

"Do you know who's with Brad?" he asked.

"Her I've never seen." She sighed. "Some people should really be more careful about their alcohol consumption."

"Oh, yeah." Except he knew Nikki could drink an entire bottle and still scale a wall. "Maybe someone should call her a cab."

"It looks like Brad has it handled." She sipped from her glass. "I guess the excitement is over."

"You were hoping for more?"

She chuckled. "These events can be so tedious. Every now and then, it's nice if something happens to break up the monotony."

"It was nice to meet you."

"I'm sure we'll run into each other again."

As Kira walked away, Wade stepped forward as Brad wrapped an arm around Nikki and led her from the room. She threw her arm on the man's shoulder and glanced behind her. Catching Wade's eye, she winked.

Still playing the game. He followed to see where they were going. Sure enough, at the base of the stairs, Brad waved off security, explaining that Nikki had had a little too much to drink and needed to lie down.

She was as good as ever. She was getting access to the part of the house no one else was permitted in. The painting he needed was probably up there. He rushed forward.

"Hey," he called to Brad. They didn't stop. "Brad."

The man paused on the second step.

"Need a hand?"

"No, man, we're good. Thanks. I'll be back in a bit to catch up."

"Yeah, buddy. We're good," Nikki added with a slur for effect.

Crap. He was out of luck here tonight. Maybe his buddy and business partner Boone would have information on the painting that Dodger hadn't bothered to get. When the old man had finally caved and called Wade for help, all he'd said was that he needed to steal a Devereaux painting from Max Ingram's house. Wade had tasked Boone with finding everything he could about Ingram and the painting.

Having his own security firm definitely came in handy when he needed to access information.

Not that Dodger would ever appreciate it.

Knowing that he wouldn't be able to get anywhere tonight, he decided to leave. On the way home, he'd hit Boone up and they'd start fresh in the morning.

Damn Nikki. Even when she wasn't in his life anymore, she still had a way of screwing up everything for him.

THREE

NIKKI DIDN'T KNOW why she thought this was a good idea.
Brad Ingram was too handsy. Maybe she should've let
Wade help them upstairs. But there was no way she
wanted his help. She knew better than to trust him. Besides, she could handle herself.

It didn't help that Jared and Mia were both in her
ear muttering about her being a drunk. Everyone was
starting to piss her off.

"We have a guest room right at the top of the stairs,"
Brad said as his hand slipped over her boob again.

She brushed it away with another giggle. "I'm sure
I'll feel sooo much better if I just lay down for a bit.
One too many glasses of champagne. Ooops!"

At the top of the stairs, she looked sharply down the
hall, looking for evidence of security. Motion detectors
on both ends of the hall. This job kept getting worse.

"Meet us at the door," Jared said in her ear. "Next
time, no drinking on the job."

Nikki pressed the button so Jared would hear her
laugh. As if she would give up drinking at his command. Then she slipped the comm out. She needed to
focus.

Brad nudged a door open and guided her to the bed.
Then, of course, he sat beside her.

"How about I help you get more comfortable?" He reached behind her for the zipper on her dress.

Nikki pressed a hand to his chest. "Actually, maybe point me to the bathroom?" Then she let out a loud belch and held a hand on her stomach. Then for added effect, she lurched and heaved a little.

"Oh, man. Yeah." He jumped up. "Right through there." He pointed at a door on the adjacent wall.

"Thank—" She heaved and half belched again before rushing across the room.

"So, uh, I'm gonna head back downstairs. I'll come back to check on you in a bit. Okay?"

She waved at him over her shoulder as she pushed into the bathroom. Then she proceeded to make some retching sounds to make sure Brad got the hint that he would not be getting busy here. She messed up her hair a bit and wet a washcloth in case Brad had decided to be a decent human being and wait for her to come out. Opening the door, she saw that she'd been right about Brad. Dude was a douche.

She replaced the comm in her ear and before she could even take a breath, Jared was talking again. "Where did you go, Nikki?"

She pressed the button on the comm allowing her to talk. "I'm fine. I'm doing recon upstairs."

"Upstairs? Security—"

"Let me walk right past because I was with Ingram's son."

"Walking is generous. He was practically carrying you," Mia's voice added.

"I was acting. Jeez, people, give me some credit. We needed eyes up here and now we have them. If you'll all shut up, I'll get the information we need and get out of here."

Thankfully, they quieted without further comment. There wasn't much she hated more than people underestimating her.

She slipped her heels off so she could move around silently upstairs. She carried them by the straps in case she needed to play stupid drunk again, and peeked out the bedroom door. No sign of cameras in the hall. Just the motion detectors, and the alarm obviously wasn't set since she and Brad just walked through.

Sliding along the wall, she tried the knob of the next door. Then she peered in. A bedroom. Based on the lack of personal touch, another guest room. How many freaking guests does one family get at a time? The next door was locked. She tiptoed across the hall. This door was open and it was the jackpot. Ingram's office.

Two more motion detectors in here. On the wall opposite the door was the painting Mia wanted. The last known piece of art created by Devereaux. Nikki stepped closer and pulled out her phone. She'd seen pictures of the painting, of course, but seeing it up close was different. It was a self-portrait and the artist was obviously a severely unhappy woman. In the painting, she was spilling out of her top, breasts practically lying on the table in front of her as she gripped a bottle of wine in one hand. Her other hand reached out toward the viewer, as if pleading for something.

Nikki snapped pictures from every angle. Then she felt over the frame, looking for trip wires. Nothing.

It seemed a little too easy.

She lifted the edge and saw the problem. Ingram

was using the painting as the cover for his safe. Silly man. Did he think this was a movie? Who covered a safe with a painting?

She swung the painting wide and took pictures of the hinge. One more complication. Then she studied the safe. This guy probably had jewels and stacks of cash sitting right there. Knowing Wade, that was what he was after. Never too imaginative. He kept it simple.

Nikki, on the other hand, liked a challenge.

Of course, sometimes that meant she completed a challenge and didn't actually make anything for it.

But she had one hell of a good time.

She took a few moments to study the safe in addition to the painting and the frame. Before backing out of the room, she took photos of the overall layout, including the windows. They might be her point of ingress and egress given that she could avoid the dogs. Putting her phone back in her clutch, she found the stupid soap dish that she'd snagged from the bathroom.

Part of her wanted to keep it, but if the security guy at the bottom of the stairs wanted to search her, she couldn't risk it. She wiped it clean and set it on the bookcase. Someone would notice and assume a partygoer was playing a prank. She scooped up her heels again and cracked the door open.

No one in sight, so she hurried to the end of the hall and attached a small camera to the motion detector. Now, they would really have eyes up here. Then she stumbled down the stairs. At the bottom, the dog turned its attention on her, sniffed and let out a growl.

"Miss," security guy said, "Mr. Ingram said you needed to rest. You're in no condition to drive."

"Isn't that sweet," she answered. "But I called a car. I can't sleep in a strange bed. And once I puked everything up, I'm doing so much better. Thanks." She waved and stepped wide to get around the dog.

"Ma'am."

She paused and turned. "Yes?"

"I hate to do this to you, but I need to check your bag. The upstairs is supposed to be off limits, but Mr. Ingram brought you up and left you unattended."

"Oh, sure, honey. You're just doing your job." She opened her clutch, which really didn't have room for much.

"All good. Thank you. Have a good night."

"You too." She handed the man a business card with her number. "Can you please pass this along to Brad and let him know I appreciate his kindness?"

"Sure thing."

She scurried out the door as quickly as possible to disappear before Brad or Wade got any funny ideas.

Outside, she tapped her ear again. "I'm heading out. See you all tomorrow."

"Tomorrow?" Jared asked.

"I need to think and process this shit show." She walked down the drive and called a car for real, although she was totally tempted to steal one from under the valets' noses. When she got down the block where the car would pick her up, she pulled the wig off and let her hair down, pulling pins out and letting them drop on the sidewalk.

She shook out her hair as her ride pulled up. She glanced at the car and the driver to make sure nothing shady was going on before getting in the back seat. She wasn't sure she wanted to go back to the River North apartment where Jared expected to her stay, or if she wanted to decompress with the company of strangers.

"Good party?" the driver asked.

"Not so much. Bunch of phony rich people. Plus, my ex was there."

"Oh. That's gotta be rough." She glanced over her shoulder at Nikki with a sympathetic look.

Nikki sighed. *Rough.* That was one way to put it. She hadn't seen Wade in years. When she'd first left, she'd always expected him to pop up. They ran in the same circles, knew the same people, but she'd successfully avoided him. Tonight had taken her off guard and that didn't sit well with her. "Haven't seen him in years and had no idea he'd be there."

"Did he talk to you or pretend not to know you?"

"He cornered me to talk but didn't say much." *Good to see you.* What was that supposed to mean?

"Who did the breaking up? You or him?"

"I guess I did, but he could've stopped it."

"Well, then, since he's a dude, he wouldn't say anything to make himself vulnerable. Guys like to make sure you know they're okay without you. A breakup's no big deal."

But for him it had been a big deal. He'd called hundreds of times asking her to come home.

"What'd he say? Tell you how great his life is? All about the hot new chick he's with?"

"Nope. Just said it was good to see me."

"Oh, girl, that was an invitation."

"What?" She excelled at reading people. There was no invitation.

"If he was still bitter, he'd want to show you he doesn't care about you. He was opening a door."

Nikki let that sit a minute. If Wade did open a door, she could walk through to find out what he was after. *Yeah, like knowing what he wants to steal is your top priority.* She rolled her eyes at herself. Open door or not, she couldn't afford to let Wade back in her life. Because where Wade was, Dodger was lurking in the shadows.

"You gonna call him?"

"No way. Too much baggage." Baggage by the name of her father. She'd sworn she wouldn't let Dodger get to her. She'd given enough of her life to him.

She was her own woman now.

THE FOLLOWING MORNING, Wade parked in the lot of the nondescript strip mall where he and his partners rented space for their security firm. He grabbed the coffees and whistled to get Flynn to jump out of the truck to follow him. Wade went into the storefront, where they sold security gear like nanny cams, pepper spray, and rape whistles. He greeted Meg, who was working the counter, handed her a coffee, and then continued on through the back and up the stairs. The real work happened in the office space on the second floor. As soon as the door was open, Flynn went galloping in to say hi to Boone, who was sleeping on the couch.

"Ugh! What the hell, Wade? I thought we agreed you'd keep this beast on a leash." Boone sat up and wiped the slobber from his face.

"I can't help that he loves you."

"He won't keep loving me when I knock him out."

"Aw, you wouldn't do that. You love Flynn, too." He

set a coffee on the table next to Boone. "Why are you sleeping here anyway?"

"Worked late." He picked up the coffee Wade brought and gulpcd.

"I hope that means you got me information." He sat next to Boone's desk.

"I got some information. I don't think it's enough to run this." He scrubbed a hand over his face, scratching at his reddish five o'clock shadow. Before standing, he rubbed Flynn's belly, proving why they were friends. "I think we should read Devon in."

Devon James was their partner, the face of the business as well as the brawn, while Wade was the brains—not that Devon was stupid. It was just that Devon was former military, so he did things by the book. Wade saw things as a thief would. Devon was aware of most of Wade's past, but Wade had never told him everything.

Boone, on the other hand, knew everything. They'd met not long after Nikki left and Wade struggled to work alone. They'd done some jobs together, but when they began to toy with the idea of going straight, they developed the idea of building a security company. Who better to test your security than thieves?

"I can't risk it. If I go down, you guys can keep the business going. I don't want to ruin your lives for Dodger."

Boone sank into his chair and put on his ball cap backwards before booting up his computer. "I don't think you should ruin your life for Dodger either. When was the last time that man did anything for you?"

It was a fair question, but Wade couldn't answer. It wasn't so much when Dodger had done something as how much Dodger had done. Boone wouldn't get it. "This is it. The last one. I'm done after this."

"Uh-huh. I'll believe it when I see it." Boone tapped away on the keyboard. "So I guess last night was less than fruitful? You couldn't get Ingram to give you a tour?"

"You could say that." He took a healthy drink of his coffee and let out a deep breath. "Nikki was there."

Boone froze, fingers midstrike. "*Nikki* Nikki?"

"The one and only."

Boone twisted in his chair and wheeled closer. "And?"

"And nothing. She's working a job, but I don't know what she's after."

"But she saw you? You talked?"

Wade nodded.

Boone smacked Wade's leg. "Well? What did she say?"

"Not much. She said she was working. She'd overheard me talking with Ingram, so she knew I was doing the same. That was it."

"Seriously?"

"What did you expect?"

"I don't know. Everything you've told me about her, I expected fireworks. Excitement. Loss of clothes. Anything more than *I'm working*. Didn't you expect more?"

Had he? In truth, he'd been so shocked to actually see her that he couldn't think clearly. "I guess we've both moved on. It's been years."

"Time doesn't really heal everything, no matter what they say. The pain fades, but it doesn't go away."

"Yeah, well, I don't have time to dwell on Nikki. She

made it clear last night that she was there for a job, and she didn't care that I was there."

Boone went back to his keyboard. "Here's the painting you're after. I ran routine security and did some searching. Ingram had it at his corporate office until last year when he retired. Then he took it home with him. If you didn't see it while you were there, it's on the second floor, probably in his office. It could be in his bedroom, but I can't imagine this thing looking good in a bedroom. It's dark and kind of creepy. It's just a picture of a woman, a bottle of wine, and she's reaching out. If it was in a horror movie, you'd think she was gonna snatch your soul."

"That's what I was afraid of. I couldn't get upstairs without suspicion. They had it guarded. And since I wasn't a drunk, half-passed-out woman, I couldn't go up."

"Huh?"

Wade shook his head. "Nikki faked being drunk and needed to lie down. She had access to the second floor. What else is up there?"

"Dude. I have no idea, but what if she's—"

"Don't say it. I don't need that complication."

"There's one way to find out."

"I am not calling her." He refused to make that mistake again. He'd called her too many times after she left. She never answered. Never returned his calls. It looked like Dodger wasn't the only one comfortable with cutting people out of his life. "Regardless of where the painting is or what Nikki is after, I need to move fast. Two thieves hitting the same place is a problem for whoever goes in second. When I steal that painting, security is going to tighten even more than it is now. I have to beat her to the job."

Boone chuckled.

"What?"

"It's just that with everything you've ever said about Nikki, I find it funny that you're so sure you'll beat her to the punch."

As if he needed the reminder from another person that Nikki was the better thief. "I don't have a choice. For her it's a score. For me, it's Dodger's life."

"What if you told her?"

"I don't know that it would matter." The thought twisted in his gut. Nikki had always been able to show a cool exterior, but she'd been fiercely loyal and loved wholly. But the Nikki he'd seen last night didn't hold any emotion. He wasn't sure it was only a façade. When she walked out of the bathroom, it had felt like he was no one to her, so he couldn't imagine how she would treat Dodger.

FOUR

MIA, JARED, AND AUDREY were waiting for her in the living room to talk about getting into Ingram's house. But Nikki was hungover and really didn't want to deal with people today.

The bedroom door flung open and Audrey stood there with a steaming cup of what smelled like coffee. As she neared, she narrowed her eyes. "What's wrong?"

"Hungover." She reached out for the coffee.

Audrey sank to the edge of the bed. "I'm not buying it. I've seen you drink until *I* was ready to puke. Other than looking a little rough in the morning, you've never shown signs of being hungover."

"First for everything." She took the aspirin Audrey offered and downed the tablets with a swig of scalding caffeine. Bitter and strong, just the way she liked it.

Audrey said nothing for a moment. She sat and studied Nikki.

"What? So I drank too much. Give me five and I'll be fine." She shoved back the covers, irritated now that Audrey might see something Nikki didn't want her to.

"Who was the guy last night?"

"What guy?" Nikki took another gulp of coffee and twisted to get out of bed.

"You went silent when you were in the bathroom. I don't think Jared and Mia noticed, but I did."

"No one."

Another full minute of silence as Nikki grabbed clothes from the dresser. "I'm going to shower. Then I'll be ready to strategize." With a bundle of clothes in one hand and her coffee in the other, she turned back to Audrey. "And you can let them know that going into Ingram's is going to screw us."

She stood under the jets of the hot shower and willed herself to be normal. *Get your act together. Dodger and Wade are not going to ruin your life.* She finished her coffee and became a little more herself with the caffeine infusion. She pulled on a tank top and shorts, knowing they always made Jared uncomfortable. That would be one less person looking at her.

She made her way to the kitchen and refilled her cup.

"It's about time," Mia said.

"Whatever. I don't see what the rush is. This job is fucked. Ingram has two dogs, motion detectors in the second floor hall, and another two in his office. And the cherry on top of this messed-up sundae? He's using the painting as a cover for his home safe. It's in a hinged frame. Like I said, we're screwed."

Audrey wheeled around behind her desk. "Okay, let's unpack all that. I have all the pictures you guys all took last night. Let's see what you have."

Audrey tapped away on the computer and photos began filing across the TV screen in front of her. Jared walked away from his post at Audrey's desk and neared the TV. Audrey flipped through all the photos once to give them an overview. Nikki didn't pay much attention since she'd taken a good number of the pictures. Instead she focused on her coffee.

"Who is this guy?" Jared asked.

Mia said, "I have no idea." She paused and then told Audrey, "Send us through the slideshow again."

Audrey set the slideshow of photos in motion.

"He's all over the place. You don't know him?" Jared reiterated to Mia incredulously. "You know everyone."

Without looking up, Nikki knew they were talking about Wade. "He's a thief."

"What?" Jared and Mia both asked.

Nikki stretched out her legs and set her cup on the table beside the couch. "He's a thief. He's there working Ingram as a mark."

"And you know this how?" Mia asked.

"How do you think?"

Mia just stared at her.

"I know him. We've done jobs together."

"What is he after?" Jared asked.

Nikki lifted a shoulder. "No clue."

"Why didn't you ask?" Mia asked.

These people are so freaking clueless. Nikki snorted. When it seemed that Mia seriously wanted an answer, Nikki responded, "If I asked him about his job, it would put me in a position to tell him about mine. I figured that would piss you off, and you know how much I try not to do that."

Her thirst for alcohol came back even though she still had a slow thud behind her eyes. Mia and Jared didn't understand her world. Audrey got it.

"Maybe we can figure it out." Audrey tapped away on the computer and started a new slideshow, this one like an homage to Wade. She'd selected only the photos where Wade appeared.

Seeing his face over and over made her want to drink to oblivion. That face had haunted her dreams last night, which was why she'd tried to chase them away, to no avail. She knew the pictures wouldn't tell them anything. Wade was too good. He wouldn't be caught studying the item he planned to steal.

"Look for whatever he's *not* looking at," she said.

"Huh?" Audrey said, pausing the photos.

"He wouldn't case the house by studying the thing he wants to steal. He'd avoid it. He'll look at every other thing in the house except the one item he wants. He wouldn't want to draw attention to his interest."

"Smart," Jared said.

"Thieving 101," Nikki added.

They flipped through the photos again and nothing stood out. Nikki shrugged. "Maybe he's not planning on stealing anything. He might be running a con."

"Either way, it's a complication we can't afford," Jared said.

"Good point. I say we move on to the next mark on the list."

"No. Ingram is next," Mia said.

"We can come back to him after things cool down," Audrey offered.

No, we can't. Wade will ruin it.

"If this guy steals something from Ingram, the security will increase, making it more difficult than it is now," Jared said.

Mia added, "Taking this will be a big hit to our fathers. The Devereaux is worth more than the last three items we took. This will make them hurt."

The bitterness in Mia's voice caught Nikki's attention. She was used to Mia being an ice queen, but the animosity had notched up over the last few jobs. By stealing from their fathers' friends, Mia and Jared were taking money from men who profited from their fathers' scheme. The money collected from the sales of stolen art paid restitution to their fathers' victims. And the cherry on top was that Mia and Jared believed the art they were stealing was part of their fathers' contingency plan for a nest egg.

Nikki returned her attention to the screen. There was another face she didn't recall noticing at the party. He was a tall man and in at least two shots, he was looking at Wade.

"Who's he?" Nikki climbed off the couch and stepped closer to the screen. "I don't remember seeing him yesterday."

She studied the man. The suit was off the rack, but his beard was meticulously trimmed. His smile was wide, but his eyes sharply focused. Something wasn't right about him, but Nikki couldn't pinpoint it.

"He's the guy who flirted with Mia," Audrey said.

"What?" the woman sputtered. "He did not."

Audrey laughed. "Yeah, he did."

Mia shot her a dirty look.

"Maybe you didn't notice because you were so focused on the job," Audrey added.

No, Nikki thought, *she noticed. She just doesn't like being called out on it.*

At least everyone was looking at him now instead of Wade. She needed to figure out what Wade was up to, especially since Mia was adamant about moving forward. She couldn't afford Wade getting in her way.

"His name is Logan," Mia explained. "He works in insurance."

"That's all you got?" Nikki asked.

"It was a casual conversation. What else would I have gotten?"

Nikki caught how uncomfortable Mia had become. "Is he good?"

"What?"

"You look like you wanted to get a piece of him." Nikki pointed at a photo where Mia and Logan were talking. "I totally hope you acted on that."

"I have no idea what you're talking about."

Jared chuckled. "Leave Mia alone. Let's figure out a plan."

Nikki raised her hand again. "What is an insurance guy doing at a social function?"

"He said that he'd been by to talk to Ingram earlier in the day while they were setting up, and Max invited him."

It was fishy, but Nikki couldn't afford the brain space on some guy who wanted to get with Mia. Wade was already using up too much room. "Back to the plan."

The three of them stood together in front of the TV with Audrey running the tech behind them.

"Even if you don't know what this guy—what's his name?"

"Wade."

"Even if we don't know what he wants, can you gauge when he might make a move? How well do you know him?"

"I know him well enough. If I had to guess, he'll

move fast. And given that he knows I'm working a job, he might move up whatever timeline he had."

Mia went from being irritated over Nikki's teasing to deflated with this additional information. *Maybe I can get her to back down now.*

With a deep inhale, Mia lifted her chin. "How fast can we move?"

"All we have to do is beat him in, right?" Jared asked.

"I guess, but there are so many moving parts."

"I have the alarm figured out," Audrey said quietly from the other side of the room. She stood and joined the group in front of the TV with a tablet in her hand.

"Really?" Nikki asked.

Pointing at the screen, she swiped on her tablet. The picture of the keypad appeared. "The alarm is old. It was top-of-the-line like five years ago, but he hasn't done much to update it. I can control it whenever I want."

It was almost too easy.

"What about the dogs? I don't do dogs."

"We can lock them up."

"And the hinged painting?"

"I got nothing for that," Audrey admitted.

"As soon as I saw your photos, I sent copies to London to get ideas. She's working on it, but she's leaning toward replicating the frame with the hinge," Mia said.

"That's not gonna work. Taking the whole thing off and hoping I can reattach the new one will take too long. Plus, a new hinge is going to stand out as obvious. I think popping that thing out is still our best bet. But it's big. We might have to cut it like we did for the one at Scott's."

"See?" Audrey bumped her shoulder. "Not a shit show. We got this."

Jared studied the picture of the hinged frame. "We run the risk of Ingram noticing that we made a swap every time he opens this, though. What if he sees the cut marks in the frame?"

Nikki hadn't thought about that. It had worked at Randall Scott's house because the painting hung on a wall. No one would notice until they went to move it. Which they had, not long after Nikki had made the switch.

"Maybe we can use his hinge and I can mount the new frame. Can London match it?"

"I think so," Mia said.

"What about the guards? Does Ingram only employ them for parties or are they on staff all the time?"

"Events only."

"Good." She sighed. "Then Wade is the only wild card."

"Since you know him, can't you talk to him?" Mia asked.

"He wouldn't tell me the truth. He's not trustworthy."

"No honor among thieves?" Jared asked.

"Not when it comes to him."

"But whatever he does tell you would give you insight into what he's doing, right?" Audrey asked. "You said look at whatever he's not looking at. It should work the same for what he says."

Nikki debated her next move. Reaching out to Wade made the most sense. But she didn't want to give him that hold over her.

She was better than that.

WADE STUDIED THE floor plans for Ingram's house to find the best way in. He couldn't focus. Thoughts of Nikki getting in the way distracted him at every turn.

Boone was right. He needed to know Nikki's plan. If he treated this like any other business transaction, it might appeal to her.

He sat at his desk, Flynn collapsed on his feet. He stared at his phone trying to figure out the best way to reach out to Nikki. He typed and deleted four messages before he finally settled on being honest.

Hey—It was great seeing you the other day. I'd love to buy you a drink and catch up.

When his phone vibrated with a message, his heart stuttered. Then he looked at the screen. Dodger.

Got a plan yet?

Working on it.

They're not playing with this deadline.

Wade wanted to scream. Dodger had been in trouble with every bookie in the city over the past few years, but this felt different. He was also pretty sure Dodger was still holding something back.

I know.

What're you going to do?

We'll talk later. As if he'd lay out his plan via text.

When the phone vibrated again, his irritation with Dodger grew, but this time, it was Nikki. No conversation. Just an address and a time. He Googled the address and found it was a hole-in-the-wall bar.

He nudged Flynn off his feet. "Sorry, bud. I've got a date."

No, not a date. Business transaction. He and Nikki had always worked well together, so maybe he could convince her to team up. Just for this one job. They could both walk away with what they wanted and maybe get some closure.

He grabbed the keys for his truck and Flynn trotted next to him. "Nope. You're not going this time."

Flynn flopped back on the floor. Wade turned the TV on and flipped to find *Law and Order*. For some reason, Flynn seemed to like the show in all of its iterations. As soon as the telltale *dum-dum* sounded, Flynn hopped on the couch and relaxed.

Wade drove to the bar and thought about what he would say. So much had happened since she left. Of course, some things, like Dodger, stayed the same. Mostly he wanted to know what she'd been doing. She looked good, so she must be doing all right for herself. Not that any of that was surprising. Nikki had said she could run her own show, and he'd never doubted her. What would his life look like now if he had followed her?

Part of him had hoped she was done stealing. Like maybe if she had a big enough score, she would've retired. But he knew better. For Nikki, the money was only part of it. She craved the challenge and excitement. She got off on the rush of doing the unthinkable.

He had to stop thinking about Nikki like that. Business. This had to be a business transaction to work. He pulled up near the bar about thirty minutes later and slowly rolled down the block. He wasn't sure what he was looking for, but her agreement to meet him happened fast. As much as he'd like to believe she missed him, his gut knew better. He needed to make sure there was nothing suspicious about this place.

The bar's door was open and music was blaring. The

immediate neighborhood consisted of a lot of apartment buildings, so maybe they weren't bothered by the noise. And it wasn't all that late. If a crowded bar was where Nikki wanted to meet, at least it would give them both a sense of anonymity.

He squeezed his truck into a spot in the small lot across the street from the bar and he sat for a few minutes to watch the comings and goings of patrons. Mostly guys in T-shirts and jeans and women in tank tops and shorts, all going out for a regular night in their neighborhood.

Did Nikki live around here? Was that why she chose this place?

It didn't matter. He didn't care where she lived. He just needed to find out what she was after and try to talk her into working together. One last heist as partners.

He stepped from the truck, smoothed his hand over his hair, and straightened his shirt. Walking into the bar, he scanned the area. It was crowded, but not wall-to-wall people. He could see all the tables and booths, and it only took a moment for his gaze to find her.

She sat with her back to him, in direct contrast to what they'd been taught. *Always face the door so you can see who's coming at you*. But Nikki liked to laugh in the face of rules.

Or maybe she just didn't care.

He slid into the booth across from her. She already had a bottle of beer waiting for him. He took her in for a moment. Her long dark hair was down, cascading over her shoulders, and in her silk blouse she was dressed better than most of the patrons milling around. Her makeup was impeccable. She was in full armor.

Casual, off-the-clock Nikki was a messy ponytail and an old tank top.

"Thanks for coming."

She looked up from where she was peeling the label from her bottle. "I figured we had things to discuss."

"How have you been?"

"This isn't a social call." She took a pull on her beer, and he stared at her long neck as her throat worked. If he didn't know better, he'd think she did it for effect.

He cleared his throat and refocused. "I know. But I'm curious. We haven't seen each other in a long time, and we have a lot of history."

"Yeah, but it's just that—history."

He took a deep breath. He didn't know why he thought she'd make this easy on him. Easy wasn't her way. "I figured since we're both looking to hit the same house, we could work together. Plan the heist so we can both get what we want."

She tilted her head and her dark eyes settled into a penetrating stare. Nikki had never liked a long con—she was a get-in-and-get-out kind of girl—but she had the ability to see right through people that would make her an excellent grifter. And Dodger had always known it.

"What are you after?"

"A painting."

"Fuck," she said under her breath as she looked up at the ceiling.

Unease slithered through him like tendrils of ice. Ingram had multiple paintings, right? This couldn't really be happening.

"The Devereaux," she said, no question involved.

Boone had cursed him by mentioning the possibility. "Fuck," he said, too.

She gulped the rest of her beer.

FIVE

THE BEER DID nothing to quench Nikki's thirst. Her throat still felt dusty. She couldn't believe that Wade was after the same painting she was. Over the years, she'd crossed paths with other thieves who wanted what she planned to steal. She never lost.

But everything about this was different.

She waved the waitress over and ordered another beer. Wade had barely touched his.

He sat across from her, shock filling his face, as if he couldn't believe she'd mentioned the Devereaux.

"What would it take to get you to walk away?" he asked.

Nikki burst into laughter as the waitress delivered her fresh bottle. "That's not gonna happen." She took a long drink. Setting her bottle back on the table, she asked, "What would it take for you to back off?"

"I'd love to, but I can't."

Her heart lurched. She knew. As soon as he answered, she knew this was about Dodger.

"I have a buyer who has a huge budget. He's paying over market for the thing. I can't let that go."

He was lying. He was such a bad liar. At least to her. He could convince a mark of pretty much anything and had the patience to string them along, but she'd always known when he was lying.

"This is it for me, Nikki. One last job and I'm done for good."

"I have a client, too, so walking away isn't an option. You can choose something else for your last score." She drained her second bottle. If she didn't leave soon, she was going to get drunk here with him and that wouldn't be a smart move.

His blue eyes pleaded with her, just like they had when she'd caught him stealing from her when they met. "Come on. You can go anywhere and get anything."

"I want this thing."

"Ingram has a lot of security. This can't be a smash and grab."

She chuckled. "I'm not a teenager."

"What about the dogs?"

She swallowed, wishing she hadn't finished her beer. "What about them? Just another obstacle."

"I thought you didn't do jobs with dogs."

"It's been a long time. Things change." She rose and slapped some cash on the table. "You might as well start looking for a new score."

The corner of his mouth crooked up. "What makes you think I won't beat you to it?"

"Seriously? We both know I'm better than you."

He rose and stood toe-to-toe with her. If she took a deep breath, their bodies would brush. "Like you said, things change."

He scooped up her money and tucked it in the front pocket of her jeans, sending a betraying tingle through her. "I said I wanted to buy you a drink."

Fortifying herself against whatever lusty power he

still held over her, she said, "Well, it wouldn't be the first time you went back on your word, would it?"

She took a step back, but he grabbed her hand.

"Nikki." Her name sounded strangled.

When she looked at their hands and then into his eyes, he dropped the contact.

"I waited for you to come back. I thought you would."

"I told you I was done. I couldn't keep living that life with him."

"Dodger needed us. I couldn't walk away. I owed him everything."

She wanted to scream and rail against him. *What about me? Did I mean nothing?* Instead, she said, "Yeah, I get it."

"I don't think you do."

"I was there, remember? When will it be enough for you? He's toxic."

"He misses you."

His words were a stab to her heart. She knew when she decided to leave Dodger that he'd cut her out of his life. She'd be dead to him. It was not an empty threat on his part. She had been willing to live with that because she'd believed she would have Wade.

"I guess he shouldn't have been such a jerk then. Live and learn." She turned away. Over her shoulder, she added, "See you around."

Out on the street, she sent a text to everyone. Now that she had confirmation that she and Wade were both after the Devereaux, their timeline had to move up. Then she called a ride share to pick her up on the next block. Her brain spun in circles on the whole ride to the apartment.

She was the first to arrive, so she pulled up the footage they had of Ingram's hall. The camera didn't offer the best picture, but it was enough for her to get a feel for the comings and goings of the family. She was more than halfway through the recording when Jared and Audrey came in.

"What's the problem?" Jared asked.

"Wade—the other thief at the party? He's after the Devereaux. We need to go in first if you want to make sure you get it."

"Damn," Jared said.

Audrey scooted behind her desk. "How good is this guy?"

"Very."

"As good as you?"

Nikki sniffed. *As if.*

Mia came through the door and set her purse on the table. She took in the scene. "Last I checked, I was in charge. I don't get summoned."

"I know how your panties get in a bunch when you don't know what's going on, so I wanted you to be in the loop. But by all means, carry on with your b.s. while this heist goes up in flames."

Nikki's outburst was enough to have Mia's eyes pop.

"I don't get it," Audrey said. "If you're better than him, what's the worry?"

She didn't want to tell them that she'd tipped her hand and Wade knew she planned to steal the painting.

"Someone please explain what is going on," Mia said.

"Wade is after the Devereaux," Jared said.

"So we need to move up our timeline to get it first," Nikki continued.

Mia crossed her arms and pressed her lips together. "Maybe we shouldn't."

An eerie relief swept through Nikki. She'd been sure Mia would never walk away. If for no other reason, this was *her* plan.

Jared stared at Mia like he didn't know her. "But Ingram—"

With a wave of her hand, she cut him off. "I still want it. But what if we let this guy steal it and then take it from him?"

"He'll move it to his buyer fast. We wouldn't have time to plan for it," Nikki said.

"And there wouldn't be a forgery in its place. Ingram would collect from insurance," Jared added.

Mia looked at Audrey. "You could hack into his account and take the money, though, right?"

"Of course."

Mia took a deep breath.

"This will draw a lot of attention," Nikki said.

"That's my main concern. We still have more art to steal," Mia reminded them.

"It'll get their guard up," Audrey added.

"And it might be too suspicious on the heels of Scott's forgery being discovered," Mia mused.

They all sat in silence for a minute, waiting for Mia to make her call.

"Are you ready?" she finally asked Nikki.

"I will be." *I have to be. Wade will not best me on this one.*

"Okay," Audrey said. She turned to Mia. "Does London have the painting ready?"

"I believe so. She just needs to work out the frame."

Audrey nodded and continued, "I've looked through everything the camera has captured and the good news is, the only time the dogs are upstairs is when Mrs. Ingram takes them with her. She treats the guard dogs like her little babies."

"Vicious babies with sharp teeth," Nikki muttered.

"My point is, as long as Mrs. Ingram is out with her husband, the dogs will be downstairs."

"What if they hear me upstairs? Isn't that going to make them come running?"

"I really don't think so. That's why they have motion detectors in the hall and in the office. If the dogs had the run of the house when no one was home, they'd trip the alarm all the time."

"Unless they don't use those motion detectors."

Audrey sent her a look with one raised eyebrow. "I've been watching them log in and out of the system. They don't bypass anything. Fully armed when they're away and when they're in bed. Keypad in the master bedroom and in the foyer."

Nikki snickered because Audrey said *fo-yay* simply because it irritated her every time Mia used the word. Audrey gave her a sly smile. She'd missed having someone to share inside jokes with.

"I still need to deal with the animals. Can we get something to drug them? Some laced treats or something?" She looked around the room, and no one answered. "Seriously? None of you have any ideas?"

Audrey shrugged. "I can go to the store and buy regular treats. If you give them a treat, they probably won't attack. Plus, you can throw them and the dogs will run away."

"What if I give them human drugs? Like some Xanax or something. You got any of that, Mia? I don't want to kill them, but I don't want to take any chances either."

Mia's face pinched. "Sorry, no, I'm not your drug dealer."

Audrey tapped away at her computer. "Xanax isn't a good choice. It takes like thirty minutes to kick in and has some horrible side effects."

Nikki groaned. "Regular treats it is, I guess." She quickly scanned her memory in an effort to recall any vets she might've dated at some point. Someone who could give her doggie sedatives. She came up empty. "Do we know when we can go in? When is the house empty?"

"That's a totally different hurdle," Audrey said. "Although their kids are adults, they're always showing up at the house. They have people coming over all the time."

Nikki looked at Mia. "Any big social event that will get everyone out?"

"I can't do much about the children, but…" Mia spoke as she scrolled through her phone, tapping away. "I just sent the Ingrams an invitation to a private event at the museum. Mrs. Ingram loves the arts."

"When is it?"

"The day after tomorrow."

"You think they'll go?"

"Most likely. It's a small event by special invitation. Only the biggest donors are coming. They'll be lured by the thought of being considered among the most generous people in the city."

"Then I have work to do. Can you have London bring the painting here so I can get it ready?" Nikki looked at Audrey. "Kiss your boyfriend goodbye. You need to help me plan this."

"We're all on the same team," Jared said.

"Yeah, but all the kissy-face action is distracting. This whole job is a mess. You go deal with your buyer. We can't have this thing sitting around any longer than necessary or Wade might get the same idea Mia just had."

"I'll call the Ingrams and make sure they understand the importance of the invitation," Mia offered as she picked up her purse.

Jared grumbled but gave Audrey a lingering kiss and then he left with his cousin.

When they were both gone, Audrey asked, "Are we really that distracting?"

"No. I just needed them gone." She debated coming clean to Audrey. The woman had had her back for weeks, through all of the heists they'd done for Mia. Would having knowledge of Nikki's relationship with Wade change how they approached this?

Ultimately, it shouldn't. But it might make Audrey feel sorry for her and that was something Nikki didn't want. So for now, work as usual. "Let's figure out how I'm getting in."

WADE WENT TO the office and picked up the information on Ingram that Boone had gotten for him. Then he went home to plan. He didn't want to leave evidence that would connect the heist to the office. Since Nikki refused to walk away from the job, he knew he'd have to move fast. She'd move up any timetable she had just to beat him. Part of him wanted to let her. But another part of him wanted her—and Dodger—to know that he was every bit the thief she was.

On his visit the night of the party, he'd gotten the specs on the alarm system and he was friendly with Max Ingram by way of his son Brad—whom Nikki had been falling all over at the party. His biggest problem was that he didn't have time to run a full con. Doing so would make his life easier. He could get Ingram to give him access to the house. Nikki preferred to break in, so he'd have to do the same.

Unless he could get Brad to invite him over when his parents weren't around. The house had a pool. Maybe he could suggest an impromptu pool party. Brad was a grown man who still used his parents' house as if he lived there. If enough people were wandering around, he'd have the coverage he'd need to get the painting.

And Brad loved to be surrounded by pretty women, as evidenced by him leading Nikki upstairs. Wade scrolled through his phone looking for women he could invite. He found a picture of him and Sasha and Amy hanging out at a bar. He'd met Sasha and Amy while running a con a long time ago and they were always up for a party. Of course, it helped that they were hot and they knew him as Walter. He texted Brad.

Some friends are looking to hang out this weekend, but it's gonna be a scorcher.

It only took a few moments for Brad to respond. My parents have a pool. I bet your friends look good in bikinis. Party time!

Saturday work for you?

Sounds good.

Shouldn't you check with your parents?

They won't care. Plus, they're probably going out.

Okay. See you then. I'll bring friends.

Brad sent a string of emojis related to drinking and girls like he was still seventeen and throwing a house party. Wade was counting on that working to his advantage. Now he just needed to figure out how to get the painting out without being noticed.

As he planned what he'd need to bring with him and studied the pictures he had of Ingram's house, his mind kept going back to Nikki. Even as standoffish as she'd been, he'd seen hints of the woman he'd loved for years. Lord, how he'd missed her. He'd been able to shove those feelings down, but seeing her face-to-face brought it all back.

Once this job was done, maybe they could spend time together.

He shook his head. "Sure. If you get the painting and show her up, she's gonna want to go on a date."

Flynn looked up from his spot at Wade's feet. Wade bent and scratched the dog's ears. "No worries. I'm just talking some sense into myself. It's a no-win situation. If she gets the painting, something bad will happen to Dodger and that would hurt her, even if she'd never admit it."

Maybe he should come clean and tell her why he needed the painting. He didn't *have* to prove himself on this job. But what if she really didn't care anymore? He'd be in the same spot he was now.

He needed some air to flush Nikki from his thoughts, so he might as well get some recon in.

"Come on, Flynn. Time for a ride." Wade grabbed his car keys and Flynn waddled next to him.

He and Flynn drove back to the far north suburbs to Ingram's neighborhood to scout. He parked his truck and hooked a leash to Flynn—not that Flynn ever tried to run away—and tucked his drone under his arm. He wanted confirmation of the location of the painting in Ingram's house.

They walked past Ingram's property and Wade looked up at the windows. After turning the corner, he set up his drone, turning on the light and camera and let it fly up to the house. No lights were on in the second floor, so he guided the ship to the first window. The curtains were pulled closed, so he had no idea what room it was. He moved to the next window and tried to see past the shadows. All he saw were bookshelves. Bingo. Looked like an office.

Then he angled the drone to face the other wall and there it was. The Devereaux painting was in an ugly gold frame hanging behind Ingram's desk. Boone had been right. He flew the drone around the rest of the house to make sure he hadn't miscounted cameras and then brought it back.

His phone pinged with messages from Sasha and Amy saying they'd love to come to a party. He forwarded Ingram's address. It was nice when a plan came together.

In fact, he was feeling smug enough to text Nikki as he and Flynn walked back to his truck. I have my plan. How about you?

Working on it.

Want to compare notes?

Why would I let you cheat off me? This isn't grade school.

Maybe you'd be the one cheating off me and I'm being generous.

She sent the crying laughing emoji.

He got Flynn settled in the passenger seat and started the engine. Still can't convince you to back off, huh?

Not a chance.

I'd be willing to trade.

What could you possibly have to offer for the Devereaux?

Has it really been so long that you can't remember what I can do for you? He knew he was overreaching, and he wished he could see her face, but he couldn't help himself.

Don't flatter yourself.

Are you implying I'm not good enough?

A long pause, following by the telltale bubbles appearing and disappearing. And again. He had her. She couldn't claim he was bad in bed because it would be an outright lie, but she didn't want to give him an inch either. He was about to give up and go home when she finally responded.

Who's to say you're as good as you once were? Even at your best, I'm not sure you were worth a Devereaux.

Now it was his turn to laugh. If you want to take me for a spin, I'm available. But we both know how well I can drive.

At first, he wrote it as a teasing joke, but once it was sent, he realized that he would go to her if she asked. Even though it would be a mistake. Even though it would ruin his plans.

He would always go to Nikki.

Thankfully, she didn't respond.

SIX

Nikki readied her gear for getting into Ingram's house. Everything felt off. First it was Wade and his silly banter full of invitation. Not that she was tempted. Not really anyway.

Then London had insisted on making some tweaks to the painting, but she neglected to say that the thing might not be dry in time.

And to top it off, she received a text from Brad inviting her to an epic pool party—at his parents' house. Tonight.

"Maybe we should scrap this," Audrey offered.

"We can't. The party is a distraction. Wade is using it to give him access. If I don't go in tonight, he'll get it."

"So then he gets it. What's Mia gonna do if we don't get this one painting? Her dad still loses the money from it. We can go in another day and steal something else."

Nikki didn't know how to explain. Audrey made valid points, but she couldn't walk away. It had nothing to do with Mia. "I have to do this."

"Your call. Are you ready?"

"As I'm gonna get." She took a shot of whiskey to steady her nerves. She normally wouldn't drink before a job, but with this mess, it was a wonder she wasn't getting blitzed.

"Do you have the dog treats for Zeus and Apollo?"

Nikki checked her bag. "Got it."

The idea of feeding those beasts had the whiskey in her stomach sloshing. *I can do this. Audrey said the dogs are never upstairs when Mrs. Ingram isn't home.*

She picked up the painting and inspected it to make sure it was dry. Then she slid it into the canvas bag she'd use for transport. Her tools settled comfortably in her belt at her waist. She was antsy waiting for the sun to set. Her original plan had been to go in while the Ingrams were with Mia. Now that there was a party, she preferred to have darkness to help keep her hidden.

"Come on," Audrey said. "London should be here with the van."

"You know, London wouldn't have to do that if you just drove."

The other woman chuckled. "Trust me. You don't want me to drive."

"It's gonna feel weird doing a job without Mia or Jared in my ear." For the first time, it seemed as if Mia was trusting them to run the job without being baby-sat. Mia was doing her thing at the museum and she was probably more focused on work, but Nikki would like to believe Mia trusted them.

"I think it'll be freeing," Audrey responded.

"You mean having lover boy in your head isn't fun?"

"I was thinking about you and how often they piss you off."

She had a point. Every time Mia and Jared were on the comms, they constantly butted in, wanting a blow-by-blow description of events.

When they got downstairs, London was idling at the

curb in the same van they'd been using for jobs when necessary.

"Have you taken possession of this thing?" Nikki asked as she climbed in the back.

"It only makes sense. I have a place to park it off the street and I'm the only one who drives it. Where to?"

"Ingram's house."

"No. I mean for food."

"I'm fine." She angled the bag beside her, taking up the space behind London, and leaned back in the seat.

London put the van in drive, but stopped. "What do you mean, you're fine? You're always hungry. You want to hit a drive-thru every chance you get."

"I guess I could eat. You pick." In truth, she wasn't hungry, but she didn't want to have to explain.

"It'll be fine. You can probably walk right in the house since Brad is having a party. That saves you a trip up a wall to climb in," Audrey said.

"It also puts me in a position to have to dodge dogs."

"What's your problem with dogs anyway?" London asked.

"I was bitten a long time ago. It was supposedly a friendly dog. It wasn't." She'd been so mad at Dodger for the lie. He kept saying that he was sure it was a friendly dog. As long as she talked nicely to it, it would lie down and she'd be able to do the job. Instead, it bit her thigh and wouldn't let go until Wade smacked it. "And these dogs aren't supposed to be friendly. Their sole purpose is to be vicious."

London hit a drive-thru and handed her a hot dog. After the first couple of bites, Nikki realized it settled her stomach.

Treat it like any other job.

By the time they arrived near Ingram's house, Nikki was more herself. They drove down the block and noted the slew of cars already lining the driveway. Nikki leaned over Audrey and pressed the button to roll down the window.

"Hey." Audrey shoved at her. "You could've just asked. I would've rolled it down for you. I didn't need a face full of your boobs."

"I have luscious boobs. You should feel lucky," Nikki said as she continued to lean out of her seat to hear out the window.

"Dude!"

"Shh! I want to hear how rowdy the party is."

Squeals and voices could be heard from the street. That's all she needed. "Okay, girls, let me out and go find a place to park."

She opened the door and grabbed the handle of the bag as she got out. As she stepped in the shadows of the bushes and trees on the beautifully manicured front lawn, the van pulled away. Sticking to the edge of the property, she checked out her options. She waited on the fringes as another car pulled in. Two tall women stepped out and walked around the house instead of going to the front door.

That answered one question. Of course she wouldn't be lucky enough to be able to walk in the front door. She went to the side of the house below Ingram's office, tucked safely behind a row of bushes. From her bag, she pulled her rope and grappling hook and tied the rope to the bag. After a quick look around, she shot the hook up until she had it settled on the roof.

Then she took off her black T-shirt, revealing her sports bra, and let her hair down so she would blend in more with the guests. She also removed her tool-belt and shoved it behind the painting in the bag on the ground. She wandered to the back of the house, scooped up someone's drink on the way, smiled at a few women—they far outnumbered the men as far as she could see—and kept walking until she was through the kitchen door.

As she stepped into the kitchen, a woman left carrying a tray of Jell-O shots. Nikki waited until the door closed behind her. She set the drink on the counter and glanced around. A hastily made sign with an arrow pointing to the bathroom was hung on the wall. Liquor bottles lined the counter. A blender that desperately needed to be cleaned appeared to have some leftover margarita in it.

No one else was around, so she tried the knob of the door she hoped led to the upstairs. It wasn't locked. Silly Brad. She slunk up the stairs, sticking close to the wall, so she could feign intoxication if need be. At the top of the stairs, another door, also unlocked. She eased it open. She was at the opposite end of the hall from where she'd come up with Brad.

She made it halfway down the hall toward Ingram's office when she heard the growl.

The treats were in the bag below the office.

How could she be so stupid to leave those? She could improvise a lot of things on a job, but a dog treat wasn't one of them.

In her ear, Audrey said, "Everything okay?"

Nikki froze, afraid to even inhale because she had

no idea where the dogs were. Audrey said the dogs were kept downstairs unless the wife was home. Sweat pricked her hairline. A slow deep inhale and she forced her feet to move. From around the corner came the two black beasts.

She swallowed the yelp and jumped into the nearest room, which unfortunately wasn't Ingram's office. A spare bedroom. She closed the door and leaned her forehead against it. Blood rushed through her body, and her heart thundered in her ears. Her mouth hung open as she gulped air.

"Nikki. Are you okay? Talk to me." Audrey's voice in her ear kept her conscious.

Movement behind her pulled her attention, but she couldn't focus enough to put on an act. She couldn't even make herself turn around.

"Figures you'd choose tonight."

Wade.

Swallowing hard, she turned to face him, while still leaning against the door. It might've been the only thing to keep her upright.

"What? No snarky comment?" he said and then paused, studying her. "Are you okay? What's wrong?"

"The dogs are outside."

"Okay."

In her ear, "I know you can't talk to me now, but give me a sign if you want me to come in."

"No." She hoped Audrey got the message. "I mean, the dogs are outside this door. Right now."

"Oh." He neared, and she was able to make him out in the moonlight. He wore a hideous Hawaiian shirt and long shorts. Maybe they were trunks. He looked utterly ridiculous.

Reaching up, he smoothed her hair back from her face where it was sticky with sweat. She wanted to knock his hand away, but the contact was soothing.

"You're really freaked out."

"Dogs," she pushed out.

As if on cue, the animals snarled and barked on the other side of the door and she sank to the floor. Putting her arms across her raised knees, she laid her forehead down. *Calm down. Get a plan. Wade being here doesn't change that.*

"What can I do to help?"

"Nothing."

He walked away and she heard water in the bathroom. When he came back, he sat beside her. He pushed her hair to the side and placed a cool washcloth on her neck. "I didn't realize they still terrified you."

"Yeah, well." She didn't have anything else.

The growling subsided, and she imagined them lying in wait to attack as soon as she opened the door. Her heart rate kicked up and her mind filled with images of their vicious pointy teeth sinking into her flesh.

Wade's hand landed on her back and moved in small circles. She closed her eyes and willed herself to relax.

"If I distract them, can you get out?"

She turned her face without lifting it. "Why would you do that?"

He sighed and broke contact. "No matter what went down between us, I still care about you. I never stopped."

Even though he didn't continue, she heard the words. *I never stopped loving you.*

In the quiet room, the truth was plain on his face, in his eyes. He'd grown into a good liar, but when it came to her, his eyes always betrayed him. She raised her head and carefully plucked the comm from her ear so Audrey wouldn't hear anything else incriminating before looking at him fully.

"I've missed you," she whispered, hating her honesty in this moment of weakness in the dark.

"All I had to do was scare you to get you to admit that? I wish I'd known. I would've done it a long time ago."

"Funny."

"I've missed you, too. It's not the same without a partner."

"You have Dodger."

He scoffed. At the same time, they both said, "Not *we*."

They chuckled quietly because they always joked that every time Dodger wanted something done, it was always, "*We* have to do this. *We* have to get that done." But Dodger was never part of the *we*.

Silence settled over them. Sounds from the party below seeped through the window. Nikki gestured to the window. "Pretty good plan to get access."

"It was supposed to give *me* access. Not you."

"I wasn't going to walk in. I was ready to climb through a window, but you made it easy."

"Feel better?" he asked.

"I guess. What do we do now?"

He stood up and held a hand out to help her. She hesitated because she knew the feel of that hand, the warmth it would give her, the connection she'd pretended to forget. Gripping his hand, she let him pull her to standing.

He pulled so hard, she crashed into his chest, and she was suddenly aware of how little she wore on top. His hands settled on her bare lower back, right on the curve of her hip, to steady her. They stood nose to nose, hip to hip, chest to chest. He pressed her closer, just a flex of his fingers on her skin, and his mouth was on hers.

Time both stopped and moved in reverse. The familiarity provided comfort. Their lips moved and opened, tongues tangled and in seconds, Nikki was breathing hard again for a totally different reason.

A loud scream and splash from outside brought Nikki back to the present, and she backed away from Wade. They both licked their lips as if to remember the taste of each other.

"If I distract them, you're okay to get out?"

Nikki nodded.

"Okay then."

"Aren't you afraid they'll attack you?"

He reached into his pocket and pulled out dog treats. "I stopped in the kitchen and grabbed some of their favorites. I'll get them downstairs so you can move."

Wade reached for the doorknob and she touched his arm. "Thank you."

He winked. "No big deal."

A moment later she heard Wade making a ruckus down the hall and the clicking of dogs' nails on the stairs. She slid from the bedroom and hustled across the hall to the office, stopping to grab the mini-cam she'd attached to the motion sensor. She figured she had about five minutes before Wade came back looking for the painting. After she quietly closed and locked the office door—something she normally wouldn't waste precious moments on—she hauled her bag up from outside and pulled out the forgery.

Using her mini drill, she unscrewed the frame from the hinge. The whirring of the drill was quiet, but her heart raced at the thought that the dogs would hear and come running. A fresh line of sweat slithered down the center of her back. She carefully set the used screws on the ledge in front of the safe. As she attached the forgery, grateful that she'd had the foresight to predrill holes in the one London did, she silently counted the seconds she had until Wade reappeared. If he showed up now, could she stop him from taking the Devereaux from her? Luckily, she was done in three minutes. She stuck her head out the window to look for wandering guests, but all she heard was the noise from the party out back. She grabbed the rope and was rappelling down the side of the house before Wade or anyone else came around.

Once she was on the ground, she knelt behind the bushes in the cover of darkness and wrapped the painting better before putting it back in the bag. She replaced the comm in her ear and pressed the button. "Ready for extraction. Got the prize."

She listened as a couple slammed car doors and laughed. She waited, willing them to move faster, until they turned the corner. She stood and crept along the side of the house, sticking to the shadows before taking off in a dead run across the yard. She got to the sidewalk just as London pulled up. She jumped in and settled in the back seat.

"How did you pull that off? Your comm went silent and I thought for sure you were busted," Audrey said.

Guilt stabbed at her. She'd been able to pull it off because Wade rescued her. "Don't worry about it. All that matters is that it's done."

London chattered as she drove down the street filling in answers for her own questions. Nikki didn't have anything to say. Some master thief she was. Without Wade, the whole thing would've been a bust. Now, he had nothing to show for his work. His kindness had cost him.

"COME ON, BOYS. I only have one treat left for each of you." Wade tossed the treats into the pantry and the dogs followed. He closed the door and hoped nothing in there would poison the dogs. He turned to go back to Nikki, but Sasha came in through the back door.

"Walter! Where have you been? I've been looking all over for you."

"Hey, Sasha. Why don't you grab us a couple of drinks and I'll meet you out by the pool. I just have to go make a quick call. It's a work thing."

"Pooh. It's the weekend. Work can wait."

"Five minutes. I promise."

She stomped a foot and stuck out her bottom lip. "Fine." She wagged a finger at him. "But I'm holding you to that. Tick tock."

He waited for her to head back outside, then he stalked back upstairs to find the painting. And Nikki, if she was still there. But the bedroom door was wide open, so she was gone. It had been lucky for her that he'd gotten distracted and turned around when he got upstairs and ended up in the wrong room. If he had gone straight to the office, he'd already be on his way back to Dodger with the painting.

But then he wouldn't have had Nikki in his arms. He wouldn't have kissed her.

He moved across the hall to the office. His stomach flipped. He'd taken care of Nikki and part of him hoped that she was so freaked out that she just abandoned the painting. But he knew Nikki. She always finished the job. He turned the knob on the office door. Locked. He pulled out his lock pick kit and popped the lock. He opened the door slowly and peered in.

"Well, I'll be. She left it." The painting, in all its ugly glory was still hanging on the wall.

He reached to pull it off and it swung. Dodger never did his job right. How did he fail to get a vital piece of information like the painting covered a safe?

But at least this wasn't as bad as the last job he'd done with Nikki. The one that he was sure made her leave and never look back.

Dodger had cased the house and planned everything. He was supposed to have been sitting on it, but as usual, he'd gone off and disappeared, probably to get drunk. Wade and Nikki had forged ahead like they always had. They excelled at thinking on their feet, so they could work around most of Dodger's screw-ups.

They hadn't accounted for the homeowner being there. He was supposed to be gone. Dodger had told them the old man had left. Dodger had also never said anything about a gun.

As Nikki had picked the lock on the door, Wade

pointed at the sticker on the window: *This house is protected by Smith & Wesson.*

"A lot of people put those up just to scare burglars away. Plus, he's not home." The door swung open. "Let's go."

They stepped into the kitchen, which reeked of cigars and garlic. Wade took shallow breaths through his mouth so he wouldn't have to smell it.

His gut churned, and not from the stench. Something didn't feel right. The background they had on this guy said if he put up a sticker like that, there was truth behind it. But he let Nikki lead the way. The old man had piles of cash in his home safe, which was where Nikki moved to. Wade, on the other hand, checked other hiding spots, like the freezer. Sure enough, he found a stack of cash wrapped in foil sitting next to the ice cream.

He turned to go find Nikki so she could help him look in the cabinets for phony cans and came face-to-face with a gun.

The old man stood in his pajamas, barefoot, with a revolver trained on Wade's chest. Wade dropped the frozen money and raised his hands. "Whoa."

"What do you think you're doing?" the man asked.

"Let's not get hasty. How about I just leave and never bother you again?" His heart raced and he hoped Nikki had enough sense to go out the front door. No use in both of them dying today.

"I'm callin' the cops." As the man took a step back, a bottle of wine came down on him from behind.

The man crumpled to the floor, the gun clunking against the tile.

"What are you still doing here?" Wade asked Nikki, not worrying about being quiet any longer.

"Like I'm going to leave you to get shot?"

He understood. He never would've left her either. They stood over the body for a minute. The man was still breathing. "Did you draw blood?"

Nikki shrugged.

"We should call an ambulance or something."

"The guy threatened you with a gun, but you're worried about a bump on his head?"

"He's old. A concussion might do him in. That's felony murder if we get picked up."

"We don't get picked up. But fine." She tossed a bag at him. It was filled with cash. Then she reached over the old phone hanging on the wall and dialed nine-one-one.

"Hey, there's a man on the floor. He's hurt." Then she left the phone on the counter. Without another word, she pointed at the door.

Now, looking at the hinged frame of Ingram's safe, Wade shoved thoughts of Dodger's incompetence out of his head. He didn't have a drill on him, so he didn't have a way to dismantle it. Instead, he went to work on getting the painting out of the frame. It took longer than he liked, but last he'd seen, Brad was sitting in the hot tub with his arms around two women.

Once the painting was free from the frame, he wrapped it in the sack he brought and lowered it out the window to be picked up after he said his goodbyes. He locked up the window and closed the office again. Time for Walter to disappear from the Ingrams' lives.

He'd make sure the stupid Devereaux landed in the

right hands to get Dodger out of trouble and then he was done. No more cleaning up after Dodger. He could go back to his company and have a life of his own.

Maybe he could even give Nikki a call.

He should've known better than to think things would work the way he wanted.

BACK AT THE APARTMENT, London went straight to the kitchen and grabbed the bottle of champagne for their post-heist ritual. How quickly these women had become part of her tradition, her celebration. Popping the cork, London said, "Here's to another creep getting his due."

Nikki wasn't feeling all that celebratory. Even though she had gotten away with the painting, for her this job had been a failure. If not for Wade, she'd still be sitting in the guest room waiting for someone to get the dogs to move.

Or she'd be lying mauled in the hallway, her blood pooling on the carpet.

She set the painting on the table below the TV but she couldn't look at it. "I'm going to shower."

"Wait," London called. "Aren't you going to have a drink?"

"Later," she answered with a shake of her head and went to the bathroom. After turning the water on scalding, full jets, she stripped and avoided looking in the mirror, sure she'd be uneasy with what she saw.

Under the hot spray, a multitude of emotions bombarded her: anger that she couldn't handle the job alone, embarrassment that Wade had to rescue her, guilt that she got the painting he was after, but worst, desire to be near Wade again. She leaned her forearms against the cool stone of the shower stall and lowered her head to allow the water to beat on her shoulders and cascade down her back. She'd convinced herself that she was over him. They'd been young and in love, but it hadn't been meant to last.

That was Dodger's fault, the little voice in her head sneered. Dodger hadn't wanted them to be together.

It didn't matter. It was over and done.

But the kiss…

The kiss wouldn't hold any weight once he realized she'd taken the Devereaux.

She stood under the water until her skin was pink and pruney and the thoughts circled so many times through her head that she was dizzy.

By the time she got back to the living room, London was gone and Audrey sat on the couch, champagne flute in hand, staring at the painting.

"About time," she said without turning around.

Nikki came around the couch and sank into the cushions.

Audrey pointed to the other glass of champagne. "London was going to wait to drink with us, but she had somewhere to be." She took a sip and waited for Nikki to pick up her glass. When Nikki didn't move, she said, "Okay, spill."

"Spill what?"

"What's going on? This fancy champagne? It's your ritual. From what I can tell, it's your way of congratulating yourself for a job well done. What gives?"

This hadn't been a job well done. This was a disaster.

"Nothing. It was just a tough job."

"We knew that going in. We've had tough ones before. This isn't like you." Audrey stretched out and picked up the other glass to hand to Nikki. "No matter how bad it is, you did it. You got the painting."

She took a drink to appease Audrey, but the bubbles burned her throat, reminding her that she only got the painting because of Wade. *He's going to hate me now because I took that ugly thing.*

"What happened with Wade in the bedroom when your comm went dead?"

"Nothing. I took out the comm to stay focused. It's hard to concentrate when I've got you panicking in my ear. I couldn't afford the distraction."

"So sorry to worry about you."

More guilt pricked at Nikki. She was lashing out at Audrey, who didn't deserve it.

"What happened with Wade? How'd you get around the dogs? I mean, come on. The two of you were in a room together, both vying for the same object. Did you knock him out so you could steal the painting? Or did you distract him with your feminine wiles?"

Nikki snort-laughed. "While my feminine wiles have felled many men, Wade—" She stopped because she suddenly had no idea how to finish the thought. "I don't think I'm enough of a distraction for him."

"Then there's something wrong with him. You're enough of a distraction for me, and I've got a man of my own."

This time, they both laughed, and Nikki realized that Audrey was doing her best to cheer her up and figure out what was wrong.

"For real now. How'd you get the painting? This story has all the makings of a great story." She switched to talking in a theatrical voice, like a movie trailer voiceover. "Two thieves. After the same painting. Guard dogs on their heels. Who will win?"

"Hmm… I've always thought my life would make a good movie. Maybe you've found your calling for when we're done with all this."

"Yeah, I don't think so. Are you going to tell me?"

"Tell you what?"

"How you got the painting before Wade."

Nikki curled her legs up on the couch and turned to face Audrey. She debated telling the truth. Lies could slip easily from her mouth, but Audrey would understand. "He distracted the dogs so I could get out. I slipped across the hall and took the painting."

"Wow." Audrey's eyes were wide. "But—" She paused again. "Oh man. You guys had a thing, didn't you?"

Nikki nodded.

"Do you still?"

"No. Not really." She didn't know what they were anymore. "We have a past. There's still some chemistry there."

Audrey curled up, mirroring Nikki's pose. "Tell me the whole story. Where did you meet? Were you in love? How did it end? Why didn't you tell us sooner?"

She didn't know how much to tell Audrey. It wasn't that Audrey would tell anyone, not that it would matter if she did, but Nikki hadn't told anyone about Wade and Dodger since she'd left them. "My father took him in to mentor him in becoming a thief."

"So he's like your brother?"

"Eww! God no. We were eighteen when we met. He just sucked at stealing, but my father saw potential."

"Hmm. I was under the impression that you grew up alone and that's how you got here. But your dad taught you how to be a thief?"

"Yeah. He was really good at one time."

"What happened?"

"I got tired of supporting his gambling habit. I wanted out. I knew I could strike out on my own."

"What about Wade?"

"He chose my father." Verbalizing her history and the hurt that came with it was easier to say than she'd thought it would be.

That last job for Dodger was the biggest screw-up she'd ever seen. Dodger hadn't waited to make sure the house was empty and he sure didn't say anything about the man owning a gun.

She and Wade had made it out okay, but she was done. In the car on the way back to the apartment, she'd pulled out two bundles of bills and tucked them in her pants. "We leave tonight."

"What?" Wade swerved the car at her announcement.

"We've been talking about it forever. Tonight just proves that he doesn't care what happens to us."

"I'm sure it was a mistake. Everyone makes them. Dodger would never deliberately put us in any real danger."

"Of course it's not intentional. That would require him to pay attention to someone other than himself. I'm done taking risks for him." She twisted in her seat to fully face him. "Why aren't you more pissed off? You could be dead right now." She swallowed the fear and blinked back tears.

He gave her the easy smile that she loved so much. She'd never get enough of that smile. "But I'm not."

"Because I hit the old man over the head. We don't attack people. That's not who we are. We think, we plan, we execute. We don't mess up." She released a deep breath. "I'm dumping this cash in Dodger's lap, I'm packing a bag, and then I'm hitting the road."

Wade said nothing in return, which was her first sign. Dodger was passed out when they got home. Wade said they should wake him. She didn't care, and when she had her bag packed, Wade wasn't around.

Dodger was sitting on the couch, and he pointed at her bag. "Where you going?"

"I'm done with you and your half-planned jobs."

"Where are you gonna go?"

"I'll find someplace and I'll plan my own jobs."

The man had the nerve to laugh at her. As if she couldn't do it.

Her anger doubled. "You don't get it. I don't need you, old man. Every job you run is a mess. Wade and I run around cleaning up after you. I'm done."

Dodger stared at her with wide, bloodshot eyes. A flicker of some emotion raced across his features, but didn't last long enough for her to identify. She waited for a couple breaths. Waited for him to say something. To apologize. To ask her to stay. To tell her she mattered.

But he said nothing.

She stormed out and went to the beach to wait for Wade, assuming he'd huff around and then pack a bag and join her. What she got was a text.

Please come home.

Those three words were so much more devastating than Dodger's laughter followed by his silence. That message was peak betrayal. He'd chosen Dodger over her.

She'd known then that she was on her own.

"That sucks," Audrey said.

"Yep."

"Yet he distracted the dogs so you could get the painting and get away."

Nikki didn't respond. She still hadn't wrapped her head around that. If roles were reversed, she wasn't sure that she would've done the same for him.

Liar.

One of these days, she was going to learn how to silence that annoying little voice in her head.

SEVEN

Mia

MIA LOOKED AT the screen on her phone. She'd been hoping to hear from Jared about the sale of the Devereaux. *Mom?*

"Hi, Mama. What's wrong?" It was unlike her mother to call in the middle of the day. Beverly Washington respected her daughter's job and never felt the need to interrupt. Anything she needed could wait until evening.

"That's a fine way to greet your mother."

"You never call me at work."

"I'm calling because I'm worried. I just heard from both Miriam and Celeste that there has been a theft at Max Ingram's house. His most valuable painting has been stolen."

Mia's heart stuttered. Damn Nikki. They had a plan. They'd paid London to create a near-perfect forgery. All she had to do was follow the plan. Mia swallowed. "Oh, really?"

"Yes. It seems Bradley had a party at the house last night while his parents were at the gala at the museum with you. Did you see them there?"

"I had a nice chat with Mrs. Ingram, in fact. She said she was trying to convince Max to buy her a Dali."

"Dali? That would never go with her décor."

"So you called to tell me society gossip?"

"This is more than gossip. If someone is brazen enough to walk out of a party with a painting, I think we all need to be vigilant. Especially after what you told me about Randall Scott's painting. And who's to say that you're safe at work, surrounded by all the art?"

Mia chuckled. "Mama, I'm fine. No one is going to run into the museum to steal art. Anyone looking to go after art is more likely to steal from an individual collector. A house is much easier to break into than a museum."

Plus, I know the thief.

"I still worry about you."

"Thank you. But I'm fine."

"All right, then. See you for dinner this week?"

"Of course." Dinner with her mother had become a standing date every Tuesday. It was something they'd both learned to count on since her father's indictment. A quiet meal, just the two of them. At first, it had been a way for her to check in on her mother, make sure she was okay. Then it became a way for her mother to keep tabs on her love life, urging her to get on with her life.

Of course, she never let Beverly know that the shadow cast on her because of her father still had an effect. Bad men wanted her father's connections. Good men completely steered clear because she was tainted.

"See you then," her mother said and then disconnected.

Mia didn't even put her phone down. She immediately called Jared. "We have a problem," she said as soon as he answered.

"Hello to you, too."

"Mom just called to tell me there was a theft at the Ingram house."

"And?"

"Do I have to spell it out? What did Nikki do?"

"Look, we know someone else was after the painting. Obviously, he took it."

"But we have the original, right?"

"I don't see why we wouldn't. Nikki didn't say anything about problems."

"Would she?" Mia had doubts about Nikki's loyalty to their plan. As long as she was getting paid, Nikki didn't care.

"The painting is at the apartment. Go check it out."

"I will. When are you supposed to get it to the buyer?"

"Negotiations are done. I plan to ship it out tomorrow. Unless you tell me it's no good. But realistically, Nikki's not dumb. She wouldn't bring the forgery back to us."

Jared was right. Their plan was good. Unfortunately, this theft was going to bring attention to Ingram and if anyone—such as Logan the insurance man—put two and two together, the rest of their plan might go up in smoke.

And Logan was the type of man who would connect the dots. Mia thought about her dance with Logan and the conversation that followed. He worked for the company that insured both Scott's and Ingram's paintings. However, he had no reason to suspect that Scott's forgery had been a theft and that it was connected to Ingram's.

To set her mind at ease, she needed to check the Devereaux.

The faster they got rid of the painting, the better off they would be. Then they could focus on the next theft.

EIGHT

Two days and fifty written and deleted texts later, Wade sat in his office, with Flynn at his feet, trying to figure out an appropriate way to reach out to Nikki. It had been so good to be near her, to talk to her, to kiss her, that he wanted more. But she'd be pissed that she let her fear of dogs prevent her from getting the Devereaux. She'd never been a good loser.

After safely getting away from Ingram's, he'd nearly texted a picture of the painting but that would've only ensured that she'd never speak to him again. So he'd toyed with various wording to tell her that he wanted to be in her life again, but nothing was quite right.

Suddenly his office door flew open and Dodger plowed through, carrying the Devereaux, or at least what was left of the painting as it was practically shredded in his hands. The old man had new bruises on his face.

"What do you think you're playing at, boy?" His voice was raspy and his outburst ended in a fit of coughing.

"What are you talking about? And what did you do to the painting? I thought you delivered it." He rose and took the shredded canvas.

Dodger sank onto the couch. After a few deep breaths, he said, "Did you think they wouldn't get it authenticated? They're not stupid."

"What are you talking about?" he repeated.

"It's a forgery."

"What?" Wade touched the canvas pieces and laid them back in place as best he could. The slash marks cut across the painted breasts violently. It was off. He could see it now. The paint was a little too bright, a little too soft. His brain scanned for a reason. "Maybe Ingram—"

"No. I tried that." Dodger pointed to his newly blackened eye. "They informed me that the real painting had been there. Figured I was trying to scam them. Please tell me you thought that would pass and you have the original."

"I can't believe—" He stopped himself this time. He couldn't let Dodger know Nikki had been involved. Pride warred with anger and embarrassment. Nikki had finished the job, as he'd thought she would have. But now he was pissed and embarrassed that he hadn't considered she'd replace the original with a forgery. It wasn't like her.

Replacing what she stole with a forgery meant no one would know. She'd miss the thrill. She liked the mark knowing he'd lost a possession.

"I knew I should've hunted Nikki down. She would've gotten this right."

Wade scoffed. Of course Nikki would've gotten it right. She *had gotten* it right. Wade bit his tongue. Dodger didn't need the reminder that Nikki had left and probably wouldn't help him.

"Well? Any ideas?"

"Yeah," Wade said, still staring at the ruined painting. "I don't suppose they would take another painting instead, huh?"

"Of course not. They think we tried to play them. They think I have the original."

"What if we explain that we don't. That someone else made a switch. Would they take something else in its place?"

"I doubt it. And now's not the time to ask. Donny is still real pissed."

Donny Harbridge was a pain. He continuously let Dodger place bets and rack up a huge bill. No matter how many times Wade had told him to stop doing business with Dodger, he wouldn't listen. Dodger was always good for it one way or another.

"If I can't figure out where the real Devereaux is, I'll talk to Donny. You lay low." Wade pulled a couple hundred dollars from his safe and handed it to Dodger. "Go stay with a friend. I'll let you know when things are settled."

"I ain't goin' far with this."

"You don't need to go far. Crash with a friend. Use that to feed yourself. Stay away from betting. Don't draw attention to yourself. Can you manage that?"

"Yeah. I'm not an idiot. Donny's not gonna kill me. He makes too much off me."

"Sure. You keep telling yourself that. At some point everyone loses patience."

Dodger stood with a groan and hobbled out the door. Wade pulled the shreds of canvas free from the frame and bunched them up to throw out. Sitting back at his desk, phone in hand, he suddenly knew exactly what to say to Nikki.

I need to talk to you. It's urgent.

The bubbles appeared and disappeared. Then again. He gained a little satisfaction imagining her sitting there stressing over what to say just like he had. But then it was just a simple line:

When and where?

He sent her the address of the bar next door with a message to meet in an hour. It would give him enough time to walk Flynn and take him home before meeting her. Hopefully by then, he could figure out the best approach to get her to hand over the painting.

He called Flynn to follow him out the door.

Maybe if he offered her cash. Although she loved the thrill of a heist, she loved money, too. Of course, if she was getting what the Devereaux was actually worth, he couldn't match that. Then he considered offering her another painting. He could come out of retirement to help her on a big job. Something she wouldn't normally take on herself because it was too much for one person.

She was definitely a safer bet for coming out of retirement than doing something for Dodger.

After a quick walk with Flynn, Wade freshened up. Looking good for Nikki couldn't hurt either. She liked his charm, and the attraction still simmered between them. Given time, it would definitely boil. He'd take every advantage he could get.

Wade drove back to the office and headed to the bar. The summer sun was low in the sky and for a change, the weather was warm without being stifling. He stood outside for a few minutes and breathed deeply. He hated this feeling of uncertainty.

He went into the bar and looked around. He was still a few minutes early, but he wouldn't put it past Nikki to be there. No sign of her, so he grabbed a couple beers and sat at a table facing the door. He had his beer half finished when she walked in.

Without effort, her gaze met his. No searching. It was as if she knew where he'd be. Her hair was down, full makeup, and another shimmery top and short skirt. Full armor again. She was not going to give him an inch.

She slid into the chair across from him and picked up the bottle. She chugged a bit and then set it back down, condensation dripping down the sides.

"So," she said.

"I need the painting, Nikki."

She snorted.

"I'm serious."

"Don't be a sore loser."

"This isn't about winning or losing."

"Don't fool yourself. It's always about winning." She picked up her beer again and drained the bottle.

Wade watched her every movement. She was nervous. He waved a waitress over and ordered two more bottles.

He debated how much to reveal to her. If he told her about Dodger's debt, would she laugh and walk away or would she offer the painting to get him off the hook?

"All cards on the table. When I saw the painting was still there after you left, I figured you didn't take it."

She snorted again. "You should know better."

"Yeah, I should. Since when do you work with forgeries? You were always about making sure the mark knew how good you are."

"It was a requirement of my client. Unfortunately, you screwed that all up."

"Like you, I was doing my job."

"A job you're retired from."

He offered her a halfhearted smile.

NIKKI STARED AT WADE, waiting for the punch line. When Mia first told her Wade stole the forgery, she'd had a good laugh. Until Mia pointed out that Ingram's house was under a microscope between the cops and the insurance company. And Mia was more than a little mad that Ingram was going to be able to claim the insurance money.

As she stared at Wade, she realized he wasn't joking. Something serious was going on. He looked a little frazzled, instead of his usual cool, charming demeanor.

"All banter aside, I need the painting."

Something in the weight of his words speared through her. "I don't have it. I handed it off to my client and it's been sold."

Wade only answered with a quiet "Fuck."

He drained his first beer and looked everywhere but at her, as if trying to make a decision. Wade didn't get upset over a job. Everything rolled off his back. Nothing ever bothered him.

She reached across the table and covered his hand with hers. "What is it?"

"I have to get that painting." He turned his hand over and held tight to hers.

"What's the big deal? Just tell your client you can't get it." She slid her hand away.

"It has to be that one. Especially now because they

think I was trying to pass a forgery. You could've warned me."

"I thought you left!"

"Why would I leave after luring the dogs away for you?"

The implication was there—she only got the painting because he'd rescued her. The irritation at herself for her stupid fear and the fact that he was lording it over her now bubbled up, but she shoved it down, reminding herself that Wade wouldn't be acting that way without reason. *People change*, the little voice in her head whispered.

"Talk to me, Wade."

"It's Dodger."

"No way." Nikki pressed back in her chair as if that could create enough distance between her and her father.

Wade leaned forward, arms on the table. "No, it's serious this time. Like I've never seen. Donny beat the crap out of him twice. Ruined your really good forgery, too."

"Donny Harbridge?"

Wade nodded.

"Some things never change. Tell Donny to go screw himself."

Wade shook his head. "There's something at play that Dodger isn't saying. What would Donny do with a Devereaux?"

He made an excellent point. Donny Harbridge was a mid-level hustler and bookie, but he had no use for art.

"You have no idea what he's gotten into?"

"I'm not even sure Dodger knows what he's gotten himself into."

"You're still lying to yourself. That man knows exactly what's going on. He's just not telling you." Nikki knew her father. Wade always gave the man more credit than he deserved. Dodger put himself before everyone and everything. It was the single biggest reason she'd left.

"I told him this was the last time, Nikki. I told him I'd get the painting. I can't go back on my word."

You went back on your word to me. You let me go. Alone.

She wanted to yell but knew it wouldn't make a difference. She took a swig of beer to push her heart back into her chest. Clinging to past hurts wasn't going to help here.

"I don't know what to tell you. I don't have it." Another sip. "And in all honesty, now that I know it's for Dodger, I don't know if I would give it to you even if I did."

"What'd you sell it for? Any chance I can buy it back?"

She laughed so hard she almost spewed beer on him. "Since when do you have the kind of money to pay for a Devereaux?"

"It's not like you got full value for it."

"I got paid a flat fee for the job. I worked for a middleman." She couldn't tell him about Mia and company.

"Can you at least tell me who does have it?"

"I don't know. Like I said, middleman." But she could find out. Audrey could access the information.

Dodger wasn't worth risking her newfound team. Was Wade?

They sat in silence, staring at each other. Not in the stubborn way they had years ago when they disagreed. The air was thick with longing and regret and lusty pheromones she'd been sure she'd forgotten.

He did a slow roll of his tongue across his lips. Nikki was fixated on the movement.

She stood abruptly. "Sorry I couldn't be more help. See you around."

"Will you?"

She paused, staring at him, knowing he wanted more from her. "Probably not. It's just something people say, right? To ease the discomfort of letting go."

Wade slid out from his seat and stepped close. "Who says we have to?"

"Have to what?"

"Let go."

"We've been down this road. It didn't work out so well for me."

"Me either."

He brushed his fingers down her arm, sending a thrill through her entire body. She let her eyes close for a moment.

"We both made our choices," she whispered.

"Things change."

Reopening her eyes, she said, "Not really. You're still taking care of Dodger." She placed a hand on his chest. "You haven't figured out he doesn't deserve you."

She stepped away and Wade grabbed her hand. "Don't go."

"What's the point?"

"Can't we just take tonight? Just for us. Pretend that no one else matters."

His offer was so tempting. His thumb stroked her knuckles, and then he tugged her close again. Kissing her temple, he said, "Stay with me tonight."

"It's too complicated. We have our own lives now. Tangling them together isn't smart."

"I think we've established that I do plenty of things that aren't smart. One night."

She swayed toward him, her body answering what her mind wouldn't allow her to admit. "I can't."

"My office is next door. I won't ask questions. I won't follow you. I'll stay out of your life if that's what you want. Just one night." His breath fluttered against her hair. His other arm came around and pulled her to his body. His heart thumped.

They could have the closure their younger selves never got.

She wrapped her arm around his neck and pulled him into a kiss. Their bodies pressed together and the heat of his skin radiated through their clothes and into her system. The planes of his body were familiar yet different. His taste full of comfort. She didn't want this to end.

With her eyes closed, the rest of the world ceased to matter, to exist. In that moment, they were young thieves, ready to conquer the universe. Together they could tackle anything.

When she finally pulled away, they were both breathless, chests heaving. She stepped back, allowing her fingers to trail down his arm, not fully separating until the last possible moment. "Goodbye, Wade."

She turned and left the bar, forcing herself to not look back, not give in to the longing and desire he brought out with a simple glance. *Keep moving forward.* It was how she lived her life now.

No matter how hard it became.

NINE

NIKKI ROLLED OUT of bed and shuffled to the kitchen. As she poured a cup of coffee, Mia's irritated sigh sounded from the other side of the apartment. No one expressed irritation quite the way Mia did when people were late for Mia-mandated team meetings.

After gulping half a cup of the scalding liquid that wasn't nearly strong enough for her liking—Audrey must've made the pot—Nikki refilled her cup and made her way to the living room. Audrey and Jared were at the desk making googly eyes at each other. Mia stood near the window staring out at the street.

"No London today?" Nikki asked, trying not to be jealous of Audrey.

You could've had that with Wade. He offered.

He offered one night. One.

Great. Now instead of just that one annoying voice in her head, she had two arguing. This was not the picture of positive mental health. Maybe she should add a shot of whiskey to her coffee.

"London doesn't need to be here for this," Mia said, turning away from the window and crossing the room.

Nikki perched on the arm of the couch and waited for Audrey to cue up the usual slideshow of art to steal and the slimeball they were taking it from, but the TV remained black. "Well? Who's next?"

"That's what we need to discuss. After this debacle at Max Ingram's, Jared and I think it's in our best interest to take a break." Mia stood stiffly in her usual spot in front of the TV, her arms crossed, irritation rolling off her.

"What? I thought we needed to move fast because these guys were liquidating." She was hungover again, so maybe she wasn't thinking clearly, but this didn't make sense.

"That was the plan. But having all of this attention brought to Ingram, immediately after having Randall Scott questioned by his insurance company because his painting is a forgery, is a bit much. Everyone is hypervigilant."

"So? I can still sneak their artwork right out from under their noses."

"But they'll be looking for trouble now. We need to give them time to relax back into comfort."

"What if they sell everything in a panic instead of being lulled into a sense of security?"

Mia inhaled deeply and Nikki braced for a scathing comment. But all Mia said was, "I don't know."

Jared came from behind the desk. "We've hit four people in about as many weeks. We're not abandoning the mission. We're just stepping back to assess. See who the new players are. Determine if we need to change our operations."

"How long are you thinking?" Audrey asked.

"A week? Maybe two," Mia answered. "That should be enough time for us to suss out what the police know and whether the rest of the men on the list are suspicious."

A week. Maybe two. With nothing to do. The boredom would likely kill her.

"Can you manage to stay out of trouble?" Jared asked.

Nikki swung her head to look at him and immediately regretted the act. "I make no guarantees. You told me not to take on other jobs while I'm working for you. Two weeks is a lot of nothing."

"Take a vacation."

She snickered. "Haven't you ever heard that if you do a job that you're passionate about, it's not really work? Who needs a vacation?"

"London is working on new pieces, so when we're ready to pick up again, there won't be any additional delays." Mia stood in front of the TV and glanced at each of them in turn.

Nikki had no idea how to read the woman. She was irritated, which Nikki had initially attributed to her tardiness, but now it felt like more. "What aren't you saying?"

"What do you mean?"

"I thought you agreed to keep us in the loop. You're not telling us something and I want to know what it is."

"There's nothing. Jared and I are going to gather information. We'll let you know if we find anything out."

She was too tired to wade through Mia's secrecy. If Mia wanted to keep them in the dark, screw it.

The room fell into silence. Finally, Mia picked up her purse. "If there's nothing else, we'll call when we're ready for the next job." She nodded to Jared and slipped out the door.

Nikki slid onto the couch and stretched her legs out to rest on the coffee table. "What will I do with a week or two off? Paris? Milan?"

"Chicago," Jared said from behind her.

"You said vacation."

"I guess I should've said stay-cation. You can't leave the country."

"Why not?"

"I don't want Interpol breathing down our backs next."

"Whatever." She waved her hand at him.

Audrey hung her bag across her body. "I'm going to go see Gram. You want to catch a movie or something later?"

"Maybe."

"Okay. I'll swing by here."

"Have fun with Gram."

"You want to come with me?"

"Why?"

"So you have something to do. So you're not alone."

"I'm fine alone. See you later."

After Jared and Audrey both left, she sipped her coffee and considered her options to keep herself busy. Her mind kept going back to Wade and his offer last night. Two weeks. Two weeks was better than a night.

Then she thought about everything else he'd said. About Dodger. About how bad things were. Wade was probably exaggerating. Or Dodger was.

But hell. She had time. Maybe she'd go make sure.

TWO HOURS LATER, dressed in an oversized T-shirt and some ratty cargo shorts, she pulled the ball cap off her head and stared at the bar across the street. She'd checked out all of Dodger's usual hangouts and had come up empty. He was nowhere to be found. Which was not like Dodger at all. He liked to be out and be seen, life of the party. If he was on a winning streak, his money poured everywhere, buying drinks as he told stories of his victory. If he was losing, he was quick to share his misery, convincing people to buy him drinks.

Of course, she could've probably asked any of his running buddies where he was, but then word would definitely get back to him that she was looking. She didn't actually want to interact with him. She just wanted to verify that he and Wade were full of it.

So she paced across the street from The White Pony—a bar she'd been to with Dodger only a handful of times in her life—waiting, based on a hunch that Wade might've told Dodger to lay low. But Dodger wouldn't have it in him to really disappear.

Finally she saw him. She put her cap back on her head, brim low enough to shadow her face as she studied Dodger. He looked bad. He walked with a partial limp, which he could fake for half a block, but this felt real. His face was mottled with bruises of varying shades. His eye was still puffy, probably from being swollen shut.

He paused outside the bar and glanced around, first over one shoulder, then the other. She ducked beside a light pole and held her phone in her hand to blend in.

Wade hadn't been lying. Something serious was going on.

Estranged or not, Dodger was still her father.

AFTER NIKKI LEFT him at the bar last night, Wade had gone home but had no chance of finding sleep, so he brought Flynn back to the office to run searches to try to figure out where the Devereaux painting had gone. He'd also tried to find who Donny Harbridge was mixed up with. He'd come up empty on both fronts. He didn't know where to go next.

Devon had connections in law enforcement, but since Wade was the one who stole the painting, cops didn't have anything to go on. He needed to find the underground sale, and the dark web was just too vast. It wasn't like he could just Google "Buy a stolen Devereaux."

A quick rap on his office door startled his exhausted brain. He didn't even have a chance to answer before the door swung open.

Boone lumbered through carrying a coffee. "You look like crap."

Flynn waddled across the room to greet Boone. After setting a cup in front of Wade, Boone folded himself in half to reach down to pet Flynn. "Been here all night?" he asked.

"Mostly. What time is it?"

"Almost eleven. I'm guessing things with Nikki didn't go well."

Wade shook his head. "She worked for a middleman. Painting's gone and she doesn't know where it is. I spent the night searching, trying to find some mention of who's been looking for a Devereaux. I had even less luck trying to find out who's pulling Donny Harbridge's strings."

"I know nothing about art, but thugs I might be able to help with."

Picking up his cup, Wade took a long drink. "I appreciate the offer, but I told you I want you guys to stay out of this."

"This is no different than any of the other searches I do."

Boone had a point. And he really could use all the help he could get.

"Okay. You know Donny. He's in it for a quick buck. He bankrolls the deadbeats in the neighborhood. Small scores. That's it. So there's something about him demanding that Dodger steal a Devereaux that doesn't sit right with me. If he told Dodger to knock off a bank, I'd believe it. But a Devereaux? Especially this one. Because it's the last known painting, it's worth more than her others."

"So lowlife Donny Harbridge has a sudden interest in high-end art. Any ideas where to look?"

"I've used all my ideas. I can't think of anyone who would want to control Donny and who also has a thing for art."

"Maybe it's more Donny than the art. What does Donny have that someone else doesn't? If it was about the painting, they could've hired another thief. But they tasked Donny—not a thief—with stealing it."

Wade didn't know if he was just too exhausted or if Boone really was making sense, but it sounded like a new direction to take. "Run with it."

The phone on his desk buzzed. Meg only called him when a customer wanted information on something special. He checked the security camera as he picked up the phone. "Damn."

"Uh," Meg said.

At the same time, Boone asked, "What?"

"Not you. Sorry, Meg." He held up a finger to tell Boone to wait.

"There's someone here asking for you."

"Yeah, I see her. I'll be there in a minute." He hung up and looked at Boone. "It's Nikki."

Boone was a big man, but he moved fast to get behind the desk to look at the monitor. "How do you know that's her? You can't see her face or anything."

"I know." He knew the shape of her. The way she stood. The way she avoided cameras. He couldn't imagine what she was doing there.

"Get moving," Boone said, poking his shoulder.

As Wade walked from his office, Flynn at his heels, Boone settled in his chair to watch on the monitor. "My life isn't a soap opera."

"So you say," Boone retorted.

He jogged downstairs and paused at the door to the shop. Nikki's back was to him and he took that moment to gather himself and school his features. Even if he was excited that she'd sought him out, he couldn't reveal that to her. "Hey."

She turned. "Hey."

She took a step and Flynn came running at her. Nikki jumped back and Wade scooped up a wiggling Flynn in his arms.

"What is that?"

"Flynn, my dog."

She flicked her wrist toward the back door. "Could you get rid of him?"

He turned. "Meg, can you take Flynn upstairs and ask Boone to keep him up there?"

"Sure." She took Flynn in her arms and the dog immediately started licking her face. "Oh, Flynn. You sure know how to make a girl feel special."

"Sorry about that," Wade said to Nikki. "He goes

most places with me. I didn't think when I came down-stairs."

"It's fine."

He scanned her features, expecting to catch her in a lie, but she was fine. No sign of the fear he'd seen at Ingram's house. "So it's just big dogs?"

She chuckled, a dry lackluster sound. "I don't like little ones either, but those I figure I can stomp on if need be."

"You'd never have to do that to Flynn. He's a lover not a fighter."

"I'll have to take your word for it."

They stood awkwardly in silence. Wade hated every second of it. This woman had been his best friend and lover for years. They'd never been awkward with each other.

"So, you're doing security work, huh? That's a heck of a gig. I bet you made Dodger real proud with this scam." She walked to the wall of items ranging from rape whistles and pepper spray to mini-cameras.

Pride rose in his chest until she finished her statement. "This isn't a scam. It's a legitimate business."

She tossed a glance over her shoulder. "Do your customers know you're a thief?"

"Former thief. And no, but my partners do. We use our gifts on the other side of the law now."

"Well, we both know that's not entirely true."

"What do you want, Nikki?"

Her shoulders sagged. She didn't turn around. "I found Dodger."

"I told him to lay low."

"He is. It took some doing for me to figure out where to go. He looks old."

"It's been a while."

She faced him now and asked, "Donny really did that to him?"

"As far as I know. He owes Donny, but I don't know who Donny is mixed up with. I can't believe that a Devereaux is something Donny wants. I offered to pay him off. He wouldn't listen to anything. Did you talk to Dodger?"

"No. I wanted to see if he was running a con. Trying to find a way to get to me."

"I'm worried about him. This is different than the other times."

She nodded, understanding without having been part of Dodger's life for years. "Then let's go steal a painting."

"You know where it is?"

"I can find out."

He wanted to rush to her and scoop her up in his arms but feared her reaction. He couldn't stomach her pushing him away. He swallowed hard. "If you get me the location, I'll get it. You can stay away."

She scoffed. "I'm still the better thief. And you're obviously out of practice, Mr. Legitimate Businessman."

He stepped closer. "Then we do it together. One last heist for old times' sake. Who knows? It might actually be fun."

"Yeah, sure."

Her voice said it would be anything but fun. He just wasn't sure if it was Dodger or him that fostered that reaction.

TEN

WADE WATCHED AS Nikki walked away from him again. At this point, he should've been used to her leaving, but it never got easier. He went back to his office, where Boone was waiting at Wade's desk, Flynn on his lap.

"So that was Nikki."

"Yep." He neared the desk and flicked a thumb over his shoulder to tell Boone to move.

"What'd she want?" Boone stood, Flynn still in his arms. He set the dog on the couch.

"She tracked Dodger down, saw his bruises. I guess she felt bad for the old man because she offered to help me steal the Devereaux."

"I thought you said it was gone," he said, settling beside Flynn again.

"She said she can find out where it is. In the meantime, my focus will be on figuring out who Donny's working with. Or for. Something isn't right there. This is bigger than Dodger owing him money. I need to know what we're getting into."

"About that," Devon said as he leaned a shoulder against the door frame.

Wade and Boone both turned to look at him.

"About what?" Wade asked.

Devon shot them a look filled with suspicion. "The

famous Devereaux painting that was stolen from a mansion on the North Shore. You know anything about it?"

Wade opened and closed his mouth, unsure of what to commit to.

"I guess that's my answer. Is this going to blow back on us?"

"I'm trying to make sure it doesn't. That's why I didn't tell you."

"Tell me now."

"How did you even hear about it?"

"Please. When something with a dollar value that high goes missing, I hear about it. Since you didn't mention it to me, you know, with security being our business and all, I figured you had a hand in it."

Wade should've known better than to think Devon wouldn't have figured it out. He gave Devon the basic rundown, leaving his history with Nikki out of it.

"You have no idea what Donny's into?"

"I never had reason to investigate his petty bullshit. But this isn't so petty anymore. Donny's not the kind of guy who wants art. This was someone else's job. Donny is a middleman, but I don't know for who or why."

"And you can't just walk away from this?"

Wade shook his head. "Family's family. No matter how bad." Devon would understand. Loyalty mattered.

"Okay. I'll put some feelers out and see what I can learn. You dig into Donny, so we know who we're really up against. Then we'll take them down."

"No. I just said I'm trying to keep this away from you guys and the business."

"Like you said, family's family."

They stared at each other for a long minute.

Boone stood. "I'll handle Donny. I still have some shady friends in the area. Someone's gotta know something."

Wade stood and tucked his hands in his pockets. He couldn't ask for better guys to have at his back. "Thanks."

"No problem," Boone answered. Flynn stretched and lifted his head to see if it was worth following.

Devon stepped aside to allow Boone to head to his office. "You should've come to me with this. We're a team."

"I was trying to protect the team."

"This works because we handle things together. We're stronger as a team."

Wade nodded. A stab of guilt hit him. He knew this. He'd never been as successful alone as he had when he'd been with Nikki.

"Next time, come to me."

Wade chuckled. "There won't be a next time. This is it. No more Donny. And if Dodger doesn't change, I'll cut him out, too."

Devon offered a small smile. "Easier said than done, man." He turned and left Wade's office.

Didn't he know it? He'd thought he was ready to leave with Nikki. And after that last heist and having a gun pointed at him, he'd planned to join her. But when they'd gotten home that night, and Nikki went to pack her bag, he jostled Dodger from sleep. He couldn't just sneak away while Dodger was passed out. He wasn't a coward.

When Dodger sat up, the bag of cash slid off his chest. He groaned as he bent to pick it up. "You did it. Told you it was a big score."

"You also said the mark was gone. The house was supposed to be empty. He was home and pulled a gun on me."

Dodger looked remorseful for a moment. Then he reached out and tapped Wade's leg. "But you're all good."

"Old man, you don't get it." Wade rose and paced. "We're leaving. Nikki's packing now. She's done."

Dodger blinked and scrubbed a hand over his face. "What?"

"She knocked the guy out to save me. But I've never seen her so pissed."

"She can't leave!"

"She is."

Dodger stood and grabbed Wade's arm. "She's all I have. If she leaves, I'll be alone. What am I supposed to do?"

"Why don't you try asking her to stay? Actually follow through and do what you say you will? Let her be in charge."

The old man scoffed. "She's not ready to run things."

"Then I guess we'll see. Because she'll be doing it on her own."

They stared at each other for a full minute, and Dodger's eyes filled. Sure, the man was probably still drunk, causing his emotions to run high, but he was lucid. "Please don't take her."

"I'm not taking her. This is her idea." Wade's heart tore. He'd never cared about anyone the way he did the Russos. Dodger was family, but Nikki was his life.

Dodger rubbed his eyes. "She'll stay if you stay. She loves you."

"And I love her." He hadn't known what love was

until he had her. He couldn't imagine doing this without her. Couldn't imagine a life without her.

"I never asked you for much, Wade. I took you in when you had nowhere to go. I taught you how to run a good con. I gave you a home and a family. Let you have my daughter. Don't let her go." Dodger choked on the last words.

Wade was speechless. The only emotion Dodger ever showed was anger. But this was real. He'd never seen the man break down. Panic clanged around in Wade's chest. He felt like a squirrel in the middle of the street with cars barreling down at him in both directions. He stepped away and looked around the apartment. He didn't know which way to go. "I don't think she'll listen to me. She's really pissed."

"Go for a drink or something. Leave now. She'll wait for you and have time to cool off."

Wade was skeptical, but he agreed that he didn't want Nikki rushing to any decision. So as always, he'd listened to Dodger. This was home and Dodger was family. For better or worse.

It had been one of the biggest mistakes of his life.

Wade woke his computer and began searching to gather information on the Devereaux.

Two hours later, Devon was back in the doorway. "We have a problem."

NIKKI LEFT WADE and tried to figure out how to explain all of this to Audrey. In order for Nikki to do what she needed, she'd have to double-cross Jared and Mia. And she'd need Audrey's help. She'd have to ask her friend to betray her new boyfriend. Nikki couldn't see that going over well.

But if anyone could understand doing everything you could for family, Audrey could.

Nikki texted Audrey and asked her to meet at the apartment alone. If Audrey could just tell her where the painting was, Nikki could leave her out of the rest. Give her plausible deniability if or when the new owner went back to Jared.

She didn't want to cause trouble for Jared and Mia, but she couldn't let Wade take all the risks to save her father. The man was an asshole who ruined her relationship with Wade, but he was still her dad. He had raised her and had helped her hone all the skills she currently possessed.

After stopping at the liquor store, she went straight to the apartment. The place Jared and Mia had rented as a base of operations had become home to her.

And if she were being totally honest, she liked having people around. She was never lonely at the apartment.

That admission should've made her want to hightail it out of there. Aligning herself with people hadn't worked out so well in the past. People weren't trustworthy. They'd leave if things got tough. She knew this. Because of it, she preferred to work alone. But Audrey, Jared, Mia, and London made her want to stay.

She wished she could say it was Mia's noble cause of righting her father's wrongs, but in truth, the paycheck was really good. And it didn't hurt that they all accepted her for who she was. No sideways looks. No backhanded compliments about how she was so talented that she could be doing more with her life.

She hadn't felt this way since she'd worked with Wade.

As she approached the apartment, she saw Audrey leaning against the fence that enclosed the small patches of grass that were supposed to be the front yard.

"They still haven't given you a key?"

"Nah. I usually don't need one. I come with Jared or I take his keys when I leave."

"Been waiting long?"

"Nope. Just got here. Travel is a lot faster these days, although having someone drive me door-to-door takes some getting used to."

Nikki led the way up to the front door and unlocked it. "Rough life having your own chauffeur."

"I don't, but Jared has a car service, and he feels better if I use it." She sighed. "I'm learning to compromise."

They stepped onto the elevator together. "Seems like you're doing all the compromising, not him. You moved out of your apartment. You're working with him when we're not doing heists. Now you're using his driver. If you were anyone else, I'd say your boyfriend has a problem with control."

"He wanted me to move in with him. I still have my own place, just different than the craphole I used to live in. I work with him, but I decide which jobs I want to do. If using his driver makes him worry less, it's the least I can do."

They got off the elevator and Nikki opened the apartment. "And he's okay with you hanging out with me?"

Audrey laughed. "He doesn't get to pick my friends."

"Glad to hear it." In more ways than one. Audrey was the kind of person who was loyal. Nikki just hoped her loyalty would come in handy. She plopped on the couch, setting the bag with beer and wine on the table.

"So what's up?"

Reaching into the bag, she pulled out a bottle of beer and the wine. Audrey grabbed the beer, so Nikki took another for herself.

After popping the top and taking a swig, she dove in. "How hard would it be for you to find out who Jared sold the Devereaux to?"

"Not very. I have the screen name from the auction. I could use back channels to figure out who. Why?"

"I need to steal it back."

"What? Why?" Audrey sputtered and set her bottle on the table.

Nikki gulped more beer. She'd considered lying, but Audrey would understand the truth. She didn't need to sell this. She just needed to convince her not to tell Jared. She gave Audrey the basics about her dad and Wade and why she wanted to steal the painting.

"He's a jerk, but he's still my dad. And something's not right about this. I don't know if he intentionally got mixed up in something bigger or if he fell into it, but it's more trouble than he can handle. Wade is willing to do it himself if I give him the information, but... he's *my* dad."

"You never talk about him. You just go through life acting like the Lone Ranger."

"I pretty much am, now. But my dad taught me about being a thief. He set me up with my career. When I walked away, Wade stayed and he's taken care of him this whole time. But this is different. I don't know how to explain it, but it is."

"What's your plan?"

"We don't have one yet. I need to find out where the painting is first. Once we know who has it, we can come up with a plan."

"I'm not gonna lie—hearing you use *we* in relation to another team makes me a little nervous."

"Not a team. Me and Wade." Saying it out loud made it sound real. The team they had been. "That way, we can keep you and Jared and everyone out of it. It's just us getting Dodger—my dad—out of trouble." She popped the top on another beer. Now the hard part. "You can't tell Mia and Jared."

Audrey picked at the label on her bottle. "I have no problem keeping it from Mia. But Jared…"

"I know. But if he knows, he'll try to stop us. And that's not an option."

"After all the grief I gave him about not being honest and keeping things from me? I don't know if I can do that."

"If you can't keep it from him, don't help. I don't want to get between the two of you. But then you have to forget this conversation ever happened."

"How is that any different?"

She had a point. "I guess it's not."

They sat in silence for a minute. "I wouldn't ask if I had another way. It'll take a whole lot longer for me to track it down. Weeks. Maybe longer. Dodger doesn't have that kind of time. I don't need you to help steal it. Just point me in the right direction."

Suddenly both of their phones were buzzing with a text from Mia.

Meet at apartment ASAP.

No other information. Nikki rolled her eyes. Yeah, the woman was paying her well, but not be-at-her-beck-and-call well.

Audrey responded for both of them, letting her know they were already there. When Mia texted back, Audrey snorted. "I think this message is for you." She turned her phone to show Nikki.

Stay sober.

"Sure, Mia." Then she tipped her bottle and took another swig.

A half an hour and another beer later, Mia walked through the door, followed closely by Jared. Jared, of course, went straight to Audrey and kissed her.

Mia took her usual position in front of the TV, as if ready to launch into a business pitch. "Our hiatus is over."

"How?" Nikki asked. "I thought we had to lay low because all eyes were on Ingram and Scott."

Jared leaned forward. "That was before the insurance company found out that Ingram's provenance was bogus."

"What does that matter?"

"He can't prove he legally owned the painting, and he didn't carry title insurance," Mia said. "That means he won't be getting a payout after all. But that's not even the best part." The woman was almost giddy. Her body practically vibrated and her eyes danced. "The local art world is abuzz because the Devereaux was just donated to the Carlisle Museum. Normally, a single donation wouldn't draw any attention, but given that this was a painting that was stolen, people were looking for it."

"If Ingram can't prove it's his, what happens to it? And who buys a painting just to donate it?" Nikki's head was spinning with possibilities of what her next steps would be.

"That's the kicker. The painting was delivered with the true provenance. The father of Jared's buyer was the rightful owner. He bequeathed it to the museum. The son had tried all legal means to track the painting down, but had no record of where it might've gone or when it had been stolen."

Nikki nudged Jared's leg. "You're lucky he didn't just set the cops on your tail for selling a hot painting."

"No luck involved. The guy had been on the web looking for information. I simply suggested I knew where it was and could procure it."

Audrey leaned forward. "But aren't the cops still looking for the thief? Wasn't that the whole point of lying low?"

"Technically, it's an open case," Jared began. "But since the painting is now with the rightful owner, no one will look too hard."

"So we're back on track," Mia said. "It's time to plan the next heist."

How was she supposed to plan heists with both Mia and Wade without Mia finding out she was doing it?

ELEVEN

As soon as Mia left, Nikki gathered her things. She needed to talk to Wade to figure this out. Jared and Audrey were going to discuss the Latimer statue that was next on the list to steal from some guy named Turner. She texted Wade to tell him she was on her way to his store and he responded that he had bad news. As if she needed another round.

She filled her flask with whiskey in case Wade didn't have anything to drink. She was going to need it to get through this night.

While Jared was in the bathroom, Audrey sat behind her desk and asked, "What are you going to do?"

"Talk to Wade and figure it out." She slipped the flask into her bag.

"You can't steal from a museum."

Swinging her bag over her shoulder, she said, "I'll do whatever I have to do. Just stay out of it."

"You already brought me into it."

"I see now that was a mistake. I'm better off alone."

"That's not what I meant and you know it." Audrey blew out a breath. "If anyone can understand how complicated family is, it's Mia and Jared. I think you should tell them."

"My plans will get in the way of Mia's. At least that's

what she'll think. I don't have time for her b.s. There's a ticking clock on my father's head."

"Let me know if there's anything I can do."

"Thanks. Just forget about me and Wade. That'll be enough for now. Do your planning—internet recon thing with Jared. I'll be back in the morning to work on the plan to get the statue. Hopefully, this will be another easy one." She called a car as she left the apartment, wanting to be out of sight by the time Jared came back to the room. While he was more laid-back than Mia, he still expected her undivided attention, and her attention was split everywhere at the moment. Even though Audrey might not like Nikki taking off, she would cover for her.

She waited at the corner for the car and used her phone to get information about the Carlisle Museum. While it didn't have the presence and fame of the Art Institute, it owned many famous masterpieces, which meant they had good security. She checked the hours to plan a field trip.

The car pulled up and she gave the intersection to get her near Wade's office. She hoped he didn't have his dog with him. She hadn't packed enough alcohol to have to deal with a dog.

"I'm Trevor and I'll be your driver this fine evening. Can I offer you a water or snack?"

"No thanks." She leaned back against the headrest and closed her eyes.

"How's your day going?"

"Not great, Trevor, so while I know you're trying to be pleasant, I'll double your tip if you just stay quiet."

He offered a low chuckle and said, "Sure thing."

The rest of the ride was blissfully silent so she could think. Not that she came up with any kind of plan, but at least she cleared her head of some of the noise. When Trevor put the car in park, she thanked him and jogged down the block to Wade's store.

The lights were off and there was no bell, so she texted him. I'm here. How do I get in?

Coming.

A minute later, he opened the door. She entered the dark store and let her eyes adjust. Wade relocked the door and walked past her, so she followed.

"Can you lock up your dog?"

"He's not here. I took him home when you texted." *Well, that was thoughtful. He must live close then. Shut up. It doesn't matter where he lives.*

She followed him upstairs to a set of offices, all of which were dark except one. He turned into that one and gestured to the couch. She set her bag at her feet and sat.

"Can I get you something to drink?" He opened a small refrigerator next to his desk. "I've got water or I can make some coffee."

"Is that grape soda? You haven't outgrown that yet?" Grape soda had been the one thing he always asked for when they bought groceries. He never made any other special requests for food of any kind. Just the sickeningly sweet grape pop. He wasn't even brand loyal.

"It's still good."

She shook her head. "I know where the painting is."

"So do I."

"How'd you find out?"

"I have people who know people. The art world is small. Something like that goes missing and people talk."

"So you know we're screwed. Stealing from a museum is no joke."

He leaned against the edge of his desk and crossed his arms. "You've done it before."

"Sure. With months of planning." She grabbed her flask and took a swig. "I don't get the impression that Dodger has months."

"You're right. It gets worse." He took two long steps until he was directly in front of her. He snatched her flask, took a drink and plopped beside her on the couch.

Once he moved away from the desk, she noticed the framed picture he had. It was one of her and him. She was pretty sure the original had contained half of Dodger's face in the corner. They'd just made a huge score from a black-tie dinner. Wade was the epitome of suave in a tux. It had been one of the rare jobs Dodger planned that came off without a hitch. After the picture, Wade had put one of the stolen diamond bracelets on her wrist and taken her out dancing. It had been some crazy hot role-playing and they'd barely made it to their bed to spend the rest of the night together.

Wade broke into her memories. "Donny is tied up with Marco Wolf."

She blinked. "Am I supposed to know the name?"

Wade lifted a shoulder. "I figured you would. He runs a criminal enterprise. He's known for only hiring the best. Kind of surprised you haven't worked for him."

She took her flask back. "I prefer to work for myself."

"You're not now."

"The money is good. A lot of the legwork is done."
She wasn't ready to admit that she was stealing for a good cause.

"Anyway. Wolf is the worst kind of dirty. Sex. Drugs. Violence. He has a hand in all of it."

"What does he want with Dodger? He's not a big player in anything."

"He used to be a great thief. And I guess Wolf really wants the Devereaux."

"So we're back to just figuring it out to save Dodger." She glanced around the office. He had a Cubs World Series pennant on one wall, and right below it hung a Three Stooges poster. Not very professional, but it made her smile. That was the fun-loving Wade she remembered. "What do you do here anyway? Is this a front?"

"I wasn't lying. I'm legit. I'm working with a couple of buddies. We run a security company."

Laughter burst from her chest. "Are you kidding me? People really hire a thief—"

"Former thief."

She narrowed her eyes. "Not so former if you're planning on stealing the Devereaux. Again."

"Point taken."

"So people hire you to tell them how to keep their possessions safe?"

He nodded. "Who better to point out the risks they take and the gaps in their systems than someone who sees them as a mark?"

"How can they trust you?"

"My friend Devon is the face of the business. He sells the jobs. I just work the back end."

Another sip of whiskey. "Unlike you. You usually

enjoy being in front of everything. Using all the charm and skills of a con man, making Dodger proud."

"If I were still conning people, sure. But this is one hundred percent legit."

"But your buddies are digging around to get you information about the stolen Devereaux?"

He took the flask again. "I tried to keep them out of this. They wanted to help. Family looks out for family."

He might not have meant it as an insult, but it sure felt like one. "So what are we gonna do?"

"We have two options."

Two? Nikki was feeling a little buzzed, but she was far from drunk.

"We can figure out how to steal the Devereaux. Again. Or we let Dodger suffer the consequences of his actions."

Nikki sighed. Still only one option. "If you want to walk away, that's fine. I'm going after the Devereaux, and I'm going to make sure Donny stays away from Dodger. Dodger might be a total asshole, but he is my father."

SHE MIGHT NOT have meant to dig at him, a reminder that Dodger wasn't really his father, but that was the way Wade heard it. "Blood isn't the only thing that ties people."

"I know."

The look she gave him was full of emotion. For a blink, her barriers were down and he saw the woman he loved. The one he'd never fully get over. But then it was gone.

"Have you ever been to the Carlisle?" he asked.

"Nope. You?" She slid her flask back into her bag.

"No." He rose and went behind his desk and began tapping on the keyboard. "They're not going to put it on exhibit right away, would they?"

"No. The fact that it was missing for years means they're going to have to authenticate it." Her eyes widened. "That might work. We can buy some time if we replicate a couple of forgeries. If we have multiple people come forward with Devereauxs, the museum will take its time authenticating."

"Like the *Mona Lisa*s of 1911."

"That's urban legend. There has never been proof that the guy sold six counterfeits."

"Come on. It's common knowledge among thieves. The guy got away with selling the same painting six times and none of them were the original."

"Dude. It was one guy, supposedly, talking to a reporter. A reporter who then wrote a fantastical story about six *Mona Lisa*s and the criminal mastermind behind them. Except no one has ever met this mastermind. You've spent too much time listening to Dodger's stories."

"Where's your sense of faith? The love of a well-played heist?"

"I have plenty of my own real heists. I don't need stories. But the concept could work." She tapped a finger against her lip.

"It's a little late to flood the market with fakes. News has already broken about the Devereaux being donated."

"Now would be the time people would come forward. Why would they think they didn't have the original? There would be outrage. Indignation." She stood and pointed her finger in the air for effect as she stomped out the words.

"How does that get us any closer to stealing the original?"

"If we have two or three other people all coming forward, claiming they have the real Devereaux, the museum will have to check them out."

"No. All they have to do is verify the one they have. If that's found to be authentic, why look at anything else? That would be on the other owners."

She sank back to the couch. "I was just thinking of the distraction factor. But you're right, even if it bought us time, it wouldn't get us near the original." With her elbow on her knee, she propped her chin in her hand. "We need to figure out where they're holding it and break in."

He leaned back in his chair. "Yeah. Just like that. No problem."

"Hey. I don't see you coming up with any great ideas."

He wasn't trying to be sarcastic or negative, but things were overwhelming right now. He didn't see a way out. "I'm sorry. I don't like anything about this situation. If I learned anything from you, it's to listen to my gut. If it's bad, get out."

"Except when you can't. Then you plow through. Knowing that a ruthless crime boss is behind this makes it imperative that we get Dodger out from under his thumb." Her resignation permeated the office.

"I want to know why he's under this guy's thumb to begin with. It doesn't make sense. Sure, Dodger is lousy with bets and this time it was a hefty sum. But why get

Wolf involved? There's got to be more to the story that Dodger's leaving out."

Nikki stretched out her legs and laid her head on the back of the couch to stare at the ceiling. He studied her, always amazed at how restless her body appeared even when it wasn't moving. He never understood how she managed to stay still long enough to complete a job.

"If Dodger hasn't told you already, he won't," she said to the ceiling.

"He might for you. Have you tried talking to him?"

"No. I'm not up for that. Don't know if I'll ever be. He made his decision and so did I. He made it clear I wasn't welcome back if I left."

Wade joined her on the couch, needing to be near her. Knowing the past still rubbed her raw. "You know he didn't mean it. He's missed you every day."

"Why didn't you come with me?" Her voice was small, quiet, and unlike the usually brazen woman she showed the world. Her face was still upturned toward the ceiling, but her eyes were closed.

It killed him to think he played a role in that.

"I wanted to. But Dodger…he was always such a mess. I didn't think he'd make it on his own."

She rolled her head to the side and opened her eyes. "He's a grown man."

"I also thought that if I stayed, you'd come back. I wanted us to continue to be a family. That was all I ever wanted." He put his arm on the back of the couch and twisted his body to fully face her. "Why didn't you come back?"

She huffed out a sad laugh. "At first it was sheer stubbornness. I was going to show you both that I didn't

need you. Time passed. When neither of you came looking, I figured we were all better off."

He inched forward and toyed with her hair. "Well, we
messed that up good. We never should've let you go."

Her eyes fluttered closed again. "Make no mistake,
Dodger was okay with it. I was getting too good and
my patience for his b.s. too short."

"Have you been happy at least?"

When she reopened her eyes this time, the spark of
mischief was back and she smiled. "I've done okay."
She released a deep breath and pushed up. "You look
like you did okay for yourself, too. What made you go
straight?"

"Not having you around."

A bark of laughter shot from her. "Are you saying
I'm a bad influence?"

"We both know you are, but that's not what I meant.
It wasn't fun anymore. And truth be told, you are the
better thief. Always were."

She shifted her shoulders and then winked. "Then
I guess I better put on my thieving hat and figure out
how to steal from the Carlisle."

He scooted forward on the couch and nudged her
knee with his. "We okay?"

"Yeah."

"And after this is over?"

She shrugged again. "I don't know. One hurdle at
a time."

He didn't like thinking he was some kind of hurdle
or obstacle in her life, but if that was what he needed to
be, he'd take that on. Then he'd keep getting in her way
until she accepted that she had no reason to run again.

"I'm going to do recon tomorrow. Visit the museum."
She stood.

"You mean look for vulnerabilities."

"Same thing."

"I could do that. It's what I do for a living now." He
stood, too, putting him close enough to touch again,
but he didn't.

"You work on the Wolf-Donny angle. See what's
brewing there. I want to know how deep Dodger is in
this mess."

Then she left, but this time, Wade was okay with it.
She'd be back.

TWELVE

Mia

MIA NEEDED A BREAK. The constant hurry and worry about the heists and reparations and trying to figure out if it was having any impact at all was taking its toll on her. Her younger self would've called friends and planned a girls' day complete with spa treatments and drinking. Those days were long gone and although she'd kept a few friends—or at least what passed for friendship in her circles—she couldn't unburden herself to anyone.

So instead, she turned to art. Art rarely let her down. Even if she didn't like it, she could still admire it. Rather than go where she might run into people she knew, she went to the Addington Gallery. It was part of the gallery district, but Mia normally chose other fine art museums. Today she needed a change.

The mixed media artwork didn't hold her attention, but she always enjoyed the melted wax paintings. She turned the corner to see the new exhibit by an up-and-coming local artist and froze. Standing in front of a glorious painting of marigolds in a field at dawn was Logan, the insurance guy. She planned to back out of the room and return later in her visit, but her feet were stuck.

As he turned to move, she spun to stare at the painting beside her. It was a canvas of shades of black.

"Mia? Is that you?"

She turned and smiled hesitantly. "Yes. Logan, was it?"

He stepped closer and placed a hand on his chest. "I must've done a poor job at making a first impression if you can't remember me."

"I do. I'm just surprised to see you, that's all. When we met at Max's house, I thought you said you were from New York. I assumed you'd be back there."

He tucked his hands in the pants pockets of his not-very-well-tailored suit. "I was going to be, but then all the excitement with the Devereaux hit. I'm sure being in the local art world, you've heard about it."

"Oh, yes. Quite a situation."

"Definitely. How about you?"

Her heart stuttered. "What about me?"

"You spend every day surrounded by art, but come to a gallery on your day off?"

"When you love something, I guess you never get tired of it."

"Agreed." He pointed at the painting on the wall. "Do you have a favorite?"

"I prefer the encaustic paintings to the mixed media in the other rooms. The texture and color variance and how the artists play with light and depth and motion."

Logan licked his bottom lip before biting down on it. She'd done it again. She rambled on about things few other people were interested in.

"Sorry," she said quietly.

"For what?"

"You were asking to be polite and I gave you more than anyone ever wants to hear."

"On the contrary. I'd love to hear more." He flashed her a flirtatious smile.

She didn't know what to do with that.

"In fact, maybe I could buy you lunch?"

She laughed without thinking.

"Why is that funny?"

She shook her head and steadied a look on him. "No man asks to take me to lunch. In case you missed all the gossip after our dance at Max's house, my last name is Benson. As in Benson and Towers notoriety. My father is a criminal on the run. I'm used to people offering superficial pleasantries when I'm out in public, but I'm also well aware of what is said about me behind my back."

He crossed his arms and tilted his head as if what she'd said was confusing. "First, I'm not one for gossip. I have better things to do with my time. Second, while your father's name sounds vaguely familiar, I can't say that I followed the case. Which leads me to my third point—I asked you out because I think you're beautiful and intelligent, and I don't hold someone's paternity against them."

It was her turn to feel confused. Was it because he didn't travel in the same circles she did? Or was he just that naïve that he believed she didn't live with her father's stink hanging over her all the time?

Her upbringing caught up with her. "Thank you for the compliment, but I'm still going to decline. If you're going to be in town, you won't want to be seen spending much time with me."

He took a couple steps closer and her breath caught. He looked at her with an unusual intensity that caused a full body flush. "I do intend to be here for some time. I guess we'll run into each other again." He extended his hand.

When she reached out, he caught her hand and kissed the back of it. The warm press of his lips sending a tingle all the way up her arm. Who was this man?

"And when we meet again, I hope you won't be offended when I ask you out again. At some point, I hope you'll agree."

"I'm not really dating right now. I have a lot going on."

"Then we can make it a working dinner. I'd love to pick your brain about the forgery at Randall Scott's house. He told me he had you look at it after I had been there."

"I don't know what I could possibly offer."

"I think you have plenty to offer. I'll be in touch." He released her and turned and walked away.

As interesting as the man was, Mia did not have time for such distractions. And spending additional time with a man who was investigating the thefts and forgeries she had masterminded was not a smart move. No matter how charming the man was.

THIRTEEN

NIKKI HAD APPROXIMATELY two hours to case an entire museum and book it back to the apartment to discuss the next heist. If she were just meeting Jared and Audrey, she could push them and stall, but Mia planned to be in attendance, so Nikki had to move fast. She'd agreed not to do other jobs while working for them, so she had to keep her absences to a minimum to avoid complications.

Lucky for her, the Carlisle was a small museum. Two floors in a century-old building that once housed a telephone company. She paid her admission and walked in. No bags being checked, no metal detector. What was this place?

The first floor was open layout with clearly defined stations, mostly consisting of antique furniture being used to create spaces and showcase the workmanship of the various pieces. Couches, chairs, tables, vases. Each with a small card describing the piece, the artist, and who donated it.

As she made her way around the first floor, she saw only one security guard covering the main entrance as well as the emergency exit tucked in the corner. They did have security cameras set up, but they were directed at specific pieces. As long as a thief didn't go after those items, she could help herself to a sizeable load. Motion sensors as well, which looked like they covered the entire floor.

Very few patrons were at the museum first thing after opening, so she had ample time to wander and chat with employees. When she climbed the stairs to the second floor, she found a more traditional exhibit style with the focus being on the paintings on the walls and sculptures on pedestals. Natural light streamed in through windows about eight feet off the floor—big enough to allow for that natural light and high enough that no one would consider coming or going through it. Not that travel through the windows would be impossible, just more of a hassle.

She finally found a docent and approached. "Excuse me."

The older woman, who was probably no more than four foot ten, looked up at her. "Yes, how may I help you?"

"My friend works at the Art Institute and she told me that you guys received a donation of the last Devereaux known to have been painted. She is my all-time favorite artist and I was hoping to see it."

"I'm sorry, dear, it won't be on display for some time."

"Shoot."

"They have to do paperwork and make sure it's clean and undamaged since it's been missing for years. They have a team of experts coming in next week. By the time they finish what they need to do, it'll be some time till the public has access. They haven't even made a formal announcement yet."

Nikki put on her disappointed face and forced a pout,

when in reality, she was ready to skip. A team of experts meant strangers to this small facility. People coming and going. A process which would give her access. "Thank you so much for your help. I guess I'll have to wait."

The docent watched as she left the hall. Nikki paused and glanced up the stairs to the third floor that was off-limits to the public. That was where the work would take place. She jogged down the stairs and left the building as quietly as she came. Out on the street, she looked at neighboring buildings. Then she crossed the street and ducked down an alley.

Using a dumpster, she climbed up and yanked on the ladder for the fire escape. She climbed quickly until she got to the roof, hoping to go unnoticed. She pulled binoculars from her bag and focused on the museum. The windows on the third floor were tinted, so she couldn't see in, but what she really wanted to see was the access to the roof on that building.

The fire escape was busted, but there was a door leading to the stairwell that would get her to the third floor. She just needed to figure out access to the roof. Once there, she could go in, grab the painting, and leave.

On the west side of the museum was a low-rise office building. If she tried, she could probably make the jump, but jumping back with the Devereaux was too risky. The building on the east side of the museum was much taller, so jumping across wasn't really an option. A zipline would do it. She hadn't done a zipline in a long time. But getting down was still a problem. Gravity would take her to the museum, but it wouldn't take her back up. The familiar buzz of excitement over a challenging heist coursed through her.

Her phone rang as she climbed down the ladder. She answered using her headphones so she could continue her climb. "Yeah."

"Find anything interesting?" Wade asked.

Strange how she had gone years without hearing his voice, and she'd convinced herself she hadn't missed it, but now she felt every syllable humming in her system.

"I have a way in. There's rooftop access and I'm fairly certain they have it on the third floor for authentication and cleaning. They have a team coming in next week. That gives us a short window to take it."

"You had better luck than I have. I still have no connection between Donny and Wolf. Or any reason they want the Devereaux." He sighed heavily. "You want to come over tonight so we can start to plan this?"

"I can, but I have something else I have to take care of and I don't know how long it'll take."

"Really? You're doing another job while we're in the middle of this?"

She froze in her tracks. "Excuse me? Are you telling me that you've aborted all jobs you have scheduled?"

"No, but—"

"Have you delegated every aspect of your business to your partners so your focus isn't split?" She was really getting tired of people dictating how she spent her time. As if she wasn't a professional.

"Point taken."

"Good. I'll see you at your office tonight. I'll text when I'm on my way over."

"Actually, I'd prefer we didn't make plans here. I'm

trying to keep my business clean. I'll text you my address."

His house? Where he lived? Nikki had been doing okay being around Wade, feeling those feelings that she preferred to ignore, but to be in his personal space… "What about your dog?"

"Flynn is harmless."

"Does he have teeth?"

"Yeah."

"Then he's not harmless."

"I can lock him up. If he gets too close to you, you can definitely outrun him."

She almost laughed at the image of the pudgy thing trying to run to keep up with her. "Fine."

They disconnected and she texted Audrey to let her know she was en route to the apartment. If her brain didn't explode by the end of the week, it would be a miracle.

WADE SPENT THE rest of his day doing his best to put Nikki and Dodger out of his head. He spoke to clients, made plans for a networking event with Devon, and took Flynn for a walk to the pet store for a new toy since he was going to be locked up for part of the night.

But Nikki was always there in the background. Hell, she'd been in the background for all these years—she was just a sharper image now. He called Dodger to warn him to do a better job of lying low.

"What are you talking about? This is as low as I can get."

"You can do better. You're easy to find. People have seen you."

"What people?"

"I'm not at liberty to say." He didn't want to out Nikki for being around. If she wanted to talk to Dodger, she would.

"Must be Nikki then."

"What makes you say that?"

"There's no one else in this world you feel the need to protect more than her. Especially when it comes to me."

"I don't know why you think Nikki would be looking for you. And if she ain't looking, and just happened to find you, that's a bigger problem. Either way, you need to stay away from your usual haunts."

"Donny's not gonna bother me. He knows you're on it. I won't push my presence in his face. So I'm safe. For now."

His cavalier attitude was really pissing Wade off. Dodger just expected Wade to fix this for him. And he was stupid enough to do it. "This is the last time, old man. You need to stop screwing up like this. This entire situation is getting out of control. Donny's in bed with Marco Wolf. Did you know?"

"I've heard rumors. I can't control who Donny works for."

"You can stop gambling. Stop making promises you can't keep."

"Whatever, kid. You got a plan to get the painting yet?"

"Almost. We'll be done with Donny and Wolf by the end of next week."

"I'll come over and you can fill me in on the plan."

"Not gonna happen. I'm keeping you as far away from this as possible. I'll handle it." The last thing he needed was the added stress of Dodger questioning every move he made. "Just stay out of sight."

"Yeah, sure. I'm still capable of pulling a job, you know. Better'n anyone you got."

"So you keep telling me. I'll be in touch." He disconnected and then he went home to print out the layout of the museum and hang with Flynn until Nikki showed up.

When he walked through the front door, Flynn came jogging around the corner to greet him, and Wade looked around trying to see it as Nikki would the first time. The living room was lived-in. His TV remote sat on the arm of the couch. An empty beer bottle from the other night was still on the table beside some files he had from work.

But he knew Nikki would see the lack of him in the space. This room could belong to any guy. He shook his head. Years ago, she'd accused him of not having his own personality. She thought he'd grown so accustomed to playing a role that he no longer knew who he was. He'd been determined to prove her wrong. He'd been so used to being shuffled around that he learned not to have too many possessions that gave people insight. And definitely nothing that he couldn't walk away from.

It had been the first time he kissed her. She'd started to believe him then. She had to learn to look past the façade and he had to learn to leave a window for her to see through. When that became comfortable, he was an open book for her.

He scooped up the empty bottle and walked to the kitchen. Old habits and all that. No matter how much he'd changed, he still wasn't the type of person to put his life on display. Still ready to run at a moment's notice.

He wondered what Nikki's place would look like. Would she have it filled with knickknacks? Or stolen goods? She liked to show off. But she could walk away from any of it. Dodger had made sure they never got too attached. *You can always steal more.*

She would definitely have a huge couch because she liked to sprawl. And a gaming system. She enjoyed shooting and blowing things up as a relaxation technique.

His imagination was getting the better of him. He had no idea who Nikki was now, any more than she knew him. The past was the past, and there was no going back. But he wanted them to have some kind of future.

After straightening up, he took Flynn for another walk to tire him out so he wouldn't mind being locked up. Then he texted Nikki. Want me to order dinner? Get some beer?

While he waited for her response, he spread the museum's blueprints across his table and dug deep online to learn every scrap he could about the Carlisle. The sun set and his living room darkened before she texted back.

Eat without me. I might be late. A couple more hours at least.

I can wait.

What was a few more hours when he'd been waiting for her for years?

FOURTEEN

Nikki smiled at the message from Wade, but sobered when Mia shot her a dirty look. The woman needed to lighten up. Her scowl might become permanent.

A meaningless text from Wade shouldn't affect her mood. He was asking about food.

"Please pay attention, Nikki."

Mia's upper-crust voice was frosty, as usual.

"What's there to pay attention to? We've been at this for hours. Bottom line, because you decided we were on hiatus, we don't have surveillance information on Darren Turner. You haven't been to his house in over a year, so the information you do have is outdated. Once again, we're working blind. How about I just go in and steal the stupid statue?"

Mia sighed. "London is still working on the counterfeit. You can't simply go in and steal it. Darren hasn't left his house. No social engagements, no parties, nothing. How do you propose you get access?"

"I sneak in through a window, wait till he's asleep, walk out with the statue." Nikki couldn't help but look at all of them like they were a little dimwitted. "It's theft. Not rocket science."

"If you get caught, penalties are worse if someone is home. You know this," Jared offered.

Nikki snorted. As if she'd get caught.

"I think the part you're missing," Audrey said, "is that Turner is paranoid. He has booby traps throughout his house. We have to find out what they are so we can circumvent them."

Great. Now she had Audrey talking to her like a child just because she hadn't been paying attention and had missed that part.

Nikki tugged at her lip while she thought. "Who does he trust?"

Mia threw her hands up. "I don't know. Ever since the indictment for my father, Darren has been lying low."

"Maybe we should skip him for now," Audrey offered. "Let's pick someone else."

"His is the only counterfeit close to being done."

"Household help? Gardener? Grocery delivery? Someone who doesn't leave has people come to him. Find out who those people are." Nikki stood and stretched. They'd been talking in circles, and she was tired of it.

Turner's house was big, like the others, but was no special fortress. It didn't help that her focus was split thinking about Wade and the Devereaux.

"I need a break. I'll be back tomorrow to start at this again."

"Where do you think you're going?" Mia asked.

"Out."

Jared stood and pinned her with a look. "Can you manage to stay out of trouble?"

"I've been nothing short of an angel."

Audrey snort-laughed and slapped a hand over her mouth.

Nikki shot her a dirty look. "Look," she said, "we're not getting anywhere with this. I need some space and time to think. Rehashing what we don't know isn't helping, and staring at your faces isn't doing anything for me either." She grabbed her bag, considered refilling her flask, but decided against it, and then waved to the room.

Wade had already been waiting hours. It was time for her to shift gears and think about the Carlisle and how to access the painting there. Outside in the fresh air, she immediately felt better. Heavy humidity hung in the night, but it was better than the oppressive atmosphere of the apartment. A mild breeze blew in from the lake and it was enough to motivate her. She walked a few blocks and then called a car to pick her up.

While she waited, she mapped Wade's neighborhood. It wasn't far from his office and Google Maps showed her a satellite image of his house. A cute little place on a quiet block. So different from how they'd lived with Dodger. Different than how she continued to live.

He'd laid down some real roots. Made a life for himself away from Dodger. She'd created a life, too, but hers was more of the same. Always looking for the next big score, the next payout, the next spark of excitement. Wade had traded it all in for a dog, a house, and a business.

When the car arrived, she checked the driver, saw it was the right guy, and got in the back.

"Hi, I'm—"

"Really not looking for conversation. Automatic five stars if you drive in silence and get me there quick." What was with all these drivers wanting to chat? Were there people out there who actually wanted to talk with strangers?

The guy drove in her requested silence, so she continued to read up on the Carlisle, searching for a chance to get access without having to break in. They didn't host as many events as bigger museums, but they had a few fancy soirées over the summer. However, the next one wasn't until late August. She doubted Donny and Wolf would wait until then. She was back to breaking and entering, so they needed to figure out the alarm system and guards.

The driver pulled up to Wade's house and only said, "Here you go."

"Thanks." Nikki opened the door, handed the guy an extra tip, and stepped onto the curb. Quiet didn't begin to describe the neighborhood. There was no noise. No people were on the street, and even traffic from the busy intersection couldn't be heard. Wade's house looked similar to the ones on either side of it. Not quite cookie cutter, but probably one company who offered a few different styles of homes for people to choose when the neighborhood was built.

They all had chain link fences around the backyard and a two-car garage at the alley. They had equal squares of lawn in front and signs posted down the block requiring parking permits. It was all so domestic.

She climbed the steps to Wade's door and knocked. His dog didn't even bark. Had she entered *The Twilight Zone*, or what?

Wade answered the door with a smile. "You made it."

"I said I'd be here."

He stepped back to allow her to enter, but she paused

just over the threshold. Wade leaned close and spoke quietly in her ear. "Flynn's upstairs. You're safe."

She released a slow breath. "Thanks."

"He really is the most laid-back dog you'll ever meet. He's never bitten anyone. Look," he said, pointing at a dog bed in the corner of the living room. "That little stuffed animal is one he's had since he was a puppy. Three years ago. If he were a vicious animal, he would've ripped it to shreds."

"Good to know he loves his teddy bear. I'm not a teddy bear."

Wade put his hand on her lower back and guided her farther into his house. "Flynn's the teddy bear. All he wants is attention and love."

She tried to ignore the warm sensation of Wade's touch and all the images it brought. It had been years. Why did this simple touch feel like it mattered?

She scanned the room. Big leather couch. Bigger TV mounted on the wall. Coffee table. True-crime book dog-eared. The dog bed and toy showed the most personality. The rest might as well be a showroom. Some things didn't change. His office showed more about him than the place he supposedly lived in. Not that she could comment since it was still more than she had.

"Have a seat. Can I get you a beer? I ordered pizza. It's sitting in the oven."

"I told you not to wait for me."

"And I said it was no big deal. It's gonna be a long night. Might as well fuel up." He pointed to the couch. "Beer?"

"Sure." She sat on the cool leather and folded her hands in her lap, which was just awkward as hell. Then she leaned back but felt too slouchy. She stood and paced the room, glancing out the front window and wondering what else the house held.

"Here you go."

She turned to see Wade setting a pizza box on the table along with two bottles of beer. He'd already opened one for her. They sat side by side on the couch similarly to how they sat in his office, but somehow this was more intimate.

Her stomach took that moment to growl loudly enough that the neighbors probably heard. "Guess I'm hungry."

"The Nikki I knew was always hungry." He bit into a slice of pizza and chewed. Then he added, "No, not hungry. Starving. Famished. Ravenous."

She helped herself to her own slice. "Still get that way before and after a job. But like you said, it's been a long day."

They ate for a few minutes, but it was beginning to feel like a date. She couldn't afford to have those lines cross. More than they already were anyway.

"Okay. I think the best way into the Carlisle is through the rooftop entrance. We can zipline from the neighboring building and get in. The buildings are tall enough that if we go in at night, no one will even notice."

He listened intently. "What about security?"

"I don't know what they have overnight. My guess would be only a guy or two. The cameras are only directed at the masterpieces. Motion sensors throughout first and second floors, but they'll be holding the Devereaux on the third floor, waiting for the experts."

"While you were visiting, I was checking out who works there. They have a small team of curators, but they often have grad student interns who do a lot of the grunt work. I think that's a way in."

"How so? They'll notice if a grad student walks out with a painting." She slid back on the couch and drank her beer.

"True. But grad students do the manual labor of packing and unpacking things. If you can get us another forgery, that's how we get it in."

"A forgery would buy us time, but why not just make the swap when I go in to steal it?"

"I think you go in, posing as a grad student. You unbox some painting that was shipped. We have the Devereaux forgery covered by something else. While you're there, you swipe the key card. That night, I go back, use the key card to take the Devereaux, uncover the forgery, and leave."

She squinted at him. "Why are you the one stealing if I'm the better thief?"

"Because you'll be out having drinks with your new colleagues. Safe alibi and you can keep them out of the office."

"I don't need an alibi if I'm not using my name, which, duh do I ever? And since they'll never see me again, it doesn't matter." She drank her beer to cool her throat. For a man who supposedly conceded that she excelled at her job, this plan didn't sound like he believed it.

"Roberta Wolcott is the head curator, and she's the only one with a full access key card."

"Then maybe you should be the one to come in. Use

your charm and pretty face," she said, making a circle at said face.

"She is a sucker for a pretty face, but I'm not her type. You are. I doubt I could get close enough to swipe her key card and not have her notice. But you, however, could steal it, pass it off to me, and go have drinks with her. There's a lounge down the block. You can walk there and I can have the card back in your hand before she feels the buzz and thinks she might have a chance with you."

She hated to admit it, but it was a pretty solid plan. "What does she look like? She might have a shot."

WADE KNEW THE minute he had Nikki hooked on his idea. Her stiff, defensive posture melted as a spark lit her eyes. Her snarky comment was just meant to get under his skin because she didn't want to give him an inch.

"I hate running a con," she said.

"I know. But I can't run this one."

"We agree to do one last job together and we have to switch roles. Can't help but think that's some cosmic meddling b.s."

"Since when do you believe in fate or cosmic anything?"

"I don't, but what's the likelihood we get thrown together like this? Some higher power is getting even with us."

"Did you grow a guilty conscience over your past?"

"Hell no."

"No qualms about taking the Devereaux from the museum where it belongs?"

She tilted her head. "Admittedly, that's a little rougher. But I see it more as a loan. I have no intention of letting Donny or Wolf keep it indefinitely. They'll verify it and then I'll steal it back. That's got to be some kind of world record for a thief, right? To steal the same painting three times? Maybe I'll get in Guinness or something."

"Record or not, the only way to get named is to get caught and we both know you won't do that."

She let out an overdramatic sigh. "I guess it'll have to keep for my memoir then, to be published upon my death so I can't be arrested for anything."

"Good to see you're still taking everything seriously."

"I can only do so much serious in a day, man, and this one has been chockful."

"So we have a plan. Can you get a forgery?"

"Maybe. Give me a few minutes." She rose and pulled her phone out.

She paced down the hall to his kitchen as she spoke in hushed tones to someone on the other end. He didn't need to listen to the conversation because he trusted Nikki to do her job, but he liked to watch her move. For the first time since they reconnected, she was herself. Her guards weren't totally down, but she wasn't actively hiding behind her armor. Her graceful movements were punctuated by her hands moving as she spoke.

Wade leaned back on his couch and waited. She suddenly turned, phone still in hand and asked, "How good do you think it needs to be?"

He shrugged. "I guess good enough that at first

glance it won't be noticed. Obviously the experts will start to evaluate and inspect it. They'll figure it out fast."

She covered the mouthpiece of her phone. "My connection has a copy that she wasn't happy with, so she created the one we used. If we want something as good as the one you got destroyed, it'll take a while. My gut says take the one that's ready."

"That's perfect. We're just buying time anyway." The experts were coming next week. The forgery only needed to fool the naked eye for a couple of days.

Nikki returned to her call, spoke for a minute, snapped sharply at whoever was on the other end, and then disconnected. She turned back to Wade. "She wants to meet you."

"Why?"

"She knows we have history. She says we can have the forgery for free if you meet her."

"Are you prostituting me?" he asked with a raised brow.

"Stop being a perv. She's a friend and she wants to meet someone who knows me. So tomorrow night we're going out for drinks." She came back and plopped on the couch again. "In the meantime, let's figure out what else we need to make this happen."

"You need to look like a grad student. Get yourself a lab coat. I'll take care of making the fake ID badge for your first day." He rose, took their dinner mess to the kitchen and returned with his laptop. "Let's learn about your new colleagues."

"I don't need to learn. I'm supposed to be a newbie. They'll tell me whatever I need."

"But Roberta will be someone you'd be familiar with.

You also have to know about the university. Programs, classes, professors. They'll want to compare notes."

"My brain already hurts. This is why I didn't go to college for real. I don't like to study. I just do what I need to do." She grabbed her beer and drank while he pulled up photos of Roberta and the other employees.

"Since you didn't go to college, where would you like to be a student now?"

"Since this is all for show, let's go with the University of Chicago. I like to be a smarty-pants. Assuming, of course, that isn't Roberta's alma mater."

"Nope. She's from out of state."

"Then I have my school. Maybe make me a school ID while you're forging documents anyway. Just in case."

For the next few hours, they talked and planned and worked like the team they had been. They created an entire life for Alice Hyde, graduate student at the University of Chicago, and they did a dive into Roberta's personal and work history. When they were both hitting exhaustion and making silly jokes, they knew it was time to call it a day. Nikki gathered her things and called a car.

"I can drive you home," Wade offered.

"It's better this way."

She was still keeping him at a distance and it was every bit as hard as it had been when she first left.

He nodded. "I'll walk you out. Flynn needs a walk anyway."

"I'm good waiting by myself."

"He'll be on a leash." Wade jogged upstairs and put Flynn on his leash. If he wanted to have Nikki in his life again, she was going to have to get used to Flynn. He was Wade's best friend.

Flynn rushed through the house and pulled at the leash to get to Nikki. While she didn't yelp or jump, she looked like she wanted to.

"Flynn, sit." For a change, his dog actually listened to the command. "He just wants attention. He's never bitten anyone. Want to give him a treat?"

At the sound of the word *treat*, Flynn's butt began to wiggle.

"That would put my hand near his mouth. No, thanks."

"Come on, boy. Out." Wade tugged the leash and Flynn walked by his side out the front door. Nikki followed behind.

In front of the house, Flynn stretched the leash to find the best spot to pee. Nikki stood beside Wade and watched cautiously.

"What kind of name is Flynn for a dog?"

"He's named after Flynn Ryder."

"From the Disney movie?" Nikki had made him take her to see *Tangled* the weekend it opened. She'd been excited to see a princess who did just fine saving herself.

"Yeah. He's a charming thief."

"But his real name is something nerdy like Eugene."

"Take a look at my dog. It fits."

"I see the nerdiness. He's kind of ugly. I don't see the charm."

"Give him a chance. He'll grow on you."

She gave him an incredulous look, as if to say she wasn't about to give him the chance to grow on her.

After taking care of business, Flynn came and sat at Wade's feet. He pointed at the animal. "Vicious, huh?"

"They all have their moments of looking cute."

"See? You just admitted he's cute."

She rolled her eyes. A car pulled up. "That's my ride."

As she walked away, he called out, "One day soon, you're gonna pet my dog and you're gonna like it."

She turned, walking backwards toward the waiting car, and said, "That sounds like a sick euphemism. I'm not petting that animal or anything else of yours. Been there. Done that."

"Just like you to make everything dirty."

She opened the car door. "That's the way you like me." She laughed and climbed in.

She was right. He still liked everything about her.

FIFTEEN

By the time Nikki crawled into bed at the apartment, her mind was bursting with details. She couldn't remember a time that she planned two jobs simultaneously. Plan one when another was set and just needed to be executed? Sure. But the whole planning process? No way. Too easy to make mistakes.

To top it all off, having Wade back in her life was overwhelming. She didn't know what to do with him. He wasn't her competition anymore, but she didn't know if he could be more. Her partner for this last job to get Dodger out of trouble. Then what? He expected answers and he wouldn't wait indefinitely.

She'd missed him. Brainstorming with him tonight had been a reminder of how good they were together. Not just on the job either. She had a level of comfort with him she didn't experience with too many people. At least not genuinely. She could fake it when necessary, but she didn't want to fake it with him.

After little more than a few scant hours of sleep, the sun was shining through the window nagging at her to get up. Time to figure out how to steal from a paranoid recluse.

She got dressed and went to the kitchen for coffee. She stood there for a full minute before realizing that no one had made coffee yet because no one else was there.

She started the pot and looked over the research that Mia and Jared had provided. When the pot was about brewed, Audrey came through the door.

"Wow. You're up early." Audrey narrowed her eyes. "Or have you not been to bed yet?"

"I slept. Here. Alone, before you ask. A lot to do, so I'm up early. Coffee's about done. Where's Jared?"

"He went to work. I told him you and I could handle coming up with a plan."

"Does that mean they finally gave you a key to this place?"

Audrey shook her head. "I took his." She moved to the kitchen.

"Grab me a cup while you're there." Nikki stood at the table and rearranged the photos and floor plans. "How much do we know about this guy?"

Audrey returned with coffee. "Before we get into this, how arc you? You haven't been around much. I'm worried."

"I'm fine."

"You're going after the Devereaux, aren't you?"

"I don't have a choice. Wade and I have it handled. We came up with a plan. By next week, it'll be done." She sipped the much-needed caffeine. "I might need you to cover for me a little, though. Our plan is going to require me to run a con."

"I don't like the sound of that."

"It is what it is. I want to avoid Mia and Jared finding out I'm doing another job. They'd throw a fit over any job, but if they figure out I'm taking the Dev-ereaux, things will explode. I don't want you caught in the middle, so the less you know the better."

"That's considerate of you to think of me, but I can't pretend to not know. And what if Wade's not trustworthy? He might leave you hanging. We're a team." She reached out and covered Nikki's hand with hers.

"Wade wouldn't do that. It's complicated and I don't want to go into it, but he's on my team, too."

"I'm here if you need anything."

Audrey saw them as a team, and in some ways, they were, but not at the level she had with Wade. Shared time mattered and she and Wade had a ton of shared time.

"Thanks. Now, tell me about Turner."

Audrey sat on a chair and curled her legs up against the table. "Not much to tell. He's been in hiding almost as much as Mia and Jared's fathers. He used to be as social as the rest. Parties, charity benefits, lavish vacations, everything. As soon as Benson and Towers took off, Turner locked down."

"Nothing lures him out?"

"He hasn't been seen at a society function in years. If there have been family events, Mia and Jared haven't heard about them."

"What about visitors?"

"Not that we've seen. But Mia hasn't had him under surveillance all that long."

"So maybe he does have people, like friends coming over. It's possible that Mia and Jared are never invited because of who their dads are."

"Uh…wow. None of us even considered that. We've been going on the assumption that since he was in tight with Benson and Towers, he'd still be part of Mia and

Jared's life like the rest of them. But that's a point we need to consider."

"Don't get me wrong. Dude still might be crazy with booby traps in his house, but we can't count on Mia and Jared to have all the information." Nikki reorganized the papers. "How does Mia know there are booby traps? Where did she get her information?"

"Gossip, I guess. Her intel has been dead on for all the other jobs. I doubt she'd be that wrong about Turner."

"Forget this. Let's start over. What do we know? Really know?"

Audrey shuffled the papers on the table. "We have a floor plan. That's one hundred percent. We know he owns the statue because we have a bill of sale."

"Bills. Pull up his financials. That will tell us what he does and where he goes."

Audrey crossed the room and tapped away at her computer. "Jared and I looked at this, but didn't see much. His bank statement shows weekly cash withdrawals. He doesn't use a credit card. He has a landline telephone. No recurring bills."

As she spoke, banking information filled the TV screen. Nikki took her coffee to stand in front of the TV. It was here. It had to be. They just weren't seeing it.

"How does he eat?" Nikki asked.

"No clue. If he leaves, he's buying groceries with cash, so I have no idea what store he shops at. If he's ordering, there would be a paper trail. We'd see evidence."

"Wait. Go back to the top." Nikki waited while Audrey scrolled to the top of the bank statement. "That's it. He's not leaving, but he's got his daughter doing his bidding. Her name is on the account. If I had to guess, she's going to the bank, pulling out cash, buying his groceries and then giving him money for buying anything else he needs. You can order a pizza and pay cash when the delivery shows."

"Okay. But that still doesn't give us much to go on."

"Yes, it does," Nikki said, still staring at the screen. "He's not totally isolated. He interacts with at least his daughter. Probably more. We need eyes on that house."

"That's a problem, too."

Nikki turned to face Audrey. "Why can't we just go sit on the house? We've done it before."

"Look again at the property." Audrey pointed at the piles on the table. "His front yard is the biggest we've encountered yet. He's got a fence running the perimeter and a gated drive. Cameras everywhere. We can't get close enough to surveil anything."

While Audrey continued to complain about the lack of access, Nikki studied the floor plans. "Do we at least know where the statue is?"

"As far as Mia knows, it's in a guest room on the second floor. That's where she saw it last." Audrey joined her at the table and pointed to a room. "There."

They stared at the house for a moment. Audrey added, "I've hacked his exterior cameras."

Nikki's face shot to Audrey's. "Why didn't you say so earlier?"

"Because it hasn't been fruitful. It's only been a couple of days, but nothing has stood out."

"No inside cameras?"

"Not that I've found."

"Let's see it. Run it on fast forward. I want to see who comes and goes."

"Fine." Audrey went back to the computer and booted up camera footage.

Nikki didn't have time for this. She needed to get to the museum tomorrow. Wade was working on making her ID and emailing the curator to secure her position. She had to do research so she could pull off the con. She knew plenty about art in general; it was a by-product of knowing what to steal. As a thief, she learned what would bring in the most money.

A con was different. She had to express some admiration for art. She had to feign interest in the artist and how the work was done. Hell, she didn't even know what was expected of grad students who worked at museums. She assumed it was free labor. Probably the grunt work that people who had actual paying jobs didn't want to do.

Images sped by on the screen. Audrey was right. The man didn't leave and for the past two days, no one had shown up. She flipped to the live feed.

"What happens when the alarm is tripped?"

Audrey shrugged as she focused on her phone. "The police would show?"

"Would it be enough to draw him out?"

"Huh?" Audrey looked away from the screen in her hand.

"If we trip the alarm, would he just answer the phone and tell them it's a false alarm? Would he flee in fear? Would he call the alarm company for a repair?"

"We don't know."

"Let's drive him out. If we strategically play into his

paranoia, we'll either get him to leave or get us access to *fix* the issue."

Audrey's face brightened as the spark of mischief lit her eyes. "You want me to create mayhem."

"Mayhem away," Nikki said with a wave of her hand.

"I should probably run it past Jared and Mia, right?"

"Why? We told them we'd come up with a plan. This is our plan. Can you trigger the fire alarm?"

"Sure. Why?"

"If anything will get someone to leave a house, it's fire. Who wants to be burned alive? Plus, we'll find out how long it takes the police and fire departments to respond."

"You sure you want to bring that much attention to the house?"

"What else do we have?"

"Here goes nothing." A few more taps on her keyboard, and Audrey had sirens blaring at the house.

They waited for movement. No one came out.

"Are you sure he's home?"

"Recluse, remember?"

They waited more. Nothing silenced the alarm. It took five minutes for the fire truck to arrive. Another two minutes for them to figure out how to get past the gate for the driveway.

"Seven minutes is a long time. Plenty to get in and out with one measly little statue. Where is this guy, though? Is he just sitting in his living room waiting to be rescued?" Nikki's eyes remained trained on the screen, scanning all exits, searching for movement.

The front door swung open as the firefighters prepared to break it down. But no one was there.

"Did you see that?" Nikki asked. "Automatic door?"

"No way. He's probably standing behind it, afraid the aliens will see him without his foil hat."

"Uh-uh. Look at the firefighters. They're all confused, too."

"Hold on." Audrey did a quick search on a split screen and then turned on a scanner. They listened to the broadcast coming from the firefighters.

Sure enough, they had no idea what was going on. No sign of fire, but they didn't see the homeowner either. A minute later, the first men left the house, and Nikki was pretty sure they were snickering.

On the scanner, they heard the all clear. Homeowner was fine. Hiding in an upstairs room. He contacted them via intercom system. They verified there was no fire. They suggested the police stop in for a wellness check.

"That's our way in," Nikki said.

"Impersonating the police?"

"No. Feed his paranoia. Make him believe that everything he's been hiding from is coming for him now."

"That seems a little cruel."

"Desperate times, babe."

Audrey went silent and continued tapping away at her computer.

"What are you looking for?" Nikki asked.

"How did he know the firefighters were there? How did he know when to open the door for them?"

"The cameras outside."

"I think this wily old man has more. They're just normally inactive." Tap-tap-tap. "Gotcha."

The split screen suddenly showed the exterior camera as well as the hallway on the second floor, which flipped to the living room, then the kitchen.

"Wow. He's got cameras everywhere."

"Yep."

"Is there a way for you to activate them from here?"

"I hope so."

Nikki stood and stretched. "Tell Mia to come over. We're going to need her help to pull this off."

"Where are you going?"

"For a run. Clear my head. Plan the details. I'll be back soon."

"Really a run? Or going to visit Wade?"

"A run. But speaking of Wade, I'm going to need you to cover for me tomorrow. I have some stuff to do."

She didn't wait for Audrey's response. Audrey would help her. She was loyal that way. Unfortunately, it also made her a liability because she was loyal to Jared, too.

Nikki couldn't afford to waste attention and headspace on such things right now. A run would free her mind and set her restless body straight.

SIXTEEN

Mia

MIA DIDN'T LIKE being summoned to the apartment. She did the summoning. And it only got worse as she sat and listened to Audrey and Nikki lay out their plan to get into Turner's house.

"You already tripped the fire alarm, possibly alerting him to the fact that we've hacked his system, and now you want to be even more blatant about it." She couldn't believe her ears. It was mad.

"Turner is paranoid," Audrey restated. "What's the worst thing that can happen to someone like that? Their fears come true."

"He thinks he's being watched, so we let him see the spies. He thinks they're listening, we show proof of the eavesdropping," Nikki added.

"What exactly do you expect me to do?"

Nikki straddled the back of the couch. Why couldn't the woman ever sit like a normal person?

"You said Turner went all hermit after your father's indictment. You go to him and tell him that you think you're being watched. Someone's after you. You need help. He's the only one who will understand."

"Excuse me? You want me to pretend to be as paranoid as he is?" As if.

"You need to panic." Nikki snapped her fingers at Audrey. "Show him a letter that was hand-delivered to your house. An I-know-what-you-did-last-summer kind of thing."

"A what kind of thing?"

"*I Know What You Did Last Summer*? Horror movie?" Audrey offered.

Nikki waved her hand. "Doesn't matter. Even if he refuses to help you, you're planting the seeds that whatever he's been hiding from is imminent."

"How does that help us?"

"He'll either leave his house to seek safety—" Nikki said.

"Or he'll burrow deeper and try to secure what he has," Audrey finished.

"The leaving makes sense. If he's not there, you can go in, but what if he stays?"

"He'll need help to fix the problem. That's where we come in. Or he hides deeper and we go in while he's hiding. We have a list of contingencies. It'll only take a few days to figure out which way he'll go."

Why did it seem that every second job they did became more and more complicated? She'd thought it was bad when she had to start a fight in the middle of a society party. Making another woman jealous was one thing, but to pretend to be paranoid? Not her forte.

"Here." Audrey strode across the room with a piece of paper in hand. "Show him this."

Mia took the paper and read it aloud. "'You'll pay for what your father did.'" They had no idea what it had already cost her. "'I'm coming for everyone who helped him.'" She set the paper on the table. "That sounds rather sinister, don't you think? Who is it supposed to be?"

"Doesn't matter. He'll make something up in his head." Nikki swung her leg over the couch and slid onto the cushion. "If that paper gets you access to the house, you can take pictures so we can see what kind of traps he might set. If he shoves you out the door, he'll still be left with the idea that he was right all along."

Mia crossed her arms. She wasn't supposed to have a hand in any of it. She planned the who, what, and when of these heists. She was not a con artist or thief.

Audrey leaned on the arm of the couch on the other side of her. Sandwiched between these two women, Mia felt the pressure to participate.

"We can't figure out how to flush him out, Mia," Audrey said.

"Fine," she huffed and stood.

Audrey handed her the paper again. "If you could do it today, or first thing in the morning, that would be best."

"Of course it would." And now she was doing their bidding. How had this happened? Her perfectly ordered plan had disappeared and she'd become part of some kind of team.

The thing was, she was becoming used to them. They seemed to accept her as she was, no pretense. It was more than she'd gotten from anyone else in her life in a long time.

She shoved the paper in her purse. "I'll head over there after dinner. Everything is worse at night."

Nikki clapped and hooted. "See? I told you she'd get it. She's every bit as wicked as we are."

Mia couldn't help but smile. In another life, Nikki's comment might've been taken as an insult, but it no longer felt that way.

SEVENTEEN

NIKKI HAD SPENT her afternoon studying—her least favorite way to occupy her time. She was ready to become Alice, the intern. When it was time to get ready for meeting Wade and London, she changed three times before settling on a short black skirt, loose tank top and sky-high heels. *This isn't a date*, she reminded herself. But it couldn't hurt to look good to make Wade drool.

Damn London for pushing to meet Wade. Nikki preferred to keep people separate. It had been fine working as part of a team, but she had no desire to introduce this team to her past.

London wouldn't let it go, though, and they needed her forgery. One drink. She could suck down a beer and drag Wade from the bar.

She left the apartment and texted London and Wade to let them know what bar to meet at.

London sent her a winking emoji.

Wade called. "Hey, I was thinking that I could bring my friend Boone with."

"Why?" Nikki asked as she stood on the corner waiting for her driver.

"It'll make it more social."

"I don't need to be more social." *Definitely not with you.*

"It might keep business questions to a minimum.

Plus, being social will allow me to get to know your friend."

Nikki almost blurted out that London wasn't her friend, but bit the words back. She didn't know how to categorize her relationship with London. They'd worked together and gotten drunk together. That was as far as most friendships went with her. "Fine. Whatever. It's only one drink."

"As if you've ever only had one."

"Are you calling me a drunk?" Her car pulled up and she climbed into the back seat.

"You do enjoy your alcohol."

"Who doesn't?"

"Would it kill you to just relax and have fun with friends for one night?"

"I have plenty of fun. I'm just not sure that putting you and London together is a wise move."

"Is she hot?"

"Really? You were hitting on me last night, but now you're asking if my friend is hot?"

His response was a low chuckle, so she disconnected.

Her driver glanced over his shoulder at her. "No decent guy would ask about your friend unless you said you were fixing him up. Want me to drop you somewhere else? Away from your date?"

Nikki laughed. "Thanks, but he was trying to get under my skin."

"If you say so."

Ten minutes later the car stopped. Nikki climbed out and walked through the doors of the bar. It was far busier than she had anticipated, but it would be easier for them to blend in and go unnoticed. She made her way around the perimeter to see if Wade or London were there yet, and when she didn't see either of them, she grabbed a table and waved a waitress over. Just because she said she was only having one drink with Wade didn't mean she couldn't have one alone.

Before she was able to order her beer, Wade and his friend walked in.

"My friends are here," she said to the waitress. "Beer?" she called to them.

Wade nodded. He wore jeans and a blue Henley with the sleeves pushed up to his elbows. So while it wasn't a date, he wasn't afraid to showcase some arm porn.

"Three beers and a white wine."

The waitress nodded and smiled at Wade and Boone as they took their seats across from Nikki.

"Nikki, this is Boone."

"Hi."

Boone smiled, his mouth curving behind a thick beard. "I can't believe I'm finally meeting the infamous Nikki."

"Infamous?" She glared at Wade. "How about notorious? Renowned?" Then she grinned and splayed her hands in the air. "Legendary."

Wade scoffed. "In your own mind maybe."

Boone leaned forward on his beefy forearms. "I like her."

"So you work with Wade doing security? Where'd you meet?" she asked as the waitress returned with their drinks. She slid the wine next to her for London.

"We were both working the streets and decided we could go legit and make money without having to look over our shoulders forever."

Nikki picked up her bottle and drank. She'd asked the question to be polite. She hadn't expected this man to have been her replacement. He'd known Wade since she left.

London breezed in, giving her a one-armed hug, before sliding into the seat next to Nikki. "Sorry I'm late. I got caught up."

"It's fine," Nikki said. "London, this is Wade and Boone." She pointed to each man.

London reached across and shook Wade's hand and when she slid her palm into Boone's she took a sharp intake of air. "Big hands," she murmured.

Nikki snickered.

"Okay. I want to hear it all," London said.

"All what?" Nikki asked.

"I want to know all about you and Wade. How did you meet? How long were you together?"

Nikki stiffened. That got way too personal way too quick.

Wade said, "We met when I lifted her wallet."

Nikki choked on her beer. "*Tried* to lift my wallet."

"Did I or did I not walk away with a wallet?"

Nikki's head filled with images of a young Wade and his clumsy attempt at stealing. He'd been so cute and he thought he could charm her enough to not notice his hand slip into her purse. Pointing at him with her bottle, she said, "You got *a* wallet, not mine, because I let you. I felt sorry for you."

This time Wade snorted. "You thought I was cute and my charm distracted you."

"Keep telling yourself that. In reality, it was pity."

"Wow," London said.

Nikki and Wade both turned to look at her.

"This," she said flicking a hand back and forth between them. "This is hot. Tell me what happened next."

"My dad thought Wade showed promise, so he brought him in to teach him."

"Is he as good…" London paused with a glance at Boone. "As you?"

"No," they answered simultaneously.

"I've only heard stories about how great Nikki is," Boone offered. "But I've worked with Wade and he's pretty good."

"He just admitted she's better," London said.

"Maybe he's just stroking her ego."

"Hold on," Wade interrupted. "Her ego doesn't need stroking. We're both good thieves."

"But I'm better," Nikki said.

Wade sighed. "She is the better thief. I'm the better con man."

"That he is," Nikki added.

"So you're like the perfect pair then," London said.

Perfect? At one time, Nikki had thought so. "Not a team. Plus, he's legit now. I bet he doesn't even remember how to steal." She took a long pull on her beer.

"I remember *everything*," he said quietly.

The emphasis was purely for her and she knew it. Even though she'd just taken a drink, her throat was dry. Thoughts of everything he could remember from their time together had her draining her bottle.

Setting the bottle back on the table with a clink, she said, "Let's put it to the test then."

He raised an eyebrow.

She waved a hand around. "Whoever lifts the most wallets in the next hour is the supreme thief."

"Like you said, I'm legit now. I don't steal from poor unsuspecting drunks."

It was her turn to sigh. "Fine. We'll return the wallets. We lift them and then have our trusty companions here return them to their owners. Plus, London and Boone will keep count so I don't have to worry about you cheating."

London giggled. "This is better than I thought it would be. I'm in."

"I don't cheat," Wade protested.

"Just show her how it's done," Boone said.

Wade stared into her eyes and she wished for another beer. "An hour?" he asked.

"I'll even give you a head start."

"No way. I won't have you claiming I won because of a technicality. We start together."

"Your call."

"Rules?"

Nikki rolled her eyes. He couldn't even just let a bet play out without laying everything out.

"We have to return here to hand off each wallet to London and Boone. The bet is purely for the number of wallets lifted, not the contents."

"Agreed." She slipped from her seat, reapplied lipstick, and blew a kiss at him. "See you in an hour."

WADE HAD NO clue what he'd gotten himself into. None of it made sense. He knew Nikki was going to kick his butt at this challenge. At least for this hour, he could step away from her and the tension that rose thickly between them every time they were in the same room. It was becoming harder and harder for him to keep his hands off her.

She skirted around the room, laughing and touching people as she went. Before he even made it to his first mark, she had double dipped and grabbed wallets from a couple she passed by. Watching Nikki work was mesmerizing. She was smooth and sexy and watching her lift wallets was making him want her more and more. Which went against everything he wanted for his life.

Hadn't he said he was done with being a thief? Yet here he was planning to break into a museum to save Dodger again and now he agreed to lift wallets in a bar. At least there was some consolation that no one would be losing anything tonight.

Two women stood near the bar and he went to introduce himself. While Nikki was stealthy, he preferred the smooth con. He chatted up the women and once he had them laughing, reaching into a purse was easy. On his return trip to hand off the wallet to Boone, he was struck with an idea. He felt better about this venture because ultimately it was no harm no foul. What if he could do that for the Devereaux as well?

Instead of handing off a priceless painting to get Dodger out of a jam, which he'd more than likely end up doing again, why not get rid of the problem completely? Nikki had mentioned stealing the painting back a third time to get it away from Donny and Wolf, but what if they got rid of them? He slid the wallet to Boone.

"You okay? You look distracted," Boone asked.

"I'm fine. I have a lot on my mind."

"Better clear your head. Nikki already has five wallets to your one. She really is something."

"Yeah, she is." Wade didn't care much about winning. He normally did, but not this time. His brain was suddenly consumed by trying to figure out how to take them all down and keep Nikki.

That last thought was enough to cause him to stumble and drop the wallet he'd just grabbed from a guy's jacket. When it slapped to the floor, he picked it up, but the movement caught the guy's attention, so Wade handed it over.

From the corner of his eye, he saw Nikki smile at him. Then she mouthed, "Sloppy."

He had no argument there. Moving to his next target, knowing he had no chance to catch up to Nikki, he focused on the idea of keeping Nikki. What would it take to convince her to give up this life? He watched as she danced with a guy for half a song before walking off with his wallet. Wade shook his head. Nikki was a thief. For her, it wasn't just survival or a job. It was who she was. If he wanted her, he would have to accept her as is.

The problem was that he wasn't sure that their lives could mesh without screwing up everything he'd worked so hard to build. And he didn't want to go back to that life. He didn't get off on the thrill and uncertainty of it all.

At the hour mark, he joined Nikki at the table with his last lift of the hour. Nikki didn't even try to hide her glee. She'd managed to steal from twenty-five people. He'd only gotten fifteen, which wasn't bad considering how distracted he'd been.

London had moved to sit beside Boone and had fresh drinks waiting for them on their return. "To the winner," she said, clinking her glass against Nikki's bottle.

Wade slid next to Nikki and accepted the bottle of beer.

"That was almost embarrassing," Boone said to him.

"I've got nothing to be embarrassed about. I agreed she's the better thief. But for someone who was accused of forgetting everything, I did okay." Turning to Nikki, he raised his bottle. "Congratulations."

"That was fun. Pure and simple." She drank from her bottle. "Sometimes I miss something that simple. It's a nice break." She clinked her bottle against his. "Thanks for that. You held your own."

"Not really. I just didn't suck as bad as you thought I would."

Pushing up from the table, London said, "We should go get rid of these last ones. Right, Boone?"

Boone glanced at him and then Nikki before agreeing. What was that about?

He and Nikki sat in silence for a minute, watching their friends walk away to go return stolen wallets. "We never did settle on a prize for the bet."

"Huh?" Nikki said.

"Prize for the winner. What do you want?"

She gave a low chuckle. "I doubt you have anything I want."

He lowered his head and stared directly into her eyes. "We both know what I can offer. It would be a hell of a prize."

"You're full of yourself."

"I can deliver. That's all that matters."

"As tempting as you make that sound—"

"Is it? Tempting?"

She offered a slow nod. "We have too much on the line to mess around." She slid from her seat. "I'm heading out. Early day tomorrow. You'll have the ID ready?"

"Of course. You need a ride?"

"I'm okay. See you tomorrow."

She walked across the room and waved at London and Boone. He drank his beer as London and Boone came back to the table.

"What was that?" London blurted.

"What?" he asked.

"We conveniently stayed away so you two could do your thing."

"What thing, exactly?"

London turned to Boone. "Is he normally this dense?"

Boone shrugged.

"Oh my God. You two are like a couple of wires arcing, just waiting to explode."

"While I appreciate your efforts, Nikki and I have a complicated situation. The past and present. She wants to prevent unnecessary distractions." He drained his bottle. "I have an early day tomorrow. Are you guys staying?"

"I think so," Boone said.

Wade extended a hand. "Thanks for tagging along, brother."

"It was an experience." Boone hugged him with his free arm.

Wade turned to London. "It was nice to meet you. I hope I passed muster to get the painting?"

"Oh, this was totally worth the trip."

Wade waved goodbye and went home alone.

EIGHTEEN

NIKKI WAS UP and out the door early the following morning. She needed to get the forgery from London, stop by her storage unit for a lab coat, and then to Wade's to get her fake ID. At the warehouse where London worked—and maybe lived?—Nikki rang the bell. A minute later, London swung the door open and a cacophony of sounds blared from the hall.

"What is that?"

London turned and led the way to her loft. Pointing at one door, she said, "Metal band, early morning practice." Pointing across the hall, she added, "Metal sculptor."

Now the banging of tools clashing with what might've passed as music made a little more sense. London slid her door open and as soon as she closed it, the noise they left behind became muffled.

"Thank you so much for letting me have this. What do I owe you?"

London lifted a shoulder. "Nothing. I was just going to paint over it. Besides, watching you and Wade last night was worth the price of this painting."

"You sure?" Nikki asked as she watched London flip through a stack of framed canvases.

"Yeah." Holding up the forgery of the Devereaux, she said, "It's really not my best work. Any expert will realize quickly that it's fake."

"That's okay. I only need it to buy a little time." At first glance, she wouldn't notice any difference, and she'd held the real thing in her hands. It was good enough.

London handed her the painting. "I assume Mia knows nothing about this?"

"Of course not. This is personal. Without going into all the gory details, I need this to help a friend."

"You're going to steal the real thing from the museum, aren't you?"

"The less you know, the better."

"Oh," London jumped up and down, clapping. "It will be like *The Thomas Crowne Affair*. Ever since Audrey mentioned it, I've watched it probably ten times."

"No. Not like the movie. The whole idea here is that I don't get caught. That no one knows I've made another switch." She wrapped the painting up to keep it hidden from view. They would pack it in a crate at Wade's.

"Okay, so obviously, you won't get caught. But neither did he. I'm talking about the smoking hot chemistry between you and Wade. *I* almost needed a cold shower last night."

Nikki didn't want to admit she had taken a cold shower. She couldn't stop thinking about him. "Wade is a means to an end. That's it."

"Oh, girl. That's a lie even you aren't buying. No way can two people who look at each other the way you guys do be all business."

Nikki paused and almost asked how they looked at each other, but in her gut, she knew. When Wade looked at her, he *saw* her. And she was pretty sure her eyes were constantly filled with lust. She shook her head.

"Thanks again. I'll probably see you this weekend when we go after the Latimer."

"Is Turner as off his rocker as Mia said?"

"From what we can tell, yeah." The man refused to leave his house even when the fire alarm was blaring. "It'll be interesting for sure."

"Aren't they all?"

"I guess." With a wave, she left the loft and walked back through the noisy hallway.

The stop at her storage unit was quick. Once she had the lab coat, she went to Wade's office. The store wasn't open yet, so she texted him to let him know she was there. He strolled up behind her carrying two cups of coffee, luckily no dog in tow.

"You're late," she said.

"Yeah, but I brought you coffee." He handed her a cup with a smile. Then he took out his keys and unlocked the door.

They climbed the stairs to his office.

"Let's see the masterpiece."

Nikki set her coffee on his desk and unwrapped the painting.

"That looks good."

"Not good enough to pass inspection. What are we going to cover this with?"

From behind his desk, he pulled out and unrolled a canvas. "Dogs having a tea party."

"I thought dogs playing poker was bad. This is hideous."

"But it's the right size. We can stretch it over the fake Devereaux, put in a couple of staples and when I go in to make the switch, it's easily removed."

They worked together to stretch the canvas enough to cover the fake Devereaux and wrapped it for delivery. Then Wade handed her an ID.

"Aren't they going to notice that I'm an extra person?" She studied the name. Alice Hyde. She had to admit that she made a pretty cute nerd.

"Probably not for a few days. Once we establish you as an intern, all you have to do is make friends. Then we'll pick a day for drinks and making the swap."

"You always make it sound simple. Running a con is never that simple. Breaking and entering isn't that simple. I think you've spent too much time with Dodger."

"Keeping it simple is what keeps me optimistic."

She was reminded of their time together last night, her joy in the simplistic nature of lifting a wallet unnoticed. This felt anything but simple.

He stepped closer and she was sure he planned to kiss her.

"One more thing," he whispered. Then he settled a pair of bulky, black-framed glasses on her face. His fingers brushed the blond hair of her wig back as he adjusted them around her ears. The gentle touch sent a shiver down her back.

"Really? It's not enough I have to be an art nerd. I have to look the part, too?"

"These aren't just disguise. First, the reflective lenses will distort your image for cameras, so facial recognition won't work. Second, there's a small camera. It sends a wireless signal to give me a live feed."

"No mic or earpiece?"

He chuckled quietly. "I can get that if you want, but no, they're not part of the glasses."

No way would she be able to focus with his voice in her head all day. She suddenly had an inkling of how difficult it had been for Audrey to have Jared in her ear. "This is good. Thanks."

He stepped back and studied her. "Slump your shoulders a bit. Look meek. Lose some confidence."

"If I'm a PhD candidate doing an internship, what makes you think I wouldn't be confident? Smart chicks are confident."

"Smart chicks are intimidating. You want to be approachable."

"I take offense to that. I *am* approachable."

Crowding her space again, he said, "You're the most intimidating woman I've ever met."

She wasn't sure if he meant it as a compliment, but that was how it came across. For a moment, they stared into each other's eyes on the verge of conversation. The heat and sexual tension made her blood roar. She should've collected on her winnings last night.

She blinked and turned away. "I better head out. Don't want to be late on my first day."

"Good luck."

"You don't need luck when you're good," she said with a smirk.

"True. Do you want to meet after you're done for the day?"

"I'm not sure. I might have to go check on some other things. I'll let you know."

WADE SPENT HIS morning filling out reports to clients, but he was distracted. He should've sent a comm with Nikki. If he was able to hear how things were going, he'd feel better. By midday, he wasn't any better. He went to Boone's office. "Do you have the analytics on the ads we placed?"

Boone looked up from his computer. "Not yct."

"What the hell, man? The whole point of running the ads is to bring in more clients. What about the specs for the alarm on the Gorham house?"

"Working on it."

"Work faster."

"What has your panties in a bunch today? I'm working as fast as I can. If you think you can do better, by all means, show me." He wheeled his chair back from the desk with his arms raised.

Of course Boone would throw that at him. Wade had a lot of skills but data analysis was nowhere near the top of the list. He understood it, but wasn't good at generating it.

"Maybe you should've gotten laid last night. Or did Nikki turn you down?"

"Screw you." It was a little too close to the truth and he didn't need the reminder.

Boone stood and came around the desk. "What's really going on? You only snap like that when you're worried about something else. And since we don't have any big jobs going right now, it must be Dodger." He paused. "Or Nikki."

Wade scrubbed a hand over his face. "Sorry, man. Just a lot on my mind."

Nikki hated running a con. If she didn't pull this off, they would lose access to the Carlisle. Dodger would be in more trouble, if that was even possible. But his greatest fear was that Nikki would disappear from his life again. He hated that she kept him at arm's length no matter what they worked on. They wanted each other. He had no doubts there, but she continued to keep her distance.

He had no idea how to explain all of that to Boone. "Just get me the information when you can. I'm going to grab some lunch. You want me to bring you anything?"

"Nah, I'm good."

Before leaving, he stopped in to see Devon. "I'm grabbing lunch. You want anything?"

"Thanks, but I have a lunch meeting with some prospective clients. You should come. Might take your mind off…your trouble." His partner gave him a knowing look.

"I'm fine. Unless you really need me for the meeting, I'd rather not. I've got some things to take care of."

"Would one of those things be a leggy brunette?"

"Unfortunately, no. I'll see you in a couple hours."

As soon as he was on the street, he put on his sunglasses against the bright summer sun, and called Nikki. It went straight to voicemail. He tried to convince himself that she was working and couldn't take personal phone calls while on the clock. She was supposed to impress her new boss, after all.

That knowledge did nothing to ease his worry. He knew Nikki could pull a con. He'd seen her do it, but that was years ago. Even back then, she preferred a straight-up theft to a con. If she hadn't kept her skills up…

No. This was Nikki. When it came to taking what wasn't hers, she always nailed it. And if she caught wind of him being worried, she'd probably kick the crap out of him. She had no use for worry.

He sent her a text to check in. How's the new job? Hope you're having a great day.

In true Nikki fashion, she responded with a middle finger emoji.

Yeah, she was just fine.

NIKKI WALKED UP to the Carlisle with the masked painting in tow. As she struggled to get through the door, the security guard rushed to hold it open for her.

"Thank you," she said on a breathy sigh. Then she looked up at him with wide eyes and rushed the rest of the story out. "The delivery guy on the street saw my lab coat and ID and pressed me into signing for this. It's supposed to go to Roberta Wolcott. Since she's my new supervisor, I know it's the right place. I hope it's okay that I signed for it. I have no idea what protocol is here."

"I'm sure it'll be fine. Can I see your ID?"

She held it up to him. He barely glanced at it.

With a nod, he said, "You know where you're going?"

"Somewhere upstairs?" she asked with a shrug and jostled the painting.

"Come with me. I'm Jason." He waved at the clerk to say he'd be back. "Let me carry this for you."

He took the painting from her. The plan was working almost too easily. "Thank you. I'm Alice."

"I don't know if Dr. Wolcott is here yet, but someone up there will be able to get you started."

"Thank you so much for your help. I'm so nervous. I still can't believe that I'm able to intern here."

At the top of the stairs, he continued into a room that

had long worktables and various pieces of art being studied or cleaned. It was a thief's playground. Nikki refocused. She was here for one thing and one thing only. But in the back of her head, she catalogued everything she could walk out with.

A guy wearing a lab coat rushed at them. "Where are you going?"

Nikki stepped forward and extended a hand. "I'm Alice, your new intern."

The guy looked at her hand and then up at Jason. "What's that?"

"Delivery," Jason answered.

"Just set it over there against the wall. We aren't expecting anything, so we'll deal with that later."

Jason followed directions, sent a smile over his shoulder at her, and said, "Have a good first day."

Lab coat guy just continued to stare at her.

"Is there an orientation or do I just jump right in?"

"No interns jump into anything here. You're here to learn and do what you're told."

"Absolutely," she said with a tight smile. This jerk deserved a swift kick to the shins. "What would you like me to do?"

"I have no idea. Roberta—Dr. Wolcott—usually likes to deal with interns. And as it's Friday, she won't be here until later." He waved a hand. "Go over to the storage closet over there and sort through the materials. Make an inventory list."

"Okay. Is there a format you prefer? Anything specific I should know about?"

"Look. We're getting ready for a huge exhibit. Because of the attention this piece will bring, we're rearranging other exhibits. We need an accounting of what we have to work with so we know what to order or borrow to create the vision Dr. Wolcott has." He turned to walk away.

"Are you talking about the Devereaux?"

His stride hitched and he spun.

"I'm an art history major. You better believe the return of such a high-profile painting is the talk of everyone in the department."

"Yes, well, it hasn't been authenticated yet, but we're cautiously optimistic."

"Any way I can see it?" she asked in an almost whisper.

"Sorry. Roberta is the only one who can access it. It's locked up until her experts arrive."

Nikki pouted.

Dude pointed at the closet.

"How would you like me to record this inventory? Paper? Computer? Stone tablet and chisel?"

"There's a tablet on the desk over there." Now he did walk away, completely dismissing her.

She picked up the tablet and moved toward the storage closet. Once the guy was gone, she engaged the camera for Wade and did a panoramic scan of the room. Later, she'd wander around through the two other doors that she saw. Knowing that things were being shuffled and moved around worked in their favor.

Once her inventory was done, she would move the dogs painting into the closet to make it easy for Wade to find and easier for everyone else to forget about.

She opened the door to the closet, which turned out to be a complete misnomer. This was no closet. It was bigger than a typical storage shed and had things piled everywhere. At least in here, she'd be so busy she wouldn't have to worry about interacting with people.

Three hours later, she was dusty and dirty and had managed to handle no fewer than five priceless works of art—handled with gloves of course, so she wouldn't have to worry about fingerprints or damaging the artifact. Then her phone buzzed. Wade.

How's the new job? Hope you're having a great day.

Real funny. As if she didn't have about five million more important things to be doing than cleaning out a closet. She sent him her favorite emoji. Then engaged the glasses again to show him the work she was stuck with for the day and let him know that she'd yet to see Roberta.

NINETEEN

Nikki spent the bulk of her day in that storage closet. At lunch, she had a text conversation with Audrey about Mia's visit with Turner. Audrey said Nikki would have to listen to the recording herself because she could never do it justice. However, they were a go for pushing the man over the edge to gain access.

By the time the afternoon rolled around, her phone was still buzzing with texts from Mia and Audrey and of course, Wade. Didn't these people understand what it was to be busy? Granted, Mia thought she should be sitting around waiting on the Turner job, but Audrey and Wade both knew she was busy.

Finally, Roberta Wolcott came in. Nikki was still making a list in the closet when she heard lab coat guy greet Roberta. Nikki waited patiently for the man to tell Roberta that she had a new intern, but he said nothing. How was she supposed to charm the woman if they didn't meet?

Gripping the tablet to her chest, she stepped from the closet and waited while Roberta and Lab Coat talked. When the conversation died, Nikki cleared her throat. Roberta and Lab Coat turned to her. She rushed forward with her hand extended.

"Dr. Wolcott, it's so good to meet you."

As they shook hands, Roberta said, "And you are?"

"I'm Alice. Your new grad student intern."

"I don't have anyone scheduled."

Nikki forced her eyes wide with concern. "Dr. Spenser said it was all arranged. Paperwork filed and everything. I only need hours for a couple of weeks. If I can't stay here, it's probably too late to get another internship."

"Let's not panic," Roberta said with a warm smile. "I'm sure we can work something out. Come with me."

Nikki released a pent-up breath and followed Roberta to her office. When they took their seats, Nikki pulled her bogus paperwork from her pocket. After setting the pages in front of Roberta, she pushed her glasses up on her nose. "I'm sorry something fell through the cracks. I mean, I thought it was all in place. I have my ID and everything." She held up her ID badge as proof of her honesty.

Roberta inhaled deeply and read over the paperwork. Since Nikki didn't want her to look too closely, she continued to talk as an added distraction.

"When Dr. Spenser said I'd been approved to work here, I was so excited. I've wanted to work under you ever since I saw the presentation you gave at the Art Institute. And then, my excitement tripled at least when I started hearing rumors of the last Devereaux not only being found but turned over to the Carlisle. It's amazing. This is a dream come true."

"Alice, was it?" Roberta said.

Nikki clamped her mouth shut and nodded.

"I'm glad you're excited. According to this, you only plan on staying for two weeks, which is far from enough time to dig deep into anything. What do you hope to get from the experience?"

"Originally, I wanted to see your approach to running a small museum, how you decide on the exhibits, et cetera. But now, since, uh…" She flicked her thumb over her shoulder. "The guy out there…he said you were rearranging exhibits to plan for the Devereaux. I would love to see how you decide what to keep, what goes, what fills the room around the Devereaux. It's all so fascinating."

"Paul should have given you a tour and explained how things work. What have you been doing all day?"

"Inventory." She handed Roberta the tablet. "I organized everything in the storeroom by era and style and then further by medium." Her years of hanging out in museums, studying pieces paid off in an unexpected way. Back then, it had been about knowing what to steal with the bonus of having a safe place to hang out. Now she put that knowledge to use. "Paul didn't give me any parameters for the inventory, so I made up a system. I'd be happy to convert it to reflect whatever you need."

Lord, she hated being a sycophant. Every nerve in Nikki's body pulled taut. Right now, she felt as though she just spent the last ten minutes bowing to her majesty.

"Actually, this looks pretty good. Since the Devereaux is a twentieth-century piece, I'm going to want to work with other modern pieces for the exhibit. How much more do you think you have to go through to finish up?"

"I can have it all done by tomorrow. It's not so bad once you start moving and rearranging."

"Tomorrow is Saturday."

"Oh, yeah. I figured it would be okay for me to come in since the museum is open and all. I was originally supposed to start earlier this week, but then the paperwork I submitted got lost in someone's inbox and I'm just so grateful to be here. I'd gladly give up my Saturday to make up for lost time."

"Just the morning, though. I'll be here at nine and I have an appointment at two, so I have to have everything locked up by one."

"Thank you. That sounds great."

Roberta stood. "I'll let you get back to it then. When you have everything inventoried, we can go through what options we have and reach out to other museums to see if there's something we'd like to borrow. I have some ideas blooming, but we can't get ahead of ourselves. If the painting isn't authenticated, this will be a disaster."

Nikki stood and took the tablet back from Roberta. "But it's the real deal, right? You just need to have verification?"

"I think so. But it's best to have an outside, objective source authenticate it. Especially since it had been stolen and there have been a number of forgeries over the years."

"So exciting. Art theft. Forgeries. It's like being in a movie."

"I hope you don't think that's a regular time around here."

"Of course not. I love art for what it is, but who wouldn't be intrigued by the rest?"

"I'm glad to hear it." The smile she offered Nikki was friendly, if not a little conspiratorial. "And as you're working through the inventory, make a list of things you think would be good for the exhibit."

"You mean…" Nikki gulped. "I can help?"

"We'll see what ideas you have. I make no promises."

Nikki glanced over her shoulder, then turned back. "Do you think I could see it?"

Roberta's smile widened. "Why not?"

She crossed the room, swiped her ID against a lock and opened the door to an adjoining office. The room was stark—only overhead lighting, a wall of drawers and a table where the Devereaux lay.

Nikki tried to muster the energy to look surprised and enthralled. Her acting skills were definitely being tested since she'd had the thing in her hands a week ago. "Wow," she managed. "Pictures never do them justice, do they?"

"Never," Roberta agreed.

They stared at the painting for a few minutes, and Nikki was struck again by the sheer loneliness depicted on the canvas. Part of prepping for this con was making sure she understood all she could about this painting and the artist. Devereaux had a string of lovers late in life, but married none. She'd married her high school sweetheart who died in war. After his death, she created a cavalier persona that was all about having a good time. Nikki could relate.

"Who do you think she's reaching for?" Nikki asked.

"Why do you assume it's a who?"

"She's too lonely to want more things. Plus, when you've already got a bottle of wine, what more do you need?"

The conversation gave Nikki time to look for cameras and other alarms. But the Carlisle was pretty low-tech, which worked in their favor. Finally, something was going their way.

Nikki looked up to find Roberta staring at her, not the painting. Nikki smiled, putting a little flirt into it. "I should get back to the inventory. Thanks for this."

"Any time," Roberta answered.

Nikki went back to the closet. As she continued to catalogue items, her mind wandered to the real flirting she'd been doing last night. She couldn't keep pretending she and Wade didn't have off-the-charts chemistry. She wasn't sure what to do about it, though.

NIKKI WAS EXHAUSTED by the time she neared the apartment. All she wanted was a long, hot shower, an ice-cold beer, and a violent video game. She needed a break from the planning and engaging. Her brain needed to turn off.

Of course, she should've known better than to think she'd get anything *she* wanted tonight. She walked into the apartment and Mia was there with Audrey. Nikki inhaled deeply and waited for the barrage of complaints from Mia about her lack of focus.

Instead, Mia asked, "What are you doing here?"

"What do you mean? I kind of live here."

"Audrey said you'd be gone for a few days because you had some problems with your father." Mia appeared to be genuinely concerned.

Nikki felt like she'd just stepped into an alternate universe. Mia didn't care about other people's problems. "I'm handling it. Besides, we need to get at Turner ASAP, right?"

"Yes, but…"

Was that pity in Mia's eyes? Oh, no. She was not going to be the downfall of the ice queen. Nikki huffed. "What happened when you went to see Turner?"

Mia scanned her face, as if looking for some kind of sign. "It worked wonderfully. The man sucked in all of the paranoia I could muster."

"Excellent," Nikki said.

"Better than excellent," Audrey added. "He's been hunkering down even more. All we have to do is come up with a plan to drive him into his panic room, break in, and leave with the statue."

Audrey said it like it was the easiest thing on the planet. Nikki just couldn't get her head in the game. So many players to keep track of. This was why she hated the con. It was so much easier to follow and track the movements of a mark without having to actually understand them.

"I'm going to take a shower. Then we can brainstorm."

"I'll order the pizza," Audrey said.

When she got to the hall outside her bedroom, she realized Mia was following her. "What do you want, Mia?"

"I hope you don't think Audrey overstepped by telling me about your father. In fact, she didn't say much. Just that your father was in some kind of trouble and needed your help."

That was more information than she'd given anyone about her life in years.

"Let me know if there's anything we can do to help."

"Why would you help me?"

Mia gave one of her tight-lipped smiles. "We're a

team. Even though it has gone against everything I thought we needed in order to accomplish my goals, we've formed something here. Loyalty is important, but it's also a two-way street."

For the first time in many, many years, Nikki felt a pang of guilt. Mia and Jared trusted her to pull off these jobs. They *trusted* her. She swallowed the uncomfortable feeling. "Thanks."

"Besides, if anyone can understand daddy issues, it's me." Mia said it in her usual highbrow way. But it made Nikki snort-laugh.

Nikki turned and went into the bathroom. As she washed away the dirt and grime from the storage room, she contemplated what the impact of her double cross would be for Mia and Jared. And Audrey. In her gut, she knew that Jared would accuse Audrey of being disloyal if he found out she knew of Nikki's plan. Everything had become so complicated. This was why she worked alone.

After toweling off, she put on some clean clothes and went back to the living room. Mia was gone, and Audrey was on the couch with a slice of pizza in her hand.

"That was fast."

"Uh, you were in there a long time. I thought about a rescue party, but seeing as you went in sober, I figured you were fine."

Forgoing the beer she really wanted, Nikki grabbed a bottle of water. "So what do we have?" she asked as she sat on the couch.

"Lots of video of Turner's house and the audio of Mia's visit. It's a little over the top."

"Did Mia witness any of the supposed booby traps?"

"No. But in the conversation, she definitely convinced him that she feels unsafe."

Nikki chewed her pizza. What could make a totally paranoid man reveal his secrets? "Do you think he'd show her if she just asked?"

"You mean, have Mia go back and say, 'Hey dude, show me your booby traps?'"

"Kind of." She gnawed her lip for a moment to gather her thoughts. "The guy obviously doesn't hate Mia. He let her in to talk. He knows she's looking for help. What if we create the illusion of her being followed or targeted or whatever trigger words will mean something to him? If she goes to him with proof of this, and asks how she can protect herself, would he turn her away?"

"I have no idea. That would be a question for Mia."

"I have no problem triggering an alarm to make him hide so I can go in and steal the statue. But if he has something rigged beyond an alarm... I'm not willing to lose a limb for Mia and Jared."

Audrey's face scrunched up. "Ew. Mia says booby traps and your mind goes to dismemberment?"

"Well, if I'm gonna booby-trap something, it's going to be effective." Her phone buzzed with a text. *How'd the rest of your day go?*

No wonder the lines between jobs were blurring. She couldn't step back from anything.

"Wade?" Audrey asked.

Nikki nodded.

"How are things going there? Anything I can do to help?"

The guilt surged up again. "It's best if you stay out of it. It's not fair to involve you. It'll mess things up between you and Jared."

"Jared and I will be fine. And I'm sorry if you didn't want me to tell Mia about your dad. I didn't tell her about the painting, of course. Just that your dad was in trouble. I'm not a good liar, so being vague seemed like the best route to cover for you."

"I appreciate it. If I can just get to next weekend, it should all be done."

"Take the time you need. Do your thing. I'll handle this with Mia and finish gathering the info from Turner's house so we can get you in there."

A sudden weight lifted from Nikki's chest. "Really?"

"Yeah. I'll text you the info as we get it and you can let me know if there's anything else you need. Focus on getting things right for your dad." Audrey twisted on the couch to fully face her. "Are you really just going to steal it and give it to this blackmailer?"

"Yes. But then I'm going to do my best to steal it again and return it to the Carlisle."

"Wait…that's stealing the same painting like three times?"

"Yeah. It's a lot. But I can't go there yet. Unfortunately, the Carlisle is probably going to find out they have a forgery. I haven't figured out how to get them the real one back without tipping off the guys who want it." She was getting dizzy again just thinking about it.

Her phone buzzed again. She didn't even have the energy to look.

Audrey patted her leg. "Go. See what Wade wants and get that wrapped up."

Nikki couldn't help but think that Audrey was referring to more than the theft of a painting. "Thanks," she said again.

Then she texted Wade that she was on her way.

TWENTY

NIKKI HADN'T BOTHERED to answer any of his texts, but then she suddenly said she was on her way over. Wade sent Flynn out to the yard to hang out. It was a beautiful night and Flynn would probably just nap on the deck. It would give Wade a chance to ease Nikki into getting used to the idea of being around his dog. If he had his way, they would all be together a long time.

When she rang his bell, he wasn't prepared for the sight of her. Her hair was up in a messy bun and she wore leggings and a tank top. This was unguarded Nikki.

She also looked exhausted.

"Everything okay?" He opened the door wide for her to enter.

"The dog?"

"Already in the yard."

She walked past him and the scent of her shampoo trailed behind. He inhaled deeply and locked up.

"Hungry?" he asked.

"I just had some pizza. But I could use a beer."

"Sure. Have a seat and I'll grab a couple bottles." He went to the kitchen and by the time he returned, Nikki was stretched out with her head resting against the back of the couch. He'd never known stress to bother her.

He popped the top on the bottles and handed one to her.

"Thanks." She sat up and drank. "I assume you saw the footage of the Carlisle?"

"Before we get to that, what's going on?"

"What?"

"You look exhausted."

"It's been a long day. A lot on my mind."

"Is it the other job?"

She just stared at him for a minute and he could almost see her shields inching up. He sat on the couch beside her. "Come on. I know you're working on something else. You've made it clear that it's an important job that you've already committed to. I'm not asking for specifics. I'm just giving you a chance to vent a bit with someone who gets it. No judgment."

Her shoulders sagged. "It's tough. The mark is a shut-in. There's no waiting for him to go."

"He's gotta sleep, right?"

"Of course. But even if I get past the cameras and alarm system, it's rumored that he has booby traps."

Wade laughed. He couldn't help it. "Booby traps?"

She chuckled. "Crazy, right? We—I don't even know what kind."

"Maybe it's nothing more than rumors."

"My intel is pretty strong that it's not a story. I just can't get specifics."

"Anything I can help with?"

She shook her head slowly, resigned. Another drink of beer, then she asked, "Ready to hear about the Carlisle now?"

"Enjoy your beer. Relax for a while."

"I don't have time to relax. Too much to plan and do."

"Nothing more is happening tonight. Let's push it all aside for a while. Talk about something else."

She sank against the back of the couch again. "So talk."

"I'd rather hear what you've been up to for the last few years. You know what I've been doing. Not long after I realized you weren't coming back, I started building my business with Boone and Devon. That's where my focus has been."

"That and keeping Dodger out of trouble, right?"

"I obviously haven't done a great job of that, have I?" It was his turn to shake his head. "I thought he was doing better. The gambling was always there, but most of the time, I could bail him out without an issue. I don't know what he was thinking this time."

"He wasn't. I told you. Dodger doesn't think. He does what feels good in the moment and that's it."

Wade inched closer. "There was a time you lived like that, too. Are you telling me you've changed?"

"No. I still do what feels good. The difference is, my decisions don't affect other people. If I make a mess, I don't wait for someone else to fix it."

"Let's go back to the part where you do what feels good." He stroked a finger from her jawline down her neck and across her collarbone.

Her breath hitched.

"Been thinking about you a lot."

"Yeah?"

"Are you going to say you haven't been thinking about me?"

She remained silent, but made no move to stop his

light caresses across her skin. She closed her eyes and swallowed hard.

"What are you doing?" she whispered, her eyes fluttering open.

"I want to make you feel good. I think we can both use some stress relief."

"And that's all it'll be? Stress relief?"

His fingers paused. This was his chance. He could tell her that he wanted to rebuild their relationship, but he knew by the way she asked that all she was looking for was a good time. He tried not to let that sting, but it did.

He licked his lips, and her eyes tracked the movement. "If that's all you want, I can oblige."

WADE WENT UPSTAIRS and used his bathroom to clean up afterward. Then he called Flynn in and stuck him in the bedroom. After giving his dog a few belly rubs, Wade went back down to the living room, figuring he'd given Nikki enough time to settle. The look on her face when she went to the bathroom told him that she was invested, even though she didn't want to be.

Lucky for him, they still had work to handle so she couldn't run from him. He put on a pot of coffee and returned to the living room. Nikki was already sitting on the couch.

"Feel better?" he asked, not even attempting to cover his smirk.

"Yeah, smartass. You are definitely a stress reducer. Now are you ready to work?"

"I'm always ready. Coffee's on." He sat beside her,

close but not encroaching. "What happened at the museum?"

"I spent my day in their storage room taking inventory to help Roberta create the right feel for the Devereaux exhibit."

"So you got to meet Roberta?"

"Yeah. I definitely hit it off with her. She showed me the Devereaux and she was so impressed with my inventory skills that she invited me to offer suggestions for the exhibit. I don't think it'll be too difficult to get her to go out for drinks."

She pulled a notebook from her bag and began to sketch out the third floor of the museum. As she drew, Wade watched her movements, the cascade of her hair over her shoulder and brushing her cheek, the way she bit her lip in concentration, the restless jiggle of her knee. So much about Nikki was the same. She was an older version of the girl he fell in love with and stupidly lost.

"The storage room is here." She pointed to her rough sketch. "I have the forgery uncrated but still wrapped so it doesn't draw attention. Dogs sipping tea would definitely stand out. The Devereaux is in a back room behind Roberta's office. She has a standard lock on her office door, so that's an easy pick. The back room has the pass key lock. Roberta's card obviously opens it. I don't think anyone else has access."

"Do you know when her experts are coming?"

"Just vague answers of next week."

"Coffee should be ready. Want some?"

"Of course. Gotta stay sharp. Plenty to plan."

Wade went to the kitchen and poured two cups.

When he returned, Nikki had her legs stretched out to the coffee table, her head rested on the back of the couch, and her eyes were closed. She was so beautiful sitting there in his space.

Without opening her eyes, she said, "Stop staring. It's creepy."

"Sorry. After spending the day at an art museum, I would think you'd understand a person's desire to stare at something beautiful."

Nikki pushed up to take a cup and let out a low whistle. "Someone's been sharpening his compliment skills. A line like that would definitely have the power to make the right woman swoon."

What does it do to you? He stopped himself from asking, no matter how much he wanted to know. "I know better than to think you would swoon."

She took a drink of the coffee. "Mmm...good."

The low sound in her throat had him imagining her naked again, but he tried to focus. "When do you think we'll be able to go in?"

"Maybe early to mid-next week? I don't want to rush the con. I have to have time to flirt with Roberta and get her to want to have a drink with me."

"When's your other job going?"

She narrowed her eyes at him.

"I'm just asking. It's not like I'm going to crash your job. But we also don't want to plan both jobs for the same day."

She smiled. "That would be one for the books." Then she sighed. "But you're right. I don't know when that one is gonna go. I have to figure out the booby trap issue so I can go in."

"Let's run the scenario. What does the place look like?"

She tilted her head and studied him. He nudged her leg. "I'm out of the game, but I'm still a great planner. Talking through it might give you what you need."

"It's a mansion." She set her coffee on the table. "The item I'm after is upstairs in a spare room. Unfortunately, so is his panic room."

"Panic room?"

"I told you he's a recluse. We tried to drive him out, but he holed up instead. So I have to go in while he hides."

It was at least the second time she'd mentioned *we*. "We, huh? You're working with a team." It wasn't a question. Nikki would never say *we* when she meant *I*. She'd preferred to work alone. "I never thought I'd see the day."

"Things change. Besides, the money's too good."

"It's just about the money?"

She opened her mouth and paused. In that moment, he realized that it wasn't just a job and cash. There was more at play. "It started out about the payday, but it works, you know? I forgot how good it felt to have someone have my back."

He wanted to reach out and touch her, reassure her that he'd always have her back. "I get it. That's Boone and Devon for me. I'm glad you found people."

"For now."

"Let's talk booby traps. You've seen inside the house?"

"Not in person. But yeah."

He handed her the notebook again. "Draw it out. There are only so many ways a trap can work. Most people won't want a deadly trap in their house that might misfire and take out a loved one."

She accepted the pad and began drawing. She spoke as she drew lines. "I'm thinking the hallway is the most likely place. He only has one piece of furniture down the entire length. Empty space allows for damage."

"Makes sense. Knock someone out before they get to the valuables. I assume there are more valuables than whatever you plan to take."

"I'm sure, but I don't have the intel on what. The room where my…item is has nothing profoundly special."

He smiled at the caution in her words, as if they were still competitors and she didn't want him to know what she was after. "Since you said you tried to drive him out, I'm guessing you don't care if you get a little dirty."

"How?"

"What if you use a drone to shoot something off, like a flash-bang or a smoke bomb? Would that be enough to trigger the traps?"

"I have no idea. What if they're only triggered by weight? A smoke bomb won't work."

Wade rubbed his jaw. "Logically, a weight-based trip is harder to pull off. A tripwire, maybe. But what happens when you step in the wrong spot? A trap door to fall into a pit of punji sticks? The trigger causes a giant boulder to roll after you?"

Nikki burst out laughing, which was what he wanted.

"It's not Indiana Jones," he added. "I've never seen a place you couldn't get into. It's not even like you to doubt yourself like this. The Nikki I knew would just show up and improvise."

She stood and stretched without responding. "Thanks for the pep talk," she finally said. "I have to get moving. Roberta is expecting me first thing in the morning."

"On a Saturday?"

"Museum is open. I want to prove my worth."

"Can you get her to go for drinks tomorrow?"

"No. She made a point of telling me that I can only be there until one because she has plans." She pulled her shoes back on and grabbed her bag. "But we will have some alone time so I can get my worshipping flirt on."

"I'd like to see that in action."

"I'll leave it to your imagination." She bent over and patted his cheek.

Impulse propelled him up and he took her hand. "Come here when you're done tomorrow. Spend the night."

"That doesn't sound casual."

"Casual enough. We can do a whole lot if we have the entire night."

"Tempting. I'll think about it."

Wade backed off because Nikki never responded well to pressure. He even resisted the desire to kiss her goodbye. "Need a ride?"

"I'm good." She headed to the front door and paused. With a glance over her shoulder, she said, "Thanks. For tonight. I'll get my head on straight."

Wade sighed as she left and went to check on his dog. For every bit of progress he thought he made toward Nikki, she seemed to pull another step away.

TWENTY-ONE

SATURDAY MORNING, Nikki woke up, stretched, and thought about her day. She needed to get her head in the game to interest Roberta in drinks. But she also had to figure out a plan for Turner. She couldn't expect Audrey to come up with a plan alone. Even if she had help from Jared and Mia, none of them were thieves. They didn't understand what it was to sneak into someone's house undetected and walk out with a piece of valuable property.

As she got ready for another fun-filled day of inventory, she replayed her conversation with Wade about Turner's house. His idea hadn't been bad. If they ran a test to trigger the traps, even if the test didn't work, it would at least give them another variable to work with. She scribbled a note to Audrey to get a couple of smoke bombs and a drone because they had a field trip tonight.

Ever the good intern, she stopped for coffee so she could bring one to Roberta. When she walked into the museum, Jason was manning the door again, so she waved.

"My ID is in my bag." She shrugged and held up the cups of coffee.

"No problem," he answered.

As she headed to the stairs, she added, "If I had

known you were going to be here, I would've grabbed one for you."

"Thanks, but I'm good."

"Next time," she said cheerfully.

If she could walk in this easily, she briefly wondered if she would be able to pull the switch without having to fake date Roberta and swipe her card. If she came in extra early one day, hacked the alarm and made the switch, she could just put the Devereaux on the roof to retrieve later.

That thought was banished when she got upstairs and realized she couldn't access the work area. No one was there yet and it was locked up. While she could probably bypass the simple lock, a move like that would draw attention.

"I'm coming," a voice called from behind her. Roberta was hustling up the stairs. "Sorry I'm late."

"Actually, I think I was just a few minutes early." She held out a cup of coffee and the bag with creamer and sugar. "I figured if we have to work on a Saturday, we might as well start with a good cup of coffee."

"Thank you. That's very thoughtful. Let me get us in and then I'll happily take that." She jiggled a giant key ring and opened the workspace.

When Nikki handed over the coffee, she made sure to allow her fingers to brush Roberta's, just enough to make a slight contact, and then she noticeably darted her glance away, as if embarrassed.

Roberta cleared her throat. "Do you need any help getting started?"

"Nope," Nikki answered with a bright smile. "I'm

going to pick up where I left off yesterday and I've already started a list of possible exhibit ideas."

"I look forward to hearing them." With a quick nod she turned toward her office, leaving Nikki alone.

While she worked, Nikki did in fact make a list of pieces that would work well with the Devereaux. Halfway through her time, she got a text from Audrey looking for an explanation for the drone and smoke bombs. Nikki responded and Audrey immediately sent a gif of a villain laughing.

Nikki's interactions with Roberta had been few but meaningful. They talked art and joked, so Nikki knew she was on the right path to get her boss out for a drink. She'd just about finished up the inventory when Audrey texted that she couldn't find a drone that would do what they needed it to. She found some small ones that would be good for recon, but nothing that could carry or drop a smoke bomb.

Damn. Every plan they came up with had huge wrinkles. Then she had a thought. The drone had been Wade's idea. Maybe he had one.

Roberta's heels clicked across the room and the keys jingled again, so it was time to go.

"All set?" Roberta asked.

"Yes." Nikki wiped her hands on her pants and grabbed the tablet. "Do you think it would be okay for me to take this with me? I know it's museum property, but I'd like to finalize the database and maybe rethink some pieces I listed for the exhibit. I promise I'll bring it back Monday."

"I don't see why it would be a problem. It's not as if you're asking to borrow a Monet."

"I couldn't imagine."

As they headed out the door, Roberta chuffed a laugh. "Actually, back in the '50s and '60s, many museums did have a loan program. They allowed priceless works of art to be used in patrons' homes."

"No—" Nikki barely stopped herself from swearing, which would've been unprofessional.

"Yes."

"How did they stop people from stealing it?"

"I'm not sure of all the steps, but the patrons were required to carry extra insurance, and whatnot."

"That's unbelievable. I can't imagine anyone having that level of trust these days." Her thief's heart kicked up a notch at the thought of convincing museums to just hand over their art.

"Have a good weekend, Alice."

Nikki blinked at the use of her alias. "You too," she added a beat later than normal. She shook her head as Roberta stepped out of the museum.

Nikki was letting the con get away from her. Out on the street, she called Wade.

"Hello, beautiful. Miss me already?"

"Actually, I'm calling because I was wondering if you have a drone."

"Hmm… I might. I thought you said my idea wouldn't work."

"I didn't say it was a bad idea. And right now, it's all I've got. But the only drone we found can't carry or throw a smoke bomb. Do you have one that fits the bill?"

"I do."

Silence. This man and his games. "Would you let me borrow it?"

"I might. What's in it for me?"

Nikki rounded the corner and leaned against the building. Lowering her voice, she said, "What do you want?"

"You. In my bed all night."

Not a bad trade-off. She opened her mouth to answer, but then he added, "And all day tomorrow. No work. All play."

"Uh…" As tempting as a full night with Wade was, she wasn't sure if she could swing a whole day. Could she afford that time away from her jobs? Then again, why couldn't she? All work and no play made Nikki a cranky girl.

"My drone can do everything you need."

"Fine. But I'll be late tonight. I have to make sure the drone can get the job done."

"Stop by the store. I'll have it ready for you."

"Thanks."

"See you soon."

By the time she got to the store, Wade was busy with a client upstairs, but the girl behind the counter handed her a box and simply said, "Wade said to give this to you."

"Thanks." She accepted it and hopped back in the car she'd left waiting. In the back seat, she undid the flaps of the box. On top of the drone was a note written in Wade's blocky writing.

Don't get caught. This is an expensive toy. See you tonight. Have fun.

Something about the note felt overly intimate. As

if all the years they'd been apart washed away. When the car pulled up to the apartment, she was still feeling hazy about her relationship with Wade. She did her best to push it all aside and get the job done. She hadn't let a man distract her since the first time Wade was in her life.

Inside, Audrey was waiting. Nikki set the box on the table and Audrey smacked her arm. "You could've texted to let me know what was going on."

"I did. I said I was working on it. I got us a drone."

Audrey cooed as she opened the box and took the plane out. "This is top of the line. Where did you get it on short notice?"

Nikki crossed her arms. "Don't ask."

"Dude. If Mia finds out you lifted this—"

"I didn't lift it. I borrowed it." She took a deep breath. "From Wade. He runs a security store that sells spyware toys. I have to return it. But it'll work, right?"

"I guess that depends on exactly what you need it to do."

"I'm thinking that we set off the alarm at the house. Then, while Turner is in his panic room, we tap his indoor cameras, and use this to launch smoke bombs into the house. If we're lucky, we can trip the booby traps that Mia is so sure are there."

"And what if we can't? Then we've exposed ourselves to his house again."

"Better watch it. You're starting to sound like Mia. Do you have any idea how many trips I take while casing a job? Tons. Planning for every contingency. That's what makes me good." She yawned, her late night catching up to her. "I'm going to take a nap. Call London and let her know we need a ride as soon as it's dark."

Nikki grabbed her bag and headed toward her bedroom. Audrey stepped in front of her, still holding the drone. "Is everything okay?"

"Yep."

"And Wade?"

"What about him?"

Audrey studied her for a minute. Her voice dropped to a harsh whisper, even though they were alone. "Did you sleep with him?"

"What do you care who I sleep with?"

"Oh my God! You did!"

"And?"

"So much. First, was it good? But also, like, are you a couple again? Did you tell him about us? Are—"

Nikki slapped a hand over Audrey's mouth. "Yes, it was very good. No, we're not a couple. I did not tell him about you guys, but he knows I'm working with a team. Now, let me go take a nap."

She released Audrey and scooted around her. This was why she didn't have friends. They always wanted to know things. Like every single detail. The thing was, talking about Wade would force her to think about it, and she couldn't afford to think more about him.

After a quality nap she was ready to get everything done. She jumped in the shower and dressed in her running clothes so she'd be ready to sprint if necessary. She heard female voices in the living room, so she figured London was here.

"Hey, bitches," she called as she rounded the corner to get some coffee from the kitchen.

"Someone's in a good mood," London said.

With coffee in hand, she sat on the back of the couch. "It's the first time in over a week where I feel like we actually have a plan and can get this done."

Audrey looked at her from behind her desk. "You're usually all about having more time to plan, get all the pieces in place. Now you're in a rush?"

She lifted a shoulder. "What can I say? I guess you all spoiled me with these fast turnaround jobs."

"Or are you just in a hurry to get your groove on with your ex?" London asked.

"Do I strike you as the kind of woman who changes my plans for a guy?" she scoffed. "Turner is making me itchy. I don't trust someone who never leaves his house."

Audrey had the drone propped on her lap and was fidgeting with it. A moment later, it zoomed across the room. "So what's the plan?"

Her eyes were on the drone as it circled the apartment.

"I assume you have that handled?" Nikki asked.

"Oh, yeah."

The excitement in Audrey's voice caught her off guard. The drone hovered in the hallway and suddenly, it shot a can of soda down the hall. It combusted on impact, spewing soda all over the wall and floor. Audrey jumped up. "Did you see that? This is so cool."

She landed the drone and put the remote beside it. Then she scurried to the kitchen for paper towels. "Trial run," she added as she began mopping up the puddle.

"Good to know it will do what we need it to. But shouldn't I be doing the trial?" Nikki said.

"If you're manning the drone, how can you be monitoring the cameras? You need to see what he has inside. I don't."

"I'm pretty sure you can record what the cameras see." Nikki smiled. "But you go ahead and have fun with the toy."

Audrey gave a fist pump. The girl was such a nerd.

"I think we need to get to the house and set off the alarm again to drive him into the panic room. Then send in the drone. How many smoke bombs do you have?"

"Three."

"That should do it. I hope." The space wasn't that big. She just needed to know if anything would kill her. "Are you just going to smash a window?"

"Nah. It's a nice night. He has the second floor windows open. If it was hotter out, we might have an issue. But these are strong enough to bust through the screen. I'll just aim low enough that it'll be little more than a tear. What time are we heading out?"

"I think once it's full dark." Nikki glanced out the window. The sun was setting, but the sky was still filled with a pinkish orange glow. "Let's go eat."

"And she's back, ladies and gentlemen," Audrey called.

"What are you talking about?"

"You haven't been yourself lately."

"Whatever." She wasn't about to admit she hadn't been feeling like herself. Her brain was fired up for these jobs. Maybe Wade had been right. She just needed to step away and process, have a little fun.

WADE SPENT HIS day with clients, but when dinner rolled around, he decided it was time to check on Dodger. The man had never laid this low for this long in his life. He had to be itching to do something. Wade picked up some Italian and some groceries and drove to Iggy's house. When Nikki said where she'd seen Dodger, Wade knew that the old man was hanging with his old drinking buddy.

He rang the bell and got no answer, so he pulled out his phone and called.

"Yeah."

"I'm at Iggy's door. Let me in."

Dodger hung up without another word. Then the door swung open. "How'd you know where to find me?"

"It really wasn't that hard." He pushed his way in.

Dodger stuck his head out the door and looked down the block. "You sure you weren't followed?"

Wade shook his head. "This isn't TV. No one has the time or energy to follow me just to get to you."

"I've been gettin' calls and texts from Donny. He's gettin' anxious. When are you gonna get the painting?"

"I'm working on it. Soon. Within the next few days. I'll handle Donny."

"Whatcha got there?" he asked, jutting his chin toward the bag.

"I figured if you're staying with Iggy, you're probably doing more drinking than eating. I brought dinner and a bag of groceries."

"Where's dinner from?"

"Sabatino's."

"You shoulda gone to Alonzo's. They're way better."

Wade sighed and bit back his retort. This man was making it hard to remember why he was helping him. He needed to keep his cool because he wanted Dodger to finally cough up the information he'd been withholding about Donny and Wolf.

He set up the food on the rickety coffee table. "Iggy home?"

"Nah. He's at the bar."

Good. At least they had privacy.

"So how you gonna do it? What's the plan for the museum?"

"Don't worry about it. I have it covered."

"Boy, don't mess with me. Planning a job was never your thing. You're good in the moment, but you're not a big picture thinker."

"Maybe not when I was twenty, but I've made plenty of plans that didn't include you."

"Talking through it can help work out the kinks, that's all I'm sayin'." He opened the lid on his linguini calamari and took a big whiff. "Smells good."

Wade sat in his chair and waited for Dodger to start eating.

"You ain't eating?"

"I have plans later."

Dodger chuckled. "I remember those days. Plans. Hope she's hot. But smart."

"She is." No better words to describe Nikki.

"This calamari is as good as Alonzo's. I never woulda thought it. You did good."

"We need to talk about you and Donny."

Dodger shoved pasta in his mouth and then dropped his fork.

"You're not stupid. I'd hate to think that you believe I'm stupid. Donny is not an art guy. Definitely not someone who would demand a masterpiece. I know he's working with Marco Wolf. I'm assuming you know that, too. The question is, how deep are you in with them? It's more than money."

Dodger listened and wiped his mouth. "It was money on my end. More than usual, sure, but as soon as Donny was like, 'We'll work something out,' I knew there was more. He wasn't real forthcoming at first. Wolf is looking for something particular."

Wade didn't like where this was heading.

"Actually, it's a someone. A thief."

This was getting worse by the minute.

"He thinks I know where Nikki is. He wants her to come work for him."

"What?" Rage bubbled up and pummeling Dodger was starting to sound like a good idea. Even when she was no longer in his life, the man was trying to use her.

"I told him I didn't know where she was. That's what got me the first beating. Then when you gave me the forged painting, they thought I was pulling a scam."

Wade was grateful that he hadn't told Dodger Nikki was back, that he'd been working with her. More important, he was glad that *she* hadn't talked to Dodger when she'd found him. Now, if he could figure out exactly what Wolf wanted, he could keep Nikki away from all of it. "What's his endgame?"

"I don't know."

"Stop your b.s., old man. I'm risking everything for you. I think at bare minimum I deserve honesty."

"They want a thief. If not Nikki, someone as good. They're not sharing their whole plan. I'm not an inside guy. I told them I could train someone. Make a

Nikki two-point-oh. Getting the Devereaux is my way of proving it."

"What's wrong with you?"

"What? You think I don't have the chops to teach someone? I taught you when you had zero skill."

"You taught me and Nikki by showing us. You can't pull a job. And where is this thief coming from?"

Dodger shrugged.

"And what happens when the new thief fails?"

Another shrug.

"What are you planning?" He stared at Dodger until the man finally broke.

"Fine. You're right. Is that what you want to hear?" He pushed off the couch and paced the living room. "My plan is to track Nikki down. Bring her home."

"There's no way she'd work for Wolf."

"I just need her to help me teach the new one. Be a mentor."

That's when Wade noticed the softened look on Dodger's face. Yeah, he needed help to dig himself out, but he really wanted his daughter back. In the back of his head, he considered whether that would be good for Nikki. He was her father.

Wade also saw that there was no getting out from under this. Once Wolf had his claws in, Dodger would never get out. It was time for a plan B—or G or H, at this point, he'd lost count. He had to find a way to take them all down.

TWENTY-TWO

NIKKI, LONDON, AND AUDREY had a full Mexican feast at a neighborhood restaurant. Jared and Mia had plenty of faults, but Nikki thoroughly enjoyed the River North location they chose as a base of operations. Knowing what she knew now about Mia, Nikki wondered if she'd chosen the area because it was a gallery district with art everywhere.

Personally, Nikki was more concerned with the food and beverage situation. The wide selection of fabulous restaurants all in walking distance set her straight before a job. Audrey and London were laughing at some silly joke London made. The warm night breeze floated across Nikki's skin.

"Let's do this," she said, filling her lungs with air. She'd been letting too much about these jobs get to her and make her doubt everything. Enough of that. She was the best thief in this city, hell, probably the best in the Midwest. Creepy old Turner was not going to win.

Audrey and Nikki rode in the back of the van while London drove to the mansion. Since the last heist, Audrey had been busy outfitting the van as a mobile base. She had full internet capabilities, three monitors to work from, and a bunch of devices that Nikki didn't recognize. On the way to the restaurant, Nikki had sat in front, so she hadn't seen the new tech. "This is unbelievable."

"I know, right? I have everything in this one vehicle to cause all the mayhem I could ever need to." Her tone was a little maniacal. "This is what I envisioned when we told Jared to get us a van."

Nikki smiled because Jared would give Audrey anything she asked for. He was gone for her.

A block away, Audrey did her thing to trip the alarm and drive the man into his panic room. As soon as the alarm started blaring, she accessed the indoor cameras. London stopped near the neighbor's house so Audrey could jump out with the drone.

Then they took off again, Nikki staring at the center screen. She watched as Turner called out and checked the cameras himself before scooting behind a bookcase in his bedroom. "He's in," she said to Audrey on comms.

"Here goes nothing."

Nikki stared at the small screen, waiting for something—anything—to happen. Then the space began to fill with smoke. Nikki switched cameras. Then she saw them. Red laser lights across doorways and the staircase. Into her comm, she said, "He's got a secondary setup. I know how the booby traps are tripped. Throw another one in, but I need it to go straight through a doorway."

She waited again. She saw the small projectile fly though the lasers. A second later, arrows or spears careened down the hall.

What. The. Fuck.

Sirens wailed in the distance.

"I think we have what we need. Hustle back here."

At the corner, Audrey popped out from behind a bush just as Nikki flung the panel door open on the van.

"This thing is so much fun. I think I gotta get one." For the entire trip back to the apartment, Audrey regaled them with all of the specs as well as the performance of the drone. Nikki would be sure to share with Wade how very impressive his drone was.

Nikki let them into the apartment and asked Audrey to pull up the recording of the smoke bombs and traps. She seemed reluctant to give up the drone.

Nikki grabbed it. "Sorry. It's going back."

"Fine. I know what I'm asking Jared to get me for Christmas."

Nikki paused in repacking the drone in its box. Christmas was months away. She hadn't considered what her life would look like by then. They would be done with these jobs, and Mia and Jared would go back to whatever their normal lives looked like, but now Audrey would be a part of that.

And Nikki wouldn't be living in this apartment anymore. How could a place that she'd been in for less than a season suddenly feel like home?

"So what did you see?" Audrey asked.

"He's got lasers to prevent passage."

"And if you cross the lasers?"

"I need to see the video to be sure, but it looks like he's got arrows shooting down the hallway."

"No way," London said with a chuckle. "Cue it up. This'll be good." She sank onto the couch.

Nikki detoured to the kitchen and grabbed a bottle of wine for London and beer for her and Audrey.

Audrey joined them on the couch and shared her screen to the TV. The whole thing played out pretty quickly, but while she was sitting in the van, it had felt much longer. That was why Nikki preferred to be the doer, not the watcher of things. On-screen, the second canister blew past the lasers and there was only a glimpse of something in the hall because Audrey was using the camera in the bedroom where the smoke bomb landed.

Switching cameras, she replayed the shot in slow motion. The paintings on the walls across from each other dropped open and a crossbow plopped out and sent arrows sailing down the hall.

"Dude is beyond paranoid," London said.

"It looks like your options are to figure out how to circumvent the lasers or trip them and hope there's not a second round."

"I'm not *hoping* for anything when it comes to this guy. We go on the assumption there is another round. Those arrows only cover the hall and the doorways. I bet there's more in the room itself, so if by chance you get through the doorway, you get nailed in the room. I think climbing up and going through the window of the guest room is going to be the move. If you cut the power to that camera, so he doesn't see me coming, we can drive him back into his hidey-hole and I can grab the statue. Go out the way I came. There are no lasers on the windows or running in the room."

"After all of this, that seems like too simple of a solution."

"I've been saying all along that simple is best."

"The weather is supposed to shift. How are you going

to get through the window without breaking it?" Audrey asked.

"Get him to open it."

"How?"

"He's got a smart house. Hack into it. Turn on the heat instead of the air. You'll probably convince him that his house is out to get him." She laughed and then drained her beer.

"You're kind of enjoying this. The tormenting him part."

"I don't like it when people make my job difficult. There should be a cost to that. And it's not like he's some innocent."

"I know, but making him feel like his house is attacking him is a lot."

"Consider it an inconvenience charge. If the jerk would just leave his house for a couple hours, we wouldn't have to do this. I'm tired of looking at this man and his house. We have other jobs to get to."

Audrey switched to a live feed of the house, which was now swarming with cop cars. London disappeared into the kitchen and reappeared a few minutes later with microwave popcorn. The three of them sat munching snacks while watching cops comb through Turner's house. They bagged the canisters and eyeballed the crossbow booby traps.

"Man, I would love to hear what they're saying."

"Sorry. No audio," Audrey said.

Without a doubt, the cops were irritated and Turner was agitated. One cop pointed toward the hall. Nikki provided a voiceover. "Mr. Turner, you can't shoot arrows at people."

London jumped in. "But someone was in my house!"

"By all accounts, a smoke bomb was in your house and not a person. But even if it had been a burglar, we'd have to arrest you for murder."

"Murder! It's my house! I'll protect what's mine."

The cop was shaking his head. Nikki laughed. "I feel kind of bad for the cop. I should go buy him a drink."

Audrey smacked her arm. "No, you should not. That would put you on his radar."

Nikki scoffed. "First, it was a joke. Second, the only thing that would be on his radar is a hot chick buying him a beer. Trust me when I say that no cop suspects a pretty little woman to be a criminal mastermind." She shoved up from the couch. "Keep me updated. I'll be back tomorrow or Monday, depending on what happens there. Keep an eye on him. He's coming unhinged."

"And where will you be this weekend?" London asked.

"Not that it's any of your business, but the use of that drone wasn't free. I have a debt to pay." And unlike her deadbeat father, she always paid her debts.

"Oh, yeah, that sounds like a hardship. Crawling into Wade's bed. Whatever will you do?"

Nikki turned to Audrey and flicked a thumb at London. "Has she always been that snarky?"

"Uh, yeah. Where have you been?"

Nikki shrugged. "Catch you later."

She went to her room and packed a bag, making sure to snag the tablet for the museum. Even though she promised Wade the rest of her weekend didn't mean they shouldn't look over the footage she took. Work would be an added reminder for both of them that this relationship was business with a side benefit of scratching an itch and nothing more.

Unfortunately, she needed the reminder every bit as much as Wade did.

WADE TRIED TO convince Boone to take Flynn for the weekend, but his friend refused. His point was that if Wade wanted Nikki in his life, she would have to get used to the dog. Luckily for Wade, the weather was fabulous, so Flynn could stay out in the yard most of the time that Nikki was there tonight. He could only push so much on her at a time. She'd run if she felt pressured.

When his doorbell rang, he was a little surprised because it was earlier than he'd expected. He opened the door.

Nikki shoved his drone box at his chest. "Thanks. It was perfect. My friend almost didn't return it. She was having a lot of fun with it."

"Glad to be of service. I thought you were going to be late."

"It's almost midnight," she said as he closed and locked the door.

"I figured you would show up at four in the morning. Just long enough to not get called on reneging on our deal, but late enough to show that you're in charge."

She smirked at him. "Don't know what you're talking about."

"You hungry?" He put the drone in the corner.

"Nah. I ate before the mission."

"Beer?"

"If you're having one." She looked around. "Where's the beast?"

"Outside. I'll put him to bed once you're safely in mine." He went to the kitchen and pulled two bottles from the fridge. Nikki followed.

He popped the top and handed her a bottle. Raising his, he said, "To a successful heist."

She clinked her bottle to his and then drank, never losing direct eye contact with him.

"Did you figure out the booby traps?"

"Oh, yeah."

"No way. There really are traps?"

"Yep."

"Let's go sit down. I want to hear about this."

He followed her back to the couch, watching her hips sway in her tight jeans.

"The dude has lasers across each doorway, preventing easy access. When the laser is disturbed, a crossbow shoots arrows from hidden pockets in the walls."

"So it kind of is like Indiana Jones."

"Guess so."

They sat in silence for a few minutes, drinking their beer.

"What are we doing?" she asked.

"What do you mean? Drinking. Hanging out."

"You wanted me here so you could take me to bed, not hang out."

"Why can't we do both?"

"Because that's not us anymore."

"Why not?"

She slammed her bottle on the coffee table and stood. "Because we had a plan. It was going to be us. And you chose *him* over me."

Wade set his beer down and clasped his hands. Obviously, their last conversation hadn't been enough to settle this. "I was sure you were going to come back," he reiterated. "When Dodger figured out our plan, he cornered me. What I shared with you was only a snippet. He laid into me with a guilt trip of epic proportions. How he saved me and gave me a life. How he couldn't believe I was stealing his only family. That I should know how it felt to have everything taken from me."

He swallowed that pain down. Pain that he thought he'd dealt with a long time ago. He thought about that night and the look in Dodger's eyes. Utter fear.

"He was afraid, Nikki. He didn't want to lose you. It wasn't about jobs and gambling and money. You're his daughter. He wanted me to stay because he figured I could keep you here." He slowly shook his head. "We were both so wrong."

"Why didn't you tell me?"

"It wouldn't have worked. You were furious. Especially after that last job where Dodger got everything wrong. I'd never seen you that mad."

"He half-assed his part and you could've been killed."

She wasn't wrong.

"But he's still family."

"You want family who's willing to screw you over?"

He shrugged. It was messed up and he could acknowledge that. "Better than nothing."

The look in her eyes spoke volumes. She'd been alone. Too alone for years.

"Do you regret it?" she asked.

"I don't regret staying. I regret not fighting harder to keep you. I shouldn't have let you go."

The corner of her mouth lifted. "You couldn't have stopped me."

"But if I kept at it, once you cooled off, I could've convinced you to come back."

This time she shrugged. "We'll never know."

He crossed to where she stood. "Are you still alone now?"

She said nothing, but he didn't get the impression that it was because she was avoiding answering him. It was as if she was unsure. And that was a whole different kind of sad.

A whine from the back door grabbed his attention. "Flynn's ready to come in."

"Excellent timing, dog!" she yelled. She grabbed her bag from the floor. "Bedroom?"

"Upstairs." He tugged her hand and pulled her in for a kiss. "I'll be there in a minute."

After letting Flynn in, Wade locked up and gave his dog his favorite toy. "No sleeping in my room tonight, buddy. Nikki needs space. She's still not ready for you." Flynn looked up at him with his tongue dangling. Wade rubbed his belly and turned out the lights as he made his way upstairs.

In the bedroom, Nikki was splayed out on his bed. He closed the door behind him.

"Who were you talking to?"

"Flynn," he answered as he whipped off his shirt.

"You talk to your dog?"

"Of course. He's my best friend."

She laughed at his answer, but he was too distracted

to worry about why she found his relationship with Flynn funny.

Right now, he had Nikki back in his life. He'd do everything in his power to keep her.

TWENTY-THREE

Nikki's body sang with sweet exhaustion. So she was startled when she felt Wade's wet mouth on her foot. She grunted. "Since when do you have a foot fetish?" she mumbled.

"Hmm?"

The sound came right next to her head, which wasn't possible if he was by her feet. Nikki's eyes popped open and she looked at the foot of the bed. There lay Wade's slobbery dog, nuzzling her foot. She yanked her leg up and curled away from the beast.

Unbothered by her fear, the dog stretched and lumbered closer to her, settling between Wade and her. Then he flopped on his back.

"Wade."

No response.

She didn't dare yell, which might upset the dog. "Wade!" she whisper-shouted.

"Huh?"

"Your dog."

A big sigh. "What about him?"

"He's in the bed." Her heart raced and she closed her eyes. If the thing was going to attack her, she didn't want to see it coming.

"Just give him a shove. He'll move."

"And take a piece of me with him."

Wade suddenly sat up. "Oh shit. I'm sorry. He needed to go out earlier and I must've forgotten to close the door."

Nikki peeked through her lashes. "Can you get rid of him?"

Wade reached over the top of the dog and touched her arm, which was folded tightly against her chest. "Nikki. Look at him."

She opened one eye a little more. The dog had his feet up in the air, his tongue lolling out the side of his mouth.

"Touch him. You'll see that not only is he gentle, but totally harmless." He peeled her hand away from her body. With his hand on top of her stiff one, he pressed her palm to the dog's belly.

It was soft and so warm. Wade glided their joined hands across the barely-there fur. Flynn snuffed and rolled over. Nikki jerked back with a yelp.

Still oblivious to her fear, the dog flopped his head on her leg.

"Doesn't he get that I don't like him? I thought animals were supposed to have a sixth sense about these things."

Wade chuckled. "First, dogs do know. Flynn wants you to like him. That's the way he is. He wants you to know you don't have to be afraid of him. Kind of like when a dog is skittish, a person will lower to the dog's level and put a hand out palm down to show they're not a threat. This is Flynn's way of saying 'love me.'"

Nikki still hadn't touched him since he rolled over. He did, in fact, look innocent, and his big brown eyes looked at her longingly. She reached past his head, touched his back, and stroked.

Flynn let out a big sigh and closed his eyes. Nikki stared at him. "This dog is a con artist."

Wade stretched and tossed off the sheet. "He learned from the best, babe."

"He knows Cameron Burris?" Nikki tossed out, naming a mediocre con man from their past.

Wade flipped over and snatched her from under Flynn before she could release a teasing laugh. The dog huffed and climbed off the bed as Wade pinned her beneath him. "Take it back."

"Make me," she dared.

Wade kissed her over and over until she took it back.

After a short nap, they showered together and got dressed. Nikki had agreed to spend the day with Wade, but sitting in his kitchen drinking coffee felt domestic. That wasn't who they were. Definitely not under the parameters of their new casual relationship status.

She wanted to be irritated by it. She knew he'd maneuvered and manipulated the situation to get them here. He may be an excellent con artist, but she saw the con. She just wasn't sure she wanted to fight it.

"What do you want to do today? Something fun to clear our heads?"

"You get that we can't go back in time, right?"

"What do you mean?"

"Great night together, taking a day to have fun and clear our heads before a big job. That's how we used to be. We aren't those kids anymore. Pretending to be won't make it so."

"I'm not looking to go back. I want to find a new way for us to be. As we are now."

She stared into his eyes. They were full of sincerity. He wanted more than casual. "Just another con, huh? Agreeing to no strings. You used it to lure me in."

"Maybe a little."

She hadn't expected honesty.

"I agreed because spending any time with you is better than nothing. But, no. If I'm being honest, it'll never be everything I want."

She bit her lip and shook her head. This man. The thought made her freeze. He *was* a man, not the boy she'd left. His frankness was a level of vulnerability a younger Wade would never have risked.

"What are you thinking?" he asked.

She wanted him. She missed having him in her life. Until they'd run into each other again, she hadn't even known how much she'd missed him. But they were so different now. "How could this possibly work?"

"Why wouldn't it? We care about each other. We understand each other in ways no one else could."

"I'm a thief and you spend your days trying to stop people like me."

His forehead wrinkled like he hadn't considered the fact that they were on opposite sides of the law now.

"Am I supposed to fall at your feet and give up my life for love?"

He stood and came to the other side of the table where she sat. "I think we both know better than that." He took her hand and pulled her to stand. "We'll figure it out. You do your thing and I'll do mine. We just make sure our professional paths don't cross."

"Just like that. You'll be okay being in a relationship with a criminal."

He slid his arms around her waist. "I want a relationship with you. I'll take you however you are." He planted a quick kiss on her lips. "Now let's get out of here and enjoy our day."

He was delusional if he thought they could each keep their career and not have it impact their relationship. But he had a point. Taking the day to clear their heads couldn't hurt.

WADE TOOK FLYNN for a walk, and Nikki came along, although she made sure to stay on his right side, while he held the leash with his left. It was progress.

"Maybe you should run with him," Nikki said.

Wade laughed.

"He's kind of pudgy."

"That's the breed. And look at those stubby legs. Flynn wasn't made for running."

"What was he made for? Besides slobber."

"Cuddling, of course."

Nikki laughed so loud, it echoed down the street.

"What is so funny?"

"Big tough guy talking about cuddling his slobbery dog."

"Whatever." They turned at the corner to head back to his house. "What do you really want to do today?"

"Let's rob a bank!"

Wade put his arm around her shoulder. "First, it's Sunday. Banks are closed. Second, that is neither fun nor relaxing. And as much as I like you, I'm not going to prison for you."

She smirked. "Good point. A pretty boy like you wouldn't do well in prison."

"We could go to the lake. It's a beautiful day."

"I didn't pack a swimsuit and last time I checked, Lake Michigan didn't have any nude beaches."

"If it's just the rules holding you back, let me do some Googling. I'll find one."

"How about the casino? I haven't gambled in a while."

"You gamble every time you do a job."

"That's not gambling."

"Are you even allowed in a casino? You're not flagged?"

"I'm a thief, not a card counter. No one knows who I am. Besides, I've only been to this casino once. Vegas is a different story."

"Okay. Casino it is." He considered how much cash on hand he had and how much he could afford to lose. Regardless of how good Nikki thought she was, gambling was geared toward making the house money. While his business was profitable, he wasn't raking in the cash like he had when he was a thief. Nikki's lifestyle definitely had its perks.

He took the leash off Flynn as they reached his front lawn.

"Is that safe?" she asked. "We already know that beast doesn't follow rules."

"He listens just fine."

"Then why was he licking my feet this morning?"

"He's allowed in my bed sometimes. He was missing me because I left him out last night and when he came in, I left him to be with you."

"So he's jealous."

"I didn't say that." Flynn lumbered up the front steps in front of them. "He just likes to be included."

Wade unlocked the door and they all went in, Nikki trailing behind. He tossed his keys on the table. "I'll be ready to go in a couple minutes. Let me grab some cash and make sure Flynn has enough food and water."

Nikki stayed at the edge of the room, arms crossed as Flynn hopped up on the couch. The dog nudged the remote with his nose as he settled in.

Wade jogged up the stairs and called behind him, "He probably wants the TV on. I turn on *Law and Order* when I'm not home."

"You're weird!" she yelled. "And so is your dog."

When he came back downstairs, though, Nikki was sitting on the arm of the couch, on the opposite end from Flynn, scrolling through channels. "No *Law and Order*, but I found reruns of *Chicago PD*. Will that suffice?"

He chuckled as he filled the dog's bowls. "He's not that picky."

"You sure? That was a pretty specific request. For. A. Dog."

"What can I say? We spend a lot of time together." He picked his keys back up and rubbed Flynn's head. "We'll be home in a few hours. Be good."

Nikki slid from the couch. "Maybe you need to spend more time with humans."

"You just don't get it because Dodger never let you have a pet. If he had, you would understand the special bond."

Traffic out of the city was negligible, so they made excellent time getting to the suburbs and the casino.

Wade parked in the garage. As they walked to the entrance, he asked, "What kind of game are you looking for? Poker? Blackjack?"

"Slots."

"What?"

"You don't have to think when you play slots. Drop money in and pull the arm or press a button. Lights and bells and a little bit of luck and you win."

He put his arm around her shoulders again and kissed her temple. That wasn't at all what he'd expected.

"Don't get me wrong. I'll watch the machines to see which ones are more likely to pay out. And I'll probably play a little poker. I assume that's still your game?"

"The guys and I have a regular game. I don't come here to play. It's just for fun these days."

"If you say so." She pulled ahead and took his hand. Minutes later, they were walking the aisles of the slots while Nikki scanned their possibilities.

Wade, in the meantime, watched her. She acted like a kid in a toy store. She touched every free machine and eyeballed every careless patron in the place. It was as if she was torn between playing a game and lifting cash from the players. Only one guaranteed to fill her pockets, but he had a feeling it wasn't as much fun as knowing she got away with winning from the house.

She stopped in front of a machine and stroked the side. "This one."

It took five tries, but she won. Wade stood there with a stupid grin on his face as she jumped up and down over winning fifty bucks. This woman, who he personally witnessed stealing hundreds of thousands in merchandise at once, was excited over fifty dollars. It was one of many reasons he'd always loved her. She found joy everywhere.

As she waved her winning receipt, she asked, "What?"

"I love seeing you happy."

"Money always makes me happy."

"What would be enough? For you to quit?"

They turned the corner at the end of the aisle. Nikki continued to peruse the machines to find her next victim. "I don't know. I never really thought about it."

"If someone cut you a check right now, you don't have a figure in mind?"

"No. To have an amount in my head, that's like saying I'm working toward this, and then I'm done." She paused and turned her body to face him. "What else would I do?"

In that moment, he realized how messed up they were. Dodger had raised her to believe she was only good for one thing—stealing. For once, Dodger's lack of faith in Wade served him well. "You could do anything. You're brilliant."

"Well, compliments will get you everywhere, but I'd die punching a clock."

"You could work with me."

She chuckled. "I thought you wouldn't expect me to give up my life. That didn't take long at all."

"I'm not expecting anything. Just throwing out an option. You act like you've never considered anything else. I'm giving you something to consider."

A woman with silvery-blue hair skirted around them and sat at the machine.

Nikki pouted. "That was my machine."

"Let her have it. Let's go play roulette."

"I thought you didn't like games of chance."

"I like my chances with you."

NIKKI FOLLOWED WADE to the roulette table. His offer, as silly as it seemed, bounced around in her head. He was right. She'd never considered doing anything else. She was a great thief. No one asked a surgeon what else she would do.

When they got to the table, the wheel was spinning, so they waited. When the dealer opened bets, the two other players at the table played safe by betting on black or red. Wade wasn't much better by placing his chips on a dozen bet.

"You in?" he asked.

"I'll wait a turn. Pretty pedestrian bet," she whispered.

"I'm all about playing it safe."

"Then why are you with me?"

The dealer closed bets and Wade pressed his lips close to her ear. "I enjoy a little danger."

His voice vibrated through her and she tightened her grip on her chips. She closed her eyes and listened to the rolling and then pinging of the ball as it found its resting place. Wade won and shot her a satisfied grin. His fifty dollars was now a hundred and fifty.

When the dealer opened the bets again, she leaned over to slide her chips onto number thirteen, but Wade touched her arm.

"Not straight up. You know that's a losing bet."

"But if I win, it pays out thirty-five to one. You got two to one."

"I'm not saying outside bet. Just something a little safer."

She rolled her eyes. "Fine. I'll place a split." She put her chips on the line in between the thirteen and ten.

"Why there?"

"We met thirteen years ago. I fell for you three years later."

His throat worked like he was prepping for a big speech. The dealer closed bets and she turned her attention to the wheel. She couldn't believe she'd just admitted to Wade that he still had that much of a hold on her.

The ball spun and bounced.

Wade's arm came around her shoulder.

The ball landed on ten.

Her phone buzzed in her pocket.

A round of cheers rose around her as she executed a dance beside Wade. While the dealer counted her winnings, Wade pulled her into a hug.

"Seventeen to one, not bad. And much better than two to one," she said.

"But if you went straight, you would've gotten nothing. We make a great team."

Her phone buzzed again. As she fished it out, she said, "Grab my money. I gotta take this."

There was a string of texts from Audrey

Got a problem.

We're gonna need to move tonight.

She touched Wade's arm. "I have to make a call. I'll be right back."

Moving toward the bathrooms, she dialed Audrey.

"Thank God. I thought I was going to have to tell Mia you weren't responding."

"What's going on?"

"We spooked Turner all right. He fired his security company this morning. You should've heard him screaming last night at the poor customer service rep. That girl ran his complaint up the chain fast."

"What are you saying? He has no security?"

"It's still running now, but the owner of the company is coming to the house tomorrow to personally check his system. When this guy shows up, if he's any good, he'll find traces of me hacking. We need to go in tonight. I've already started adjusting the thermostat. Should be ninety degrees in there by evening. He'll be throwing every window open before sundown."

She didn't need to look over her shoulder to know that Wade had followed. She felt his eyes on her. "Okay," she said to Audrey. "I'll be there soon."

She slid her phone back in her pocket and turned around.

"Problem?"

"Only for you."

"Me?"

"I know I said I'd give you the day, but duty calls. My timeline just got moved up and I need to go."

His eyes registered a flash of disappointment, but then his face showed resignation. "We should go cash out then."

They traded their chips for cash and went to Wade's car. "Come back to my place when you're done?"

"I can probably swing that. But it'll be late."

He fiddled with his key ring until he slid one off. "That's fine. Let yourself in." He pressed a key to her hand.

She held it up. "One lock? What kind of security is that?"

"Would it do me any good to have anything else? We both know you can get in anywhere." He started the ignition. "Where do you need me to drop you off?"

She hesitated.

"Look. I know you have your super-secret life with whoever you're working for. Do you think I'm going to call the cops? You're safe with me."

In her gut, she knew that was true. And it would save her time. She gave him the cross streets near the apartment. She'd have him drop her off there and then jog down the block. He'd have a neighborhood but not an address. They drove in silence, Nikki's mind wandering from the job at hand to all the thoughts and feelings Wade had sparked.

At the corner near the apartment, he finally asked, "Where now?"

"Here's good. It's right down the block." She reached for the handle to open the door.

Wade grabbed the back of her neck and pulled her in for a kiss. "Be safe."

"Thanks. See you later." She swung out of the car and jogged down the block. From behind her, she heard Wade's wolf whistle, so she flipped him off over her shoulder.

TWENTY-FOUR

INSIDE THE APARTMENT, Audrey was on her computer, headphones on, head down, lost in concentration. Only one energy drink at her elbow, though, so that was a good sign.

"Hey," Nikki called after locking the door.

Audrey pulled her headphones off and blinked a couple of times. "Hi. You got here fast."

"You made it sound kind of urgent."

"Not an emergency, but sorry to interrupt your weekend."

"Weekends don't have the same meaning for me as they do for other people, you know that, right?"

"Normally, yeah, but you and Wade…" She lifted a shoulder and one corner of her mouth.

"Business comes first."

Audrey pressed her lips together as if she needed to prevent herself from making further commentary.

"How's our friend doing?"

"Hot." Audrey let out an evil little chuckle. "Do you have everything you need for tonight?"

"Do we have the forgery?"

"London is dropping it off soon."

"My gear is here. As soon as it's dark, we'll be good to go. I'm gonna go take a nap."

Audrey shot up out of her chair. "What?"

"I had a long night. I'm tired. Wake me when London gets here."

"You're really not going to tell me what happened?"

"What's there to tell? I went to Wade's house. Spent the night. Then we went to the casino, and I made some money on slots and roulette. Then you called."

Audrey stared at her, eyes wide. "Are you guys back together?"

"Between the sheets, you bet." Nikki added a wink for effect.

"Nice try. Sit." She pointed at the couch.

Nikki rolled her eyes, but plodded over to the couch and sat on the back while Audrey went to the kitchen to fill coffee cups.

"You can play the game with Mia and Jared if you want, but London told me about your night at the bar. She saw the two of you together. And I've seen you every time Wade is mentioned. I might not understand people as well as you, but this isn't just casual between you guys. I mean, how could it be? You have *history*."

Nikki drank her coffee while Audrey rambled. When she finally paused, Nikki wasn't sure how to respond. She and Wade did have history with a capital *H*. "He initiated. I explicitly told him we were casual."

Audrey waited in that quiet Audrey way.

"Then he changed the script. He wants us to be together."

"I knew it." Audrey leaned on the couch. "So, what does that mean?"

"I told him it can't work. I think in his gut he knows that, but he wants to hope. That's the kind of guy he is. He knows people are disappointments, but he hopes they'll be good. Like he stayed with my father even though the man will never change."

"Why can't it work?"

"I'm a thief. He's a security consultant. That's like one step down from being a cop."

"No, it's not."

"His life goals are to stop people like me from doing what I do."

"But he can't arrest you."

"I'm sure somewhere in there, he plays nice with cops. And I'm not about to walk away from my life."

Audrey sipped her coffee. With a smirk she said, "Maybe he'll leave his."

"What?"

"He used to be a thief. Maybe he'd be willing to go back if it gave him a chance to be with you."

"You're high if you think that he'd jump back into this life. He wanted out. He got out. He won't come back for me." He'd already proven that.

"Maybe you're wrong."

"Now you have the scoop. I'm going to take my nap." She set her cup on the table and crawled into bed. She dreamt of having a life where she and Wade worked together like they had ten years ago. They were a near perfect team. When she woke, however, she was filled with guilt.

What was that?

She didn't feel guilty over anything she'd ever done. Not for a single crime she'd committed. But having a life where she and Wade were happy made her feel guilty.

Screw that.

She threw the blanket off and stomped to the shower. What she really wanted was a run, but she needed to conserve her energy for scaling a wall in a few hours.

After getting dressed in her usual black gear, she went in search of more coffee. Audrey was nowhere to be seen, but London must've stopped by because the statue stood on the dining room table. The coffeepot was empty, so Nikki used the single cup maker to get a cup quickly. While she waited, she checked her phone to see if Audrey left a message.

None from Audrey, but Wade had texted a picture of himself and his dog. We'll be waiting for you to get back.

She smiled in spite of herself. Flynn is not a selling point for me to come back.

Why not? Don't you see how cute he is?

He still has teeth.

I can't believe you don't think he's proven himself yet. Trust what you see.

Nikki was struck by the idea that Wade wasn't talking about his dog anymore. She wanted to trust Wade. Wanted to believe that things would be different. But how many times in her life had she thought Dodger would change?

She grabbed her coffee as the front door opened. London and Audrey walked in carrying bags.

"We brought dinner," London announced.

"I must be getting predictable if you know what to get for me before I pull a job."

Audrey smiled. "There's not much to know. Anything greasy and calorie-laden. Other than that, you're not too picky."

London pulled out a chair and sat. "We have time for girl talk."

"We're all friends here. You guys talked me through my issues with Jared," Audrey said.

"So now that's a thing?"

"It should be," London said.

"Fine. Tell us all about your love life," Nikki prompted London.

"Ooo...you said *love*."

She threw a fry at London. "It's an expression."

London continued to stare.

"You're not going to let this go, are you?" Nikki took a giant bite of the hot dog she'd unwrapped.

"At the bar that night, watching the two of you was magical. You read each other and communicated without words."

"We have history. We worked together for years. That history gave us a shorthand." She dragged some fries through a puddle of ketchup.

"But it's been years and you still fell right into that rhythm. Some people go their whole lives without finding that."

Nikki huffed and dropped the fries. "You're right. We had it and he walked away."

"Uh..." Confusion filled London's face.

"You said you left," Audrey said.

"He was supposed to come with me. He chose to stay."

"And now?" London prompted.

Food no longer held its appeal. "Now he wants to make a go of us. Says he regrets not coming after me. But he doesn't regret staying. My father needed him." She scoffed. "But here we are years later, still fixing screw-ups for my dad."

"Take your dad out of the equation. Would you want to be with Wade?" Audrey asked.

"My dad is there."

Audrey shook her head. "Hypothetically. Like when Jared paid for Gram's care. I was so mad that he was trying to manipulate me. But then he explained that he paid so that I wouldn't feel obligated to come back. He knew the draw of the money would lure me for Gram's sake. He wanted me to choose him. If your dad wasn't an issue, would you choose Wade?"

Nikki stood and gathered her trash. "I don't know. We're still living in two different worlds." While that answer was true, it wasn't totally honest. If Dodger was out of the equation, she would pick Wade. "Are we ready to do this? Is Turner sweating yet?"

Audrey made eye contact with her and understood that Nikki needed the conversation to be over. "Oh yeah. He's called the alarm company twice this afternoon. I intercepted one call to keep suspicion at bay. Cameras are showing every window in the house is open."

She scooted back to her computer and brought images up on-screen. The exterior cameras on Turner's house showed the windows wide open on the second floor.

"Can you tap the interior cameras?"

"Sure." A few keystrokes later, they were looking

at Turner walking through the kitchen with a plate and glass. As he bent and put them in the dishwasher, Nikki stared at the man's waist.

"Shit. Is he carrying a gun?"

Audrey tapped a few more keys and then pulled up a still shot and zoomed in. The angle wasn't great, but it looked like Turner had a gun tucked into his pants.

"Maybe we pushed this too far," Audrey said. "We didn't sign on for weapons."

"It's fine. He's carrying in case someone comes crashing through the door while he's sitting in his living room. If he's in bed and the alarm goes off, we already know he'll go to his panic room. Especially if he can't use his cameras to give him the advantage."

"It doesn't seem like a good idea," Audrey said.

"I'll be fine. Let's gear up."

"You sure?" London asked.

"Yeah. We need to get this over with." Nikki pushed the empty food bags out of the way on the table and spread out the pictures of Turner's house. "You drop me off on the street. I'll let you know when I'm in place. Audrey will cut the cameras and trigger the alarm. By the time I scale the wall to climb through the window, Turner will be in his panic room. I go in, make the swap, and leave before the cops show up."

"You make it sound easy," London said.

"She always does," Audrey added.

"Let's roll."

BY THE TIME they were in Turner's neighborhood, Nikki was in the zone. She loved the rush of sneaking into someone's house. Bonus if someone was home, increasing the risk of getting caught. She knew it wasn't normal thinking, but nothing beat that kind of adrenaline rush.

London sang along with the radio, bopping in the driver's seat, while Audrey monitored Turner's security system.

"Are you sure this is a good idea?" Audrey asked.

"We need to get this done. We haven't wasted this much time on a job since the first one."

"You're the one who always complains about not having enough time to plan," she retorted.

"I'm just tired of this guy." She tugged on her gloves, which would both protect her hands while climbing and make sure she left no prints behind.

London drove past Turner's house to verify nothing strange was going on. When they were about a block away, Nikki grabbed her gear and hopped out of the van. After piling her hair on top of her head and securing it under a ball cap, she put her earpiece in and tapped it. "I'll let you know when I'm in place so you can cut the cameras and set off the alarm. Seven minutes till cops show, right?"

"Assuming they don't make it faster because he's so bitchy."

"Then I'll be out in five." Staying in the shadows, Nikki jogged down the block. It was hot enough and late enough that the streets were empty. It didn't take long before Nikki felt sweat trickle between her breasts and down the center of her back. Being covered like this in the middle of a Chicago summer was disgusting. The payout made it worth a bit of suffering, though.

She climbed the wall at the edge of Turner's property. The gray stones scraped against her gloves as she hoisted herself over. It wasn't a terribly tall wall, about seven feet. Just enough to deter most people from bothering him. She dropped down on the other side. One long, deep breath in and out. Then she called Audrey. "Let's do this."

Staying in the black outline of the big trees lining the property, Nikki trained her eyes on the house.

"Go!" Audrey yelled. A second later, the siren began to blare.

Nikki bolted across the lawn to the side of the house. She pressed herself against the brick. "Is he in his hidey-hole?"

"Oh yeah. He wasted no time today."

Nikki shot her grappling hook up to the roof and tugged. Confident it was set, she climbed the wall, feeling a lot like Batman. Her feet pressed against the bricks as she made her way up to the second floor. At the window, she let out a little chuckle because the hole Audrey had made in the screen when she shot the smoke bombs in wasn't fixed yet. The hole wasn't big enough for her to fit through, though. She jiggled the frame and slid the screen up. She adjusted her cap lower on her head to obscure her face, just in case.

Stepping through the window, she said, "I'm in."

She pulled the Latimer forgery from her backpack and held it close, which felt a little dirty. The sculpture was a small statue of Narcissus staring into what she assumed was a pool of water. Narcissus, however, was buck naked except for the wreath on his head and the dude was hung like a porn star. His position on the ground had one leg propped up, putting his junk on display for all to note. Walking past the desk, she catalogued the items—Montblanc pen, a Tiffany desk clock, and a Louis Vuitton calendar-planner thing. For a guest room. She hated rich people.

Although, when it came down to it, she was also a rich person.

"Three minutes," Audrey said.

Having a countdown clock in her ear was distracting. Her internal clock had never let her down. She tuned out the siren and turned on her penlight, keeping it low so that if a camera picked up an image, it wouldn't be her face. The Latimer stood on the top shelf of the built-in bookcase.

She had to go up on tiptoe and stretch, but she was just tall enough for her fingertips to maneuver the statue to the edge to grab. As she pulled it from the shelf, a sprinkling of dust followed. "Oh, come on," she whispered.

"What's the problem?"

"Nothing. Looks like the maid skips this room." There would be noticeable drag marks in the dust, so she pulled the desk chair over and wiped down more of the shelf. At least enough that moving the statue wouldn't be noticed.

She stepped off the chair and put it back where it belonged. Then, taking the forgery, she retraced her movements, up on tiptoe to slide the statue in place. On her way back down, she bumped a vase holding fake flowers. A cheap, ugly thing all around, which should've been her first clue.

She reached out to steady it, but by the time her brain registered the inconsistency, it was too late. Turning her head to the side, she was still caught by a blue cloud of dye.

"Damn!" she growled.

"What? What happened? You've got a minute left."

In her anger, she swiped the Montblanc pen from the desk and dropped it in her bag beside the statue. She considered it an inconvenience bill. She looked back at the vase and moved it to the floor, so it looked like it had fallen. "I'm fine."

She climbed back out the window, replacing the screen, and rappelled down the wall. At the bottom, she released her hook and it dropped down to her. She gathered the rope and shoved it in her bag. In the distance, she heard the first siren.

"I'm out and on my way to you." After reaching the corner of the property, she boosted herself over the wall again and made her way back through the shadows. Half a block down, London pulled up and Audrey threw the panel door open.

"What happened?" Audrey asked once Nikki was in the back and tossing her cap across the van.

"He had a booby trap in the room."

"Oh my God. Are you okay?" Audrey twisted in her seat and reached for Nikki.

Nikki waved her off. Her heart thundered and it wasn't the good adrenaline, job-well-done rush either. This was an I-want-to-kill-someone tension. *I can't believe I was so stupid.* She turned her phone camera on herself to see the damage.

London flipped on the interior lights, which didn't help much, but it was enough that Audrey could see.

"What is that?" She reached over and swiped a finger over Nikki's neck. Nikki flinched.

"Don't."

Audrey withdrew her finger, which now sported a blue streak. Nikki assumed she had a matching one where Audrey made contact.

"Are you going to tell us?" London asked.

"After getting the forgery in place, which required me to do some light dusting, I bumped a hideous vase on the lower shelf. It had a dye pack or something that exploded and got me." She sighed. "Just don't touch it. I think that makes it worse. I need to figure out how to wash it off."

She lifted her chin and tried to get a better look at the damage. Blue speckles coated the left side of her neck and part of her shoulder and collar. At least it missed her face. Small blessings.

When London parked the van, Nikki put her hat back on, not that anyone was on the street to notice that her skin was blue.

She unlocked the door and Audrey and London followed in silence. After setting the stupid statue below the TV, which had become the designated spot for stolen art, she turned it sideways so she wouldn't have to stare at it. Then she went to the bathroom to see how bad the dye was.

London yelled, "Want champagne?"

"No. Get me whiskey." Although she wanted to peel off her shirt and jump in the shower, she knew better. She'd made those mistakes when she was younger. Sure enough, the untouched dye remained small specks on her skin, but where Audrey touched her was a streak.

Unfortunately, her past mistakes had only taught her what *not* to do, not what she needed to do.

"Hey," London called from the other side of the bathroom door. "I don't suppose you know what the dye is made of, do you?"

"Sure. There was a nifty little label right on the shelf."

"Don't need to be a smartass. I'm Googling solutions for you. I think if we treat it like hair dye, we'll be okay."

Nikki sighed and opened the door. London handed her a glass of whiskey. After a sip, she said, "Thanks. Sorry I snapped."

"I'd snap too if I looked like a Smurf."

Nikki cringed. "It's not that bad, is it? I only saw the speckles."

"Nah. I'm messing with you." London continued to scroll on her phone. "We can try baby oil or olive oil. If that doesn't work, there's alcohol. Or, of course, you can scrub at it."

Nikki inhaled deeply and then slammed back the rest of her whiskey. As they made their way back to the living room, Audrey had the cameras on Turner's house on the screen.

"Problems?" Nikki asked.

"Just monitoring," Audrey said. "Cops showed. Banter on the scanner says they think he's a nutjob. Especially since he wouldn't leave the panic room. I turned his interior cameras back on so he could see they were cops, but he wasn't having it." Her eyes were trained on the screen, completely fascinated.

"Do they know we made the swap?"

"They're still trying to convince him to come out. They've flashed badges at every camera and have told him they've checked the whole house."

"If they leave, we're good. So let's hope they can't talk him into coming out. I have a feeling that he would notice every speck of dust that I disturbed."

The door opened and Mia walked in. For once, she didn't look completely irritated by them. She strode directly to the statue, picked it up, and inspected it. "You did it."

Nikki snorted. "You don't have to sound so shocked. Have we let you down yet?"

Mia blinked. "That's not what I meant and you know it. Last we spoke, you had me intervening and trying to convince Turner that I'm as paranoid as he is. What was the point of all that?"

Nikki leaned against the couch. "Psychological warfare. We freaked him out enough that he scurried into his panic room and still hasn't left."

Mia set the statue back in its spot and neared her. "What happened there?" she asked, pointing to the blue streak on Nikki's neck.

"Booby trap."

"Are you all right?"

Is that genuine concern in Mia's eyes? "I'm fine. Mad that the old man got one over on me."

"He's out!" Audrey yelled.

They all turned to face the screen. Turner was walking down the hall, gaze shifting between the cops on his side. They walked together room to room.

"What I wouldn't give to be able to hear this. I

should've planted a bug." Nikki watched the cops. "They believe him."

"How could you possibly know that?" Mia asked.

Nikki rolled her eyes. "If I didn't know how to read people, I would be sitting in prison right now. They're not dismissing him. They're going to start looking for evidence."

"What are they going to find?"

Nikki looked at Mia. "They'll find the vase that had the booby trap dye in it lying on the floor. There was no erasing the evidence of that, so I put it on the floor so he might think the wind knocked it over. If they're good, they'll find scrapes from my grappling hook. Or possibly notice that the screen isn't quite right. But since Audrey busted it the other day, who's to say?"

"But," Audrey interjected, "they won't think anything was stolen. We've already tormented him with the drone and smoke bombs. He thinks someone's out to get him, but the police will assume it's harassment. Especially since he can't tell them anything is missing."

Nikki thought of the pen she dropped in her bag. What was the likelihood he would notice it missing? And if he did, would it be worth telling the cops? "Good point. Although I should tell you that I stole a pen from his desk."

"What?" Mia asked sharply.

"I was mad about the vase and the dye. So I swiped a Montblanc." She waved a hand. "It's the guest room. I doubt he'll even notice it missing."

"You better hope not" was Mia's only comment.

She set her empty glass on the table. "On that note, I'm out of here."

"Where are you going?" Mia asked.

"First, to get some oil to remove this." She pointed at her neck. "Then I'm taking tomorrow off. See you all on Tuesday. I'm assuming you'll be ready to plan the next one by then?"

"Yes. Enjoy your night."

Nikki shot a look at Audrey, who understood where she was going. She got a wink in response.

In the car ride back to Wade's, Nikki tried not to let panic hit. If she had been wearing a turtleneck, this wouldn't have happened. But it was too hot to be wearing a sweater that covered all of her skin. Maybe if they hadn't jacked the heat up on Turner's place, she might've considered it.

But now she had to get this dye off before going to the museum tomorrow. Having blue skin would definitely make her memorable, and she couldn't afford that. She had the car drop her off at the strip mall closest to Wade's house. She went to the drugstore and got baby oil. As she wandered the aisles, she grabbed a bag of chips and a couple of candy bars. Then she saw a bin filled with cheap dog toys and added one to her basket.

She walked the rest of the way to Wade's house, thinking about how she could get Roberta to go out for drinks. Everything in her life would be so much better if she could nab the Devereaux and get rid of Donny.

The niggling voice in her head reminded her that she'd be getting rid of Wade, too. Not getting rid of him, but once the job was done, their arrangement was technically over. They didn't need to be around each other. She wasn't sure she was ready to walk away again, but she couldn't reconcile her desire to be with him with the idea of having Dodger back in her life.

As she neared his house, she saw the blue light from the TV flickering in the living room. He was waiting up. Her heart gave a little thump. She fished the key he gave her out of her pocket and unlocked the door.

Pudgy Flynn came running at her, but for the first time in her life, she didn't panic. Fear spiked, but she tossed the toy she bought and it distracted him enough that she could get into the house. Wade stood and smiled at her.

The fear and confusion fled her body. She stepped into his embrace, and it was better than coming home because Wade cared more than Dodger ever had.

TWENTY-FIVE

WADE WRAPPED HIS arms around Nikki. "Bad night?"

"The job went off without too many issues. I'm just tired."

"Well, since you appear to all be one piece, I'm guessing you didn't trigger the booby traps."

She chuckled. "Not the ones we knew about." She stepped back and pointed at her neck, which was all splotchy.

He put his face close to get a better look. "What is that?"

"Some kind of dye." She held up a plastic bag. "I stopped to buy oil. I heard it might help remove it."

"Smart move with the toy for Flynn." On cue, his dog came waddling over and sat at Nikki's feet. "But now I think you have a friend for life."

"I'd settle for a truce. We agree to stay out of each other's way."

Wade pulled her close again. "I think you're out of luck there, too. Flynn's a lot like me. We like to be up in your space."

She tilted her head and pressed her lips to Wade's neck. "As much as I'd like you to invade my space right now, I need to try to get this dye off. I might have a hard time explaining it to Roberta tomorrow when I'm asking her to go out for drinks."

"Then let's get you cleaned up." He stepped back, took her hand and tugged her toward his bathroom.

"I'm capable of cleaning myself."

"It's more fun with help. Just sit for a minute."

Surprisingly, she did as he said and sat on the closed toilet lid. He pulled out some cotton and opened the bottle of baby oil from the bag. She piled her hair up into a sloppy knot. The picture threw him back in time. She looked so much like the Nikki he remembered—the Nikki of his dreams—that for a moment, he had a hard time focusing.

Then she tilted her head to give him full access to her neck. The back was worse than the front, so she must've been turning when it hit.

"If you leave your hair down tomorrow, most of this will be covered."

She sighed. "Except I'm supposed to be handling priceless art. I can't have my hair getting in the way."

He dabbed and then rubbed the oil in, making her skin glisten. While his left hand applied the oil, his right slid along the other side of her neck, cradling her jaw. Her breath hitched at his touch and then evened out. Most people wouldn't have noticed, but he was well versed at looking for the slightest reaction.

She closed her eyes and leaned into his touch. He stroked her cheek with his thumb. The cotton in his other hand was turning blue but she still had streaks running over her skin.

"Do you ever think about giving this up?"

Her eyes opened slowly. "Not really."

"Not even when you're stuck in an elevator shaft for hours waiting for an office to clear out? Or when you're going out the back as the cops are coming in the front?" His heart raced at the memories of all the times he'd worried about her.

A slow smile spread across her face. "Those are the things that keep life exciting."

He turned to get a new piece of cotton.

She touched his arm. "Seriously. What else would I do? I could never punch a clock as a secretary or work in retail with people yelling at me over stupid stuff."

"You'd make a pretty good salesperson," he said with a slight laugh as he applied more oil to the ink.

"I've never known anything else. You know that."

"Neither did I until I looked for something else." It wasn't until that moment that he realized how much he wanted her to walk away from this life. It made him even more determined to settle things with Donny and Wolf and get rid of them for good. There was no way he'd stand by and let them anywhere near her.

Dodger thought he could have Nikki train a new thief. She could just as easily train security to spot the vulnerabilities she saw.

He grabbed a washcloth and wiped away the excess oil. "There's still some blue smudges, but the oil worked pretty well."

She stood, which pressed her body against his since he hadn't stepped back. She bumped him with her hip and twisted to look in the mirror. "Yeah, that's good enough. If Roberta sees it, I'll just tell her I was role-playing this weekend." She winked at him in the mirror and then turned back. "Wanna do some role-playing so I'm not lying?"

"I'll take you any way I can have you. But you're not painting me blue."

"First, I need a shower. Think you can help with that?"

"Absolutely." He pulled her close and kissed her.

THE NEXT MORNING Nikki stood in Wade's bathroom feeling exhausted. Back-to-back jobs were never a smart move. Her brain needed a chance to reset, and she didn't have time for that. Thank God that by tonight, it would all be over.

But once the jobs were done, where did that leave her and Wade? There was no way she would continue on this path, fixing Dodger's screw-ups. She'd already wasted too much of her life on that. At the same time, she couldn't leave Dodger in a position to do this to himself again. It would be so much easier if she could just hate him.

But he'd stuck around after her mother took off. He could've abandoned her, given her up. Although she couldn't quite picture what a "normal" life would've been like, Dodger had done the best he knew how. Unfortunately, he didn't really grasp how to grow and change.

"Hey, you up?" she called as she got ready for work.

"Yeah," Wade's voice came from the bed, still sleep-scratchy. The sound made her want to crawl back into bed.

"When are you making the handoff to Donny?" She walked back into the bedroom as she adjusted her wig.

Wade scrubbed a hand over his face. "Not sure. Assuming everything goes off without a hitch tonight, probably tomorrow." He sat and leaned against the headboard.

"I want in on that."

"What? I thought you didn't want Dodger to know you were around."

"You seriously haven't told him?"

"Of course not. I'll handle Donny."

She rolled her eyes. "I want to look Donny in the eye and tell him no more business with Dodger. This is it."

"I'll make sure he gets the message." He pushed out of bed. "I don't want you anywhere near Donny."

"Donny doesn't scare me." She flicked up a hand. "And before you say it, neither does Wolf."

"He should." He took her hand. "Devon gave me background on the guy. He's not someone to mess with."

She chuckled. "So even though he's all big and scary, you can talk to him because you're a man."

"It's not like that and you know it. Can we just get through today? I'll get the painting to Donny, and we'll never have to deal with him again."

He was being a little too insistent about her not participating, which made her suspicious. Part of her wanted to believe he was just doing the macho caveman thing, but that wasn't Wade's way. "What aren't you telling me?"

"Dodger and I will make sure everything is taken care of. I know you don't trust Dodger. Trust me." He kissed her softly. "Besides, you tend to rub people like Donny the wrong way."

"Are you saying that I'm not smooth enough to handle the likes of Donny?"

"I'm saying your dislike of him overrides everything, even common sense."

"I'm not twenty anymore. I can fake it with the best of them." This was one of the problems of having history with someone. Wade didn't see her as she was today; he still saw the impulsive, hotheaded girl who acted without thinking.

She wasn't going to change his mind. She let out a sigh. "I'm only supposed to be working till six. I'm going to invite Roberta out for dinner and drinks. Hopefully everyone else will be gone by then. You can grab the key and by the time you're in place, it should be dark enough for you to go across the roof unnoticed."

"Meet back here for a celebratory drink?"

"Sure." She put her lab coat and glasses on.

On her ride to the museum, Nikki did some digging to track Donny down. Luckily, thugs like him never moved too far. Wade could go ahead and make the handoff. She'd meet Donny tonight and set things straight. Then she and Wade could decide what the future held, if anything.

After a quick wave at Jason, the security guard, Nikki went upstairs and found all of the organization she'd done in the storage closet destroyed. Paul stood in the doorway, checking things off a list as other college students moved things around.

She swallowed her anger as best she could. "What's going on?"

Paul barely spared her a glance. "We're getting ready to put together the exhibit for the Devereaux."

"But Ro—Dr. Wolcott said she'd look over some of my ideas."

"Yeah, well, newbies don't dictate exhibits."

She sighed and pulled the tablet from her bag. "If you tell me what you're looking for, I can direct you to it. I did spend the last few days inventorying and organizing all of this."

He snatched the tablet. "These are not supposed to leave the premises."

"Dr. Wolcott gave me permission."

He huffed and scrolled through the tablet, stopping at the design layout she'd created for the Devereaux exhibit. Those drawings had been her plan to get Roberta out to dinner.

"Not bad," he mumbled, and she wanted to smack the tablet into his smug face.

"Where do you want me?" she asked.

"You can work downstairs today. The architect will need someone to reposition things to make room for the new exhibit."

"So, I'm moving more artifacts around?"

"If that's what he needs."

"Do you even understand what an internship is? I'm not a glorified mover."

"We all have to pay our dues."

It took every ounce of control she had not to say anything else. She spun on her heels and went downstairs.

Hours passed before she even saw Roberta. Everyone was buzzing around, and Nikki feared she wouldn't be able to get the woman to agree to drinks tonight. Rumor said that the authentication was happening within the next couple of days. Wade had to get the painting tonight.

When Roberta came to check with the designer, Nikki waited until the woman turned to go back upstairs.

"Dr. Wolcott," she called.

"Hi, Alice. How are you?"

"Good. A lot going on today, huh?"

"It's quite exciting. We're anxious to get the Devereaux on display."

"That's actually what I hoped to talk to you about. Would you be available tonight to maybe get some dinner?"

"I'm sorry, but like you said, things are hectic."

"Maybe just a drink then?" Nikki lowered her voice. "To be totally honest, I'd like to talk to you, but I don't feel comfortable speaking openly here." A glance up the stairs. "It's about Paul."

Roberta's lips thinned as she pressed them together. "It'll have to be late. Eight o'clock?"

"I'll go home and change and then come back. We can grab something at a place in the neighborhood, so you're not far from here." And it would give Nikki enough time to find Donny tonight in case Wade pushed up his timetable.

"Sounds good. Just have them page me when you get back here."

"Thank you so much."

As soon as Roberta scooted up the steps, Nikki pulled out her phone and texted Wade. We're a go for tonight.

WADE PUT ON his old blue jumpsuit that he'd used for numerous cons when he'd needed to be a serviceman no one would notice. Much like Nikki's favorite disguise of waitress, it was a costume designed to make people overlook him.

"There's no talking you out of this?" Devon asked, leaning against the frame of his office door.

"You know I have to do it."

"I'd feel better if you sent Dodger or Nikki in to do the actual heist."

"She's getting me access." Plus, he didn't want her to take any more risk.

Boone pushed past Devon and came into the room. "Tell the truth. You don't want her to do it—even though you admit she's better than you—because you still love her."

Devon straightened. "What?"

Wade shot Boone a dirty look.

"Ah, fuck me," Devon said.

"Thanks, but you're not my type." Wade zipped the uniform up and looked at his friends. "Look. She's always been the one. I never thought I'd get another chance, so I'm not going to blow it."

"She's a thief." Devon stared at him in utter disbelief.

"She is. But I'm hoping I can convince her to use her skills for good instead of evil. She would be an excellent asset here. No one is better at spotting vulnerabilities."

Devon snorted. "And you think giving a thief access to our wealthy clients, who we know don't have good security, is a smart move?"

Wade sank onto his couch beside Boone. "It's not about the money for her. It's the thrill. She's just never looked to get that thrill anywhere else."

Boone smacked his leg. "That doesn't say much for your skills in the bedroom, man."

"Shut up. We're fine in the bedroom. Dodger raised her to do this one thing. And she's the best. She never considered anything else. I at least want to make the offer."

Devon crossed his arms. "And what if she declines?"

"Then I'll figure it out." He stood and smiled at his friends. "But I can be very persuasive."

Boone stood as well. "You need backup?"

From the corner of his eye, Wade saw Devon stiffen again. "No, thanks. We got this." He turned to Devon. "This won't come back on us. I promise. I just have one favor to ask."

"What's that?"

"Your FBI connection."

Both Devon and Boone stared at him with wide eyes.

"I told you I was putting an end to this." He finished packing his tools for the job and waited to hear from Nikki about a time and place for the handoff.

He couldn't risk her getting picked up. No way would the FBI cut her a deal. She'd been suspected of too many crimes. Arresting her was an agent's wet dream. And if he told her that he'd involved the FBI, she'd probably be pissed. A pissed-off Nikki was impulsive and reckless.

Her disdain for cops was almost as legendary as her skill as a thief.

He felt bad not telling her his whole plan for tomorrow, but he had to keep her safe. They just needed to get through tonight. Then, tomorrow, when she was nowhere near Donny and Wolf, he'd make sure the Devereaux was given back to the museum.

NIKKI TUCKED HER lab coat into her bag but left her wig and glasses on. Donny might be a thug, but she knew enough guys like him to know he'd have some kind of security and the last thing she needed was evidence of her colluding with him. She strode into the dimly lit South Side bar and scanned for Donny's scrawny body. Of course, she found him in the same spot he'd been sitting in more than a decade ago when her father sent her to pay off a debt.

She walked to the corner booth, eyes checking around for anyone paying extra attention to her. One guy by the back door. The bartender. No one else even glanced in her direction. Even Donny kept his eyes trained on the TV on the wall.

The TV looked newish. That was the only thing that had changed in the years since she'd last been here. The scarred floor and busted tables were all the same. As was the clientele. She was all for hanging in a dive bar, but the amount of scum in this place would make her rethink her life choices.

Nikki slid into the seat across from Donny and waited for him to acknowledge her presence. When he finally turned to her, his sharp face creased into a lascivious smile.

"Hello, there. Can I get you a drink?"

"No, thanks, Donny. I just need a minute of your time."

"Sure, sweetheart. What's this about?"

She leaned forward on the table. "First, I'm not your sweetheart. Second, it's about Dodger."

His eyes about popped out of his head. "Ho-ly shit. It's you."

"Yeah, long time, no see, thank goodness."

"Why you gotta you be like that?"

Because you're slimy and nasty, and I would never

let you get close enough to touch me. "This is business, Donny. I know you're working with Wolf, and I'm here to let both of you know that you'll get your painting, and then you will never do business with Dodger again. Not even a five-dollar bet on a Cubs game. Even better, don't let him walk through the door. Don't take his calls."

"You want to leave Dodger out of this, that's fine. He's mostly useless these days. But I have to admit, I didn't see this coming. I never thought he'd be able to deliver."

"I'm glad we're in agreement. You get the painting and lose Dodger's number." That had been way easier than she'd expected.

"As soon as I get yours."

"You'll never need mine."

Donny's low chuckle made her stomach turn. She knew his agreement had come too easily.

"I guess Dodger and his boy left a few things out of the deal. The painting acts as proof of ability. Something to tide us over. The deal was for a thief."

Her stomach sank again. That was why Wade had come looking for her. She swallowed hard and unclenched her jaw.

"Dodger originally said he couldn't get you, but he could train one to be as good as you."

She didn't stop the snort at his comments. Dodger had once been a master thief and con man, but she doubted he had it in him to train someone else. "You'll get your painting, but you should know that Dodger doesn't negotiate for me. I take care of my own business."

She stood and turned to leave. The thug at the back door took a step, but Donny raised a hand.

"Dodger owes us. He delivers or he pays. And I don't mean with cash."

"You'll have the painting tomorrow as planned." She'd been hearing similar threats most of her life. No way was she getting sucked back into Dodger's mess. How could she have been so stupid to think that Wade wanted her to stay away from Donny and Wolf to keep her safe?

She could almost hear him now: "I know I said it was one last job for old time's sake." Then it would morph into "But we're so good together." How long did Wade think he'd be able to keep up the charade? Her blood boiled, mostly out of anger at herself.

How did I do this to myself again? I should've learned my lesson. And to make the same mistake with the same man?

Once back outside, the air felt thicker, heavier than it had when she'd entered the bar. Or maybe that was just the weight of the truth. She should just blow off Roberta tonight. It would serve them right, but she wouldn't do that. *She* had honor and would hold up her end of the deal.

Then she would disappear from their lives for good.

TWENTY-SIX

FOR THE FIRST time in years, Wade's nerves buzzed with an uncomfortable mixture of excitement and anxiety. It felt good to be back in the game. While he didn't miss the danger of the job, he missed pulling off a massive heist successfully. Who didn't love feeling one hundred percent on their game?

But breaking and entering was Nikki's thing. She was right when she said he enjoyed charming people out of their belongings. It seemed less harmful than forcing his way into a place and helping himself. Plus, she was better at it.

If she were in his position right now, she'd be bouncing on the balls of her feet, debating whether she could fit in a run before the job. Then she'd need to eat. The thought of food made his stomach flip. He was an eat-once-the-job-is-done kind of thief.

Standing on a corner waiting for Nikki and Roberta to make an appearance didn't help. The neighborhood was bustling, as the street was filled with various bistros and cafés. The museum was on the next block at the north end of the Loop. Close enough to downtown that things were accessible, but far enough that they didn't have all the same congestion. The neighborhood had a good mix of office and retail buildings. He glanced around. Many of the buildings were old, historic, and intriguing to look at.

He thought he'd timed it right, but he'd obviously walked too quickly. Now he was standing here looking like an idiot, staring at the screen on his phone, hoping no one would take note of his van parked in an alley.

Then, like a beacon, her voice echoed down the block. He heard her above the traffic and the people talking. It was as if she spoke to him. His gaze darted up and he waited for her to make eye contact. She looked at him but offered no smile, no wicked wink. Barely a glance.

In character or not, Nikki played. It was part of who she was. Something was wrong.

He stepped forward to make his pass to accept the ID card from her. He waited for some signal that they were a no-go. But then from her sleeve slid a card, down to her fingertips. He reached to take the card, make contact with her hand, as they had done hundreds of times.

But she retracted her hand too quickly. If he hadn't been paying attention, the card would've hit the ground, risking exposure. Nikki was smoother than that. What kind of message was she trying to send?

If something was wrong with the museum or the location of the painting, she would've called this off. He slid the card into his pocket and turned back to look at her.

Over her shoulder, she glared at him. It only lasted two seconds, but it was a long two seconds. She was pissed off, and he had no idea why. When she'd left his house this morning everything was fine. The only contact they'd had since was a text to let him know they were a go.

What the hell happened since then?

He didn't have time to attempt to understand the inner workings of Nikki's mind right now. He only had a small window to make the switch, grab the Devereaux and return the ID before Roberta finished her drink and headed back to the museum.

At the corner, he crossed the street and headed to the building opposite the museum. His van was already staged in the alley. He donned his coverall again and reentered the office complex with his bag of tools. He'd made his appearance hours ago and made sure security and the front office knew he was coming back. They were thrilled he'd agreed to come after hours so residents wouldn't be disturbed.

Tugging his hat low on his head, he signed in with security. They waved him on to the elevator. Two minutes later, he had rooftop access. He walked the perimeter of the roof, then dropped his coveralls and shoved them in his bag.

Nikki thought the taller building on the other side was the better choice. Mostly she just enjoyed ziplining. But he could make the jump pretty easily between the buildings, and once he had the painting, he'd go down the back of the museum to land right at his van. He pulled a mask over his face just to be sure he wouldn't be caught on camera. At the ledge, he tossed his tool bag. Then he calculated the difference, took a few deep breaths, and backed up.

One more deep breath and a loud exhale. Then he took off at a run and jumped across. He landed on the museum roof and rolled to soften the blow to his body. He lay on his back and took stock. "I'm too old for this," he said to the night air.

At least nothing was broken. He carefully turned over and stood, grabbing his bag as he went. He eased the metal door open at the stairwell. With the exception of the glowing emergency exit sign, it was pitch black. He closed his eyes and listened. He heard nothing. He slid through the opening, holding the door to prevent a bang, and reopened his eyes.

He flicked on his flashlight for a second to see the stairs, then turned it back off. He'd stay in the dark as long as possible. Making his way down the stairs to the third floor was quick. He opened the door there and found hall lights burning. There were only two doors on the floor, both closed. He went to the one Nikki said would lead to Roberta's office. Good thing he kept his lock-picking skills sharpened.

He had a hard time believing how little security some museums had. It took him three minutes in total to get in. He closed the door behind him and turned on his flashlight. If anyone on the street saw the light, they would assume it was security. Nikki had said the rooms had no cameras. Just the hallway by the stairs going into the museum proper was covered.

The storage room was unlocked and he found the dog painting. Ripping the dummy canvas off the forgery took longer than he liked. He had to be careful with the utility knife because he didn't want to mark the forgery. Something like that would stand out to Roberta. They needed a little time before the forgery was discovered.

Twenty-four hours and then they'd be free.

The same wouldn't be said for Wolf and Donny.

He carried the forgery to Roberta's office and picked that lock. He entered the room, closed and locked the door behind him. Extra steps like that were something Nikki made fun of him for. She was all about speed and chance. But locking that door would be enough to deter a typical security guard from further investigation.

He swiped Roberta's ID on the interior room. The keypad immediately lit green. This was almost too easy. He opened the door and flashed his light across the entire room, searching for evidence of another alarm. He should've known better than to doubt Nikki.

She wasn't Dodger. She didn't get things wrong.

The Devereaux was laid out on a pristine white table, just as she'd said. He made the swap and wrapped the real painting in a canvas bag to protect it.

He closed the room, locked up Roberta's office, and made his way back to the hallway. He turned off his light again and gave his eyes a minute to readjust to the dark. Opening the door a crack, he peeked out. No sound. No movement.

Back on the roof, he created a rigging for the painting to lower it down the side of the building to the roof of his van. Then he used the fire escape—which was rickety as hell—to get halfway down. Once he was deep in shadow, he waited to make sure the alley remained empty. Not even a homeless person in sight. Then he used his rope to rappel the rest of the way to the ground.

After safely securing the painting in the back of the van, he drove down the alley and pulled out on the street. He needed to park the van and get back to Nikki to return the ID before Roberta noticed it was missing.

Of course, his luck had run out. There had been an accident on the next block. The cops had the street closed off and traffic was backed up, no movement at all.

"Great," he muttered. He pulled out his phone and texted Nikki.

Stuck in traffic.

Nikki tried to focus on the text from Wade, but she'd consumed a lot of alcohol in a short period of time. "Jerk," she said to the screen.

"Is there a problem?" Roberta asked. She was a genuinely nice person.

Nikki almost felt bad stealing the Devereaux from her. Dodger and Wade didn't deserve her help. And Donny didn't deserve the painting. But she'd get it back. "Nah," she answered. "Stupid ex."

"Do you need to take that?" she asked pointing at the phone.

"No. It's definitely over. Completely. You know how it is. They betray your trust, and even if you're gullible enough to give 'em another chance, they just screw you over again." That probably was not a real professional way to speak to her boss. But given that she would be out of Roberta's life after tonight, she didn't care.

"We've all been there, honey. Want to tell me about it?"

"Not really. But I'd love another drink."

Roberta waved the waitress over and ordered another round. Nikki worked to stay in character. She inhaled a chest full of warm night air and looked around the patio for the bar they were at. The open layout would allow an easy handoff from Wade when he finally got here.

Focusing back on Roberta, she asked, "Have you always worked at the Carlisle?"

"For the last fifteen years. Prior to that, I worked at a few small galleries. Where do you hope to land after you finish school?"

Nikki widened her eyes. "I'm not sure. There seem to be so many options, but at the same time I've realized how small this world is." She sipped her drink, a margarita, wishing it were straight shots. "Really, I'll just be happy to have a paying gig. It would show my family how wrong they are."

Everyone had at least one sucky family member, right? Nikki had forgotten how hard it was to fake bonding with a stranger.

"Your family doesn't support your education?"

"They support education. They just don't see much real-world value in art. They accuse me of being…uppity, I guess."

Roberta reached across the table and patted Nikki's hand. "I'm sorry to hear that they don't see the beauty in the things we do. But don't worry. There are plenty of us out there who do place value on this. Surround yourself with people like us."

Nikki smiled. It was almost like she wanted to believe Roberta would still be in her life after tonight. How much had she had to drink that she was looking to befriend a mark?

"What period of art do you like best?" Roberta asked.

"Of course, I love the masters. But there's something about modern art that draws me in." She thought of the Banksy she'd stolen for Wade years ago. It was supposed to have been one of the things that would give them a new start, doing whatever they wanted. Now it sat gathering dust in a storage unit. "I love seeing art evolve, especially street art. As a teen, growing up in Chicago, I loved watching graffiti murals covering dilapidated buildings. Giving beauty to an area filled with despair."

"Wow," Roberta whispered. "I've never thought much about graffiti other than as vandalism, which I know is shortsighted of me, but to think about it as evidence of evolution..." She paused to take a drink.

Nikki tapped her foot under the table. She didn't know how much longer she could do this. At some point, she was going to run out of art-related things to say.

"When you asked me to meet you, you mentioned something about not feeling comfortable talking at the museum?" Roberta prompted.

Oh yeah. I had started with that ruse to get her here. Bitching about a coworker? Way easier than pretending to know art.

"Paul is..."

"Did he do something inappropriate?" Roberta asked.

"Nothing sexual. Not at all. He just..." She took a deep breath. "Every interaction I have with him he acts like I'm stupid. Like he can't be bothered to tell me where I'm needed or what I should do. I'm not normally a snitch, but I feel like I'm not as effective as I could be as an intern because I'm not getting enough direction."

Roberta nodded. "Paul is a little rough around the edges. But he's good at what he does. You could learn quite a bit from him. But, yes, I know he doesn't have patience to delegate well." She smiled. "I imagine he was one of those students who took it upon himself to complete an entire group project by himself."

"Totally," Nikki agreed.

"I've been trying to work with him on those skills. Because the museum does take on a number of interns each semester, he gets overwhelmed. The lack of consistency bothers him."

"I guess that makes sense." From the corner of her eye, she saw Wade walking briskly down the block. Finally. Time to wrap this up. "I'll cut him some slack. I hope he's willing to give me the same courtesy."

Wade brushed around her, slipping the card back between her fingers. The air around her was charged with the energy she always felt in his presence, and it almost knocked her off her game. Almost.

"I can have a talk with him again."

Him? Paul. Jeez, her brain was fuzzy. "No. That's okay. It actually makes me feel better to know that he's like this with everyone and not just me." She bent down to grab her bag, sliding Roberta's card back into her purse. "I'll square up our tab and let you get back to the museum."

"I'll take care of the bill," Roberta offered.

"No, really. I appreciate you taking time out of your busy schedule to make me feel better." She stood.

Roberta held up a hand. "Do you want me to call a car? Are you okay to get home by yourself?"

"I'm tired and the margarita is hitting a little harder than usual, but I'm fine. Thanks." She tried for a soft smile so she could break free.

Roberta stood. "If you're sure."

"Completely sure."

"See you tomorrow?"

Nikki nodded, a lump filling her throat on the lie. She left the table, went into the restaurant to find their server and paid the bill. Within minutes, her phone was blowing up with texts from Wade wanting to know if everything was okay.

No. Nothing is okay.

TWENTY-SEVEN

WADE CIRCLED THE block twice looking for Nikki, but he couldn't risk more than that. Too many places had security cameras that might catch the van. While he'd seemingly gotten away with the swap, he needed to finish the job. He texted and called, but she didn't answer and he began to worry. He took a deep breath.

Get the painting out of the van and somewhere safe. Then look for Nikki. He wasn't worried that if caught, she would give him up. She didn't have it in her to do that. He was worried that something happened to her. While she could carry a con if she had to, she didn't like it, and her disdain might've caused her to slip.

On his third call, he left a message. "Please call and let me know you're okay. I think we need some champagne to celebrate. You still do that, don't you?"

It had been a tradition she started because Dodger would never let them celebrate. He participated because it made her happy, but he'd never developed a taste for bubbly.

The rest of the ride back to his house was spent in silence, hoping for her return call. He parked and immediately noticed Boone's car two spots in front of his. Checking out the street, he saw no one, so he pulled the painting out and hurried to his house. The door opened before he had the chance to touch his keys.

Boone stared at him. "It worked."

"You don't have to sound so shocked. We're good at what we do."

Boone stepped back to let him through the door. "No Nikki?"

"I don't know where she is. She isn't answering her phone."

"You think someone figured out what you were doing?"

"I don't think so. Something was up when we made the handoff. She was pissed, but I have no idea why."

"Job pissed, or personal pissed?"

Wade shrugged. His gut said personal, but he'd done nothing. "I know where to find her. Let me handle this and then I'll figure her out."

He unwrapped the painting and took a picture on a new burner. Then he texted it to Dodger, Donny, and Wolf. "What are you doing here anyway?" he asked Boone. "I thought we agreed you guys were going to keep your distance."

"I didn't agree. And I figured Flynn would be lonely and need to go out, so I stopped by."

"Yeah, sure. My dog is the reason," he said, full of sarcasm.

"Sue me for being concerned. What's the next move?"

"Get Devon's FBI contact so I can get rid of all this trouble. Start fresh with Nikki."

Boone leaned back on the couch. "Have you talked to her about any of this? She seems to really like being a thief."

"I'll show her she has options."

"You're in deep, man. If she doesn't want to change her life, she's gonna pull you down."

"No, she won't." Boone didn't know Nikki like he did. They were meant to be.

"I'll text Devon and get you the info." He pointed to the painting. "You might want to find a safe place for that."

After rewrapping the painting and tucking it into a closet, he went to the kitchen and grabbed a couple beers. He texted Nikki again and considered showing up at the apartment he'd dropped her off at.

He handed Boone a bottle and sat next to him on the couch. He finally got a response from Nikki.

Fuck off.

Boone chuckled. "Guess that answers my question. It's personal and you pissed her off."

Wade stared at his screen. "How? When she left this morning, we were good. Made plans for tonight after the heist. We didn't even talk after that."

"She's a chick. She probably remembered something you did ten years ago that pissed her off all over again."

That wasn't it. But he knew Nikki well enough to know not to push her now. He'd let her sleep and seek her out tomorrow.

Boone's phone buzzed. "Devon. He's got the number for his FBI contact in art crime."

Wade put his beer down. "And?"

"He says text the agent right now. He's waiting." Flynn lumbered over and Boone bent and began petting him.

Using the same burner phone, he texted and waited for a call back. This was a long shot and he hadn't considered the FBI would want to move this fast. He took another sip of beer. He hated waiting. This was why he'd always preferred a con. There was always something happening, something to do. Nikki didn't mind the wait. She was like a panther on the hunt. But a heist was the only time she was patient and graceful and silent. The rest of her life was loud and carefree.

Hell, he'd missed her.

The phone rang and Wade answered without checking the screen. "Hello?"

"Hello. This is Agent Eden Stokes. With whom am I speaking?"

A female agent? He should've known.

"Why should my name matter?"

"I don't have time for games."

"You can call me Dodger."

Boone swung a look at him with raised eyebrows.

"Devon said you have information that could lead to the arrest of Marco Wolf."

"I happen to know that he will be at a meeting to take possession of a stolen piece of art. I can get you the time and place of the meeting. I can't guarantee he'll show, but at least one of his lackeys will be there."

"What piece of art?"

"The Devereaux that was just given to the Carlisle."

"I haven't seen any reports of it being stolen."

"It hasn't been reported yet. What they have in the museum is a forgery. The original is set to change hands tomorrow afternoon. If you show up, you can get Wolf on possession of stolen property."

"It's not much, but it might be enough to find more. What's your stake in this?"

"Just trying to help a friend. I don't want to land in jail for orchestrating this."

"If you're there, you'll be scooped up with the rest, but we can make a deal. What are the chances we can meet early so you can wear a wire?"

"Zero. No wire. But I will get you the meeting information in plenty of time to get there and set up before anyone else arrives. Do your own recording."

"You expect me to pull together an entire team and run an op based on your word? Why would I trust you?"

"First off, what do you have to lose? A blown op? Big deal. I'm the one taking all the risk by contacting you. Second, even if you don't trust me, I'm guessing that you trust Devon since we're having this conversation at eleven at night. So the real question is, how much do you trust Devon?"

She huffed. "I'll need at least a couple of hours' lead time to pull together a team and get to the location."

"Done. I'll text you the information first thing in the morning."

He didn't like bringing Devon into this, but if he could pull this off, he and Nikki would be free and clear. Neither of them would be on-site. Dodger would be taken in, but he'd get a deal out of it. And really, Dodger had at least that much coming.

He probably should have told Nikki, but she trusted the cops less than he did, and if things didn't go right tomorrow afternoon, she'd never trust him. Better for him to figure everything out and then come back to her.

All he had to do was keep Nikki away until after the swap.

NIKKI WENT STRAIGHT to the apartment even though Jared no longer demanded that she live there. For her, it had become a place of refuge. Somewhere she could stay out of trouble.

And right now, she was in a heap of trouble.

She let herself into the apartment, expecting to be met with silence, but the TV was on, and the smell of microwave popcorn filled the air. London and Audrey came from the kitchen carrying a bottle of wine and bowls of popcorn.

"What are you guys doing here?"

"We know how you like to celebrate after a success-ful heist," Audrey said, lifting the bottle of cheap wine.

"First, I celebrate with the good stuff. Second, what if I didn't come back here?"

London snickered. "That's why we went with the cheap stuff. If you were busy with Wade, you wouldn't miss anything here."

"Getting together with Wade won't be happening any time soon."

"Uh-oh. Trouble in paradise?" Audrey asked, taking a seat in the corner of the couch.

Nikki plopped in the middle between the two women. "Far from paradise. He used me."

"For the heist? You kind of knew that…" Audrey's eyes squinted in confusion.

Nikki swallowed and then took a gulp of wine straight from the bottle. "Wade and Dodger played me. Remember I told you that my dad was mixed up in something bad? Well, it turns out that the Devereaux wasn't really what they were after. They want me."

"What?" Audrey and London both yelled.

Nikki nodded and took another gulp of alcohol.

"Are they running some kind of sex trafficking?" London asked.

Nikki snorted. "They want me as their own personal thief."

"What are you going to do?" Audrey asked.

"First, I'm going to steal that painting again. Then…" She paused. "Back to these heists, I guess. I already told them to go screw themselves."

"How'd they take that?" London asked.

"I don't think they got the message clearly." She grabbed a handful of popcorn from Audrey's bowl. She really should've eaten something more substantial.

"Wait. Are you saying that Wade planned to hand you over to some creepy guy to be his thief?" London said.

Nikki nodded.

"I don't buy it. I saw the way the man looked at you."

"He knew about it. He had to. He's been up to his eyeballs in this mess. He has the painting and he was adamant that he take care of the handoff. I wanted to be there to make sure they got the message that this was over. Something about his reaction didn't sit right with me, which was why I went to go see the guy this afternoon."

"You did what? You said this guy was dangerous." Audrey twisted on the couch to fully face her. She was angry.

"Calm down. I went to the guy's bar. And he's the bookie I used to deal with all the time. Slimy, yes. Scary? No."

"Maybe I had too much wine," London said. "But you found out about this backdoor deal before you stole the painting? Why go through with it?"

"Because I follow through. I said I'd get the painting and I did." She might be messed up a million different ways, but she didn't go back on her word.

Audrey rubbed her forehead. "So you think Wade

made a deal with this guy to continue to use you to steal for them?"

Nikki nodded.

"How was he going to pull that off? I'm not understanding."

Nikki huffed. "It's not like he explained his plan to me, but I know Wade. He's an excellent con man. He'd use my feelings to get me to do things."

"That's really lousy," London said. "Are you sure that he knew?"

"Yep."

"Is it possible that you're misreading his intentions?"

"No. Donny said Dodger and *my boy* left out some details. There was no misreading."

"What are you gonna do now?" Audrey asked.

"I have to steal it back. They don't get to keep it. I stole it to dig my dad out one last time. For all I care, he can rot. He was gonna sell me and my skills to these jerks. I'm returning it to the Carlisle." Just saying it did something to her. What was happening to her? She didn't return stolen items. Mia and Jared and their mission to right wrongs were rubbing off on her.

"I think we should bring Jared and Mia in on this," Audrey said.

"No."

Audrey raised a hand. "Hear me out. I get it. I've covered for you. But this is bigger than just you now. It's going to get out that the Carlisle has a bogus copy. This could blow back on all of us."

"What can they do other than bitch at me for stealing it again?"

"It's still the right thing to do. They need to be prepared."

"Jeez." Nikki folded forward and held her head on her knees.

London rubbed her back. "It'll be fine. We'll figure it out together."

That's not how she did things. She handled stuff on her own. "You know there's a possibility they'll fire me over this."

"No," Audrey said.

Nikki sat back up. "Mia demanded no other jobs. This was another job. Worse, it was the same painting that almost halted her plans. This won't just be irritated Mia. This is gonna cause full-on pissed-off Mia."

"Jared won't let her fire you. You're too good. And even with stealing the Devereaux again, you still didn't get caught."

"Because I am that good. I don't get caught." *Except I do get sucked in by Wade and his lies*.

"Don't worry. I'll talk to Jared when I get home and he'll know what to do about Mia."

"Home, huh? I thought you weren't living with him."

Audrey rolled her eyes. "I'm not. Nice way to change the subject, though."

Nikki stretched. "I'm going to bed. Good thing I pack light, so if she throws me out tomorrow, it'll be quick."

"You're not going anywhere," Audrey said.

London leaned over and put an arm around her shoulder.

"We'll see." But in her gut, she didn't want to go. As someone who'd spent years alone, this apartment and these people gave her a sense of belonging, and she wasn't ready to let go.

TWENTY-EIGHT

Mia

"SHE DID WHAT?" Mia worked hard to keep her voice low, when all she wanted to do was scream at Jared. At least now she knew why he'd insisted on taking her out for breakfast. He knew she wouldn't cause a scene in public.

"I don't have the whole story. I'm not sure Audrey does. But the gist is that Nikki's father owed some bookie and this bookie is tied to Marco Wolf, who has his hand in some dark dealings. To give you an idea about him, he's one of those men I refuse to work for. They tasked her father with getting the Devereaux, so she stole it from the museum after she'd stolen it for us."

"Damn it," Mia whispered. "If she got away with it, why tell us?"

"She wants to steal it back and return it to the Carlisle."

Mia set down her coffee. "If she wants to return it, why take it? Why not offer them something else?"

Jared raised his hands. "I'm sure we'll get more of the story when we get to the apartment. I just wanted to prep you."

"You mean ambush me."

"No. You'd feel ambushed if we dumped this on you

at the apartment when you thought we were meeting about the next job."

"Are we supposed to put everything on hold so she can take the thing again? We're running out of time."

"If we don't give her time, the Carlisle will probably figure out they have a forgery. Aren't they expecting appraisers this week?"

Mia nodded and took a sip of her lukewarm coffee, her brain racing. Nikki could obviously plan multiple jobs simultaneously; she'd been doing it the whole time for the Turner job.

She tossed her napkin on the table. "Let's go."

"I want to finish my coffee first." Her cousin slowly raised his cup to his lips. As he drank, he tapped his phone to light the time.

"Seriously? What are you waiting for?"

"I'm enjoying my morning coffee." He sipped again. "And I know that if you have a few more minutes to digest the information, you'll approach the situation with logic instead of anger."

"You think you know me so well," she sneered. Of course, he was right. Which only irritated her more. She waved the waitress over to get a refill. "If I'm stuck here, I'm certainly not drinking cold coffee."

They sat in silence for a few moments, each caught in thought.

"I don't want to suspend current operations because of this."

"I know. But if we—all of us—don't help her, her attention will be split and she'll be less effective. If we remove this obstacle, everything else will go on as it should."

Mia tapped the sides of her coffee cup. "Do we know anything about this Wolf person and where he might store the painting?"

"Audrey and I set up some searches last night. If he tries to sell it online, we'll be notified."

"Then our best bet is probably divide and conquer. You and Audrey work on that piece, while Nikki and I work on the new project. She works best when she's kept busy. Hopefully, you can find where Wolf is keeping it, and we can just notify the authorities. The Carlisle has proven provenance, so no matter who is holding the painting, it belongs to the museum."

"It's a plan, but we need to convince Nikki that she doesn't need to steal it back."

"Leave that to me. I understand where she's coming from." Like she'd told their thief, she knew daddy issues, but she knew the need for revenge better. She just had to convince Nikki to be smart about it.

TWENTY-NINE

NIKKI WENT FOR a run first thing in the morning. She needed to clear her head. She hadn't misheard what Donny said. Wade knew about the deal with Dodger, and he never told her. But her heart kept scrambling for an explanation. She racked her brain to find one and came up empty.

He'd called at least twenty times last night. She couldn't bear to hear his lying voice.

Sweat dripped down her back and her hair stuck to her head. Even her ponytail was limply swaying. A seven a.m. run should've been cool, but Chicago weather. The humidity was making it hard to suck in air, so she turned back to the apartment, not feeling any better. A block away, her phone buzzed with a text from Audrey.

I think Wade was just here looking for you.

Where?

The apartment. Some guy rang the bell and asked for you.

Her heart pounded. She slowed her walk and raised her arms over her head. Half a block away she saw him.

The beat in her chest and the air in her lungs moved in slow motion. Part of her wanted to rush at him and beat him senseless. Another part of her wanted to run the other way, so he wouldn't witness her weakness.

As if he felt her eyes on him, he turned and caught her. Less than two buildings separated them now. He raised his hands. "Don't run."

He knew her too well.

"Get away from me."

"I need to talk to you."

"To spin more lies? Thanks, but I've had my fill."

"I haven't lied to you."

She searched his face, but he was too good and it had been too many years. She could no longer spot a lie in his eyes.

"I talked to Donny yesterday."

"Shit."

"Yeah, that was my thought, too. My father and the man I love were going to screw me over. Again. Too bad I saw it coming this time, huh?"

He stepped closer and reached for her, but she stopped him with a look.

"I wasn't going to screw you over. I would never let Wolf anywhere near you."

"Oh, I'm sure. You make an excellent middleman. You probably told him all about how you could get me to do whatever you want. Fool me twice, Wade." She shook her head. "I can't believe I let you suck me in again."

"Listen to me, Nikki. I would never betray you again. I'm willing to do anything to keep you in my life, and I've got a plan in motion to take care of Donny and Wolf."

"That's almost believable seeing as how you refused to tell me about the handoff so I needed to seek Donny out myself."

"I'm trying to keep you safe."

"I can take care of myself."

"You can trust me."

A laugh burst from her empty chest. "Look at where we are. You know I have other people I'm working with and I didn't want you here. Yet you're blowing any cover I might've had. Real trustworthy."

Surprise and regret flashed in his eyes. She read that without a problem. Had she been wrong? No. Donny had no reason to lie.

He rubbed a hand over his head. "I'm sorry. I just—"

"Don't. I have people I can trust. I don't need your pitiful attempts."

"Just give me the day. I'll prove it to you."

"Then why not tell me? If all these supposed plans are in motion?"

"I can't."

"Screw you. Don't ever come looking for me again." She pushed past him and walked toward the apartment building where Audrey waited for her.

"Plausible deniability. You can't know."

She flipped him the bird without even turning around. Upstairs, she let herself into the apartment. Audrey looked at her expectantly. "Not now. I need a shower."

She left Audrey in the kitchen and peeled off clothes as she moved toward the bathroom. Could things get any worse? She let the hot spray of the shower ease her muscles and if the water also camouflaged some tears, so be it. She'd survived before. She'd be just fine again.

She managed to dry off, get dressed, and pour herself a coffee before Audrey pounced.

"It was him, wasn't it?"

"Yes. He won't be back."

"Are you okay?"

"I'm fine." She took a drink of coffee and allowed the strong brew to hit her system. Audrey must've been really worried about her because she made the coffee the way Nikki liked it. Friendship, man. It had been a while. "When are Jared and Mia going to be here?"

"Soon. He took her to breakfast to tell her."

"Great. This should be fun."

A few minutes later, the front door opened and Jared and Mia strode in. Nikki studied their faces but they didn't appear to be any more irritated than usual. That was almost more worrisome than if they'd come in screaming.

For a full minute, they all just stood around their planning table, staring at each other.

"Well?" Mia finally asked. "Give us the full story."

"I don't know where to start."

"The beginning is usually best."

Nikki heaved a sigh and sat down, bringing her feet to rest on the edge of the chair, her knees to her chest. "As soon as I saw Wade at the party, I knew I was in trouble. I didn't tell you the whole story about us. We used to be a team, working for my father. We were in love." *Past tense, sure.*

Her voice cracked on the last sentence. *Damn him.* She swallowed a gulp of coffee and continued. She ran down everything that had happened, including details about Dodger, Donny, and Wolf. "And when I went to see Donny yesterday, I found out that Wade sold me out."

Jared sat across from her and Mia leaned against the back of the couch, her arms crossed. "Is that all?" Mia asked.

Nikki shook her head. "One more thing. While I was out for a run this morning, Wade rang the bell." Mia's jaw set tight. "Audrey answered the intercom and told him he had the wrong apartment. But I caught up with him outside."

"Does he know anything about what we've been doing?" Jared asked.

"No. He knows I've been working with someone, but he doesn't know who." She paused. "Correction. He knows that London made the forgery of the Devereaux because she gave us the one for the museum."

"Is that all?" Mia asked again.

"Think so." She looked over at Audrey to see if she'd forgotten anything.

Audrey sat beside her. "Nikki thinks Wade was playing her, but London and I have doubts. I think we can use him to get to the painting to steal it again and return it to the Carlisle."

Mia shook her head. "I can't believe you stole from a museum. It should be more difficult to do than you make it appear."

Was that a little awe coming from Mia?

"I wouldn't say it was easy. And it wasn't like I took it off the wall. It was still in storage."

"Is he going to be a problem?" Jared asked.

"No." Nikki was sure of that. He'd played his hand, but Wade wasn't malicious. "He runs a legit business. This was a one-off for him. Plus, I told him to never look for me again."

"What happens when Wolf realizes you aren't working for him?"

Nikki shrugged. "No idea. But no one knows about you guys. Wade said he had something in the works to take care of Wolf, but he wouldn't say what. And worst case, I can disappear."

"No!" Audrey yelled. Then she took a breath. "I mean, there's no reason for you to go on the run because some loser thinks he owns you. You're not alone."

Nikki offered her a smile that she didn't really feel.

"She's right," Mia said. "We're in this together."

If Nikki hadn't been sitting, that statement would've knocked her over. That unsettled feeling returned in her gut. This was what it was like to have family.

"I'm going to do whatever I have to in order to make sure I don't have to run."

"Jared and I discussed a plan over breakfast," Mia said. "He and Audrey will work on finding where this Wolf character might be holding the painting. You and I will begin planning the next heist."

"I can handle Wolf."

"We'll handle it together." Mia spoke as if all discussion was over.

It should've irritated Nikki, but when the sentiment behind Mia's command was born out of unity, how could it bother her?

"Once we know where Wolf has the Devereaux, an anonymous tip to the police will take care of him. The painting will be returned to the Carlisle and Wolf will go to jail—at least for a while," Jared explained.

"Hmm." Nikki bit her lip. "I was really hoping to steal it again. To steal the same painting three times from three separate locations in the same month? That's history making."

"Become legendary some other way," Mia said. "Let's get to work."

"You're the boss. Who's next?"

Mia looked at Jared and Audrey. "Ready?"

"Our next mark is Jerome Bauer and he has a Hardison painting, which is the most valuable one we've stolen," Audrey said, a little giddy.

They all moved to the couch as Audrey went to her computer and brought images up on the TV. For at least a while, Nikki could forget about Wolf, Dodger, and the Carlisle.

Wade, however, was never far from her mind. London and Audrey didn't think he'd conned her. But Audrey had never met him and London would be easily duped.

Her heart wanted to have faith in him, though. And that was the worst part.

WATCHING NIKKI WALK away again killed him. Everything he was doing was to be able to keep her in his life, to protect her.

At least he now knew why she was pissed. Unfortunately, her little visit to Donny put a wrinkle in his plan. He sped back to the office to talk with Boone and Devon. Inside, he found Boone rubbing Flynn's back under his desk.

"You still look like crap. Didn't you find her?"

"I found her. I also know why she's pissed. She went to see Donny and she knows the deal that Dodger swung with him and Wolf. She thinks I was playing her." He sank heavily to the couch and Flynn wiggled out from under Boone's foot to climb up beside him.

"You kind of are playing her."

"No, I'm not."

"You led her to believe this was a onetime thing and you've known that Dodger was hoping to bring her back. Does Dodger know?"

Wade shook his head. "He didn't. But now that Donny knows, anything is possible."

"What are you going to do?"

"Hell if I know. That's why I came back here."

"Yo, Dev, come here," Boone yelled.

Devon came in and looked at them. "Things go sideways?"

"I have the painting and I talked to Agent Stokes last night," Wade said.

"So what's the problem?"

Wade explained what happened with Nikki. "I'm open to suggestions about how to move forward. I need to keep her out of this—both with Wolf and Dodger."

Devon sat beside him and Flynn inched over to get a belly rub. Devon obliged while he spoke. "Read Dodger in. You keep saying he's not the dirtbag everyone thinks. Have him demand Wolf be at the swap. The feds will be creaming in their pants to get a crack at Wolf."

"I worry that Dodger will screw it up, and if he's in a bind, I wouldn't put it past him to give up Nikki."

"What about giving up you?" Devon asked.

"He might. I have no clue what the man is capable of when he's desperate."

"So we prep him," Boone said. "Tell him the feds are coming."

"He might tip off Donny and Wolf."

"That won't help his case with them."

"I'm talking unintentionally. I don't know that he can pull off a con anymore."

"You can't make the swap," Devon said. "You gave Eden Dodger's name like I told you to, right? By now, she would've run it and even if she acknowledges the voice on the phone didn't match the old man, she'll be looking for him today."

"Eden, huh?"

Devon rolled his eyes. "Shut up. Get Dodger in here. We'll get him ready."

Wade got as far as pulling his phone out when they heard stomping up the stairs toward them. He knew immediately it was Dodger. He was the only person who routinely sweet-talked whoever was running the front counter to let him come up to the offices. Maybe the old man wasn't totally out of con.

Dodger burst into the office and didn't acknowledge anyone. "You found Nikki and didn't tell me?"

Wade lifted a shoulder. "She found you. That she decided not to contact you is pretty telling."

"She's my daughter."

"Like that matters to you. All you've ever cared about is what she could do for you, what she could get you."

Dodger's eyes narrowed. "She's the one who stole the Devereaux, not you, isn't she?"

"No. I took the painting. Nikki isn't part of this."

"Bullshit. Donny said she came to see him and let him know he'd have the painting. Donny also pointed out that Wolf is expecting her to work for him. Where do I find her?"

"Go to hell, Dodger. She's out. Which is exactly what she told Donny. You thought you were so slick, playing every angle, and not honest about a thing." He got in Dodger's face. "You don't care about anyone other than yourself. We saved you, like always, but this was the last time. Nikki's gone because of your games. Again."

"Don't tell me what matters to me. I gave both of you what you needed to excel at life. You think you'd have any of this—" he swung his arms wide "—without me?"

Wade laughed. The man was delusional. "Everything we have, we earned in spite of you."

Dodger's face went red and he started sputtering. Devon rose and pulled Wade away.

"Look, Dodger. We have an offer for you that will take care of Donny and Wolf. But you need to do your part."

Dodger gave him the squinty eyes again. "Why should I listen to you?"

"Because at the rate you're going, you're going to lose the little support you still have. You want to prove that Nikki and Wade mean something to you? That you don't always put yourself first? This is how you do it."

"Do what?"

Wade released a deep breath. This was why he loved these guys. They had his back no matter what. "Take a seat and we'll fill you in."

When Dodger sat, they outlined the plan to take Wolf

down. To his credit, Dodger actually listened without jumping in or making faces to tell them it was a dumb plan. "Why would Wolf actually show up for this meeting?"

"You need to convince him. Or get Donny to convince him," Wade said. "Wolf is what makes the deal. You tell Donny that even though Nikki refused, you have the next best thing."

"Yeah? What's that?"

"Me." It was only a partial lie because if it came down to it, he would do whatever he could to keep Nikki out of this mess. She'd moved on and seemed to have people who cared about her. He wouldn't let Dodger bring her down.

"You ain't much of a selling point," Dodger said.

"But our business is," Devon told him. "We have access to many rich, connected people. People who trust us with all kinds of information and access."

Wade shot Devon a look, but his friend showed no doubts. He really hoped Agent Stokes didn't blow this, because right now everyone he cared about was putting their lives on the line for him.

THIRTY

NIKKI WAS RESTLESS after a long afternoon of planning. Audrey and Jared went home together. Audrey had offered to stay with her, probably because they thought she would go in search of Wade and Dodger and the painting, but she promised she wouldn't. They asked her to trust them, and although her trust was in short supply, she agreed.

It didn't help the restlessness, though, so she texted London to see if she wanted to hit a club. London declined because she had art to create, but she invited Nikki to come over. Nikki stopped to grab a couple bottles of wine to restock London's kitchen and headed out.

When London answered the door, she was covered with paint splatters. Nikki laughed. "Interesting look, even for you."

"Not funny. Mia is going to kill me. I told her I would have this painting done, but I can't get it right." She grabbed one of the bottles from Nikki. "Thanks for coming prepared. I'm gonna need this."

Once they were in her loft, locked behind a huge metal door, London asked, "How did it go with Mia and Jared?"

"Better than I expected. Mia has Jared trying to figure out where Wolf will keep the Devereaux, and instead of stealing it back, they're going to report it to the cops."

"Are you good with that?" She handed Nikki a coffee mug filled with wine.

Nikki accepted and took a sip. "I guess. It gives me the desired outcome. The Carlisle will get the painting back and Wolf will probably go to jail."

"But?"

Nikki hefted a sigh. "I'm pissed off. I can't stand cops, but I hate being played more."

"And you still think Wade played you?"

"I know he did."

"Have you talked to him?" She was almost snooty in the way she asked, as if she was sure Nikki was too stubborn to have a conversation.

She wasn't totally wrong.

"Yes. He tracked me down at the apartment this morning. Said he kept me out of the loop to keep me safe."

London smiled into her mug. "He loves you."

"He lied to me."

London rolled her eyes. "If he had come to you and told you all of this, what would you have done?"

"I would've told him and Dodger to go screw themselves." At least that was what she told herself. She'd never been able to leave Dodger in a bind. That was why she had to leave.

You can trust me. Just give me the day. I'll prove it to you.

His words echoed in her head. She wanted to believe him. "I really don't want to think about him anymore. Tell me about the painting you're stuck on."

"Hardison was a tricky one," London said. "He re-used canvases to give each painting greater depth. I think he was a cheap bastard who wanted to make it impossible to forge."

"What do you mean?" Nikki followed London over to a collection of canvases.

"He used a canvas to practice various types and styles of art. Then he'd paint over them with white and create something new."

"I thought a lot of masterpieces were done like that."

"Well, yeah, some, but it wasn't intentional. They were poor, starving artists, hoping and waiting to make it big. This dude keeps doing it. I think he has a collection of canvases he painted when he was three just sitting in Mom's garage waiting for him."

Nikki plopped down on the floor and crossed her legs. "Does it matter what's behind the painting you're doing for us?"

"Maybe. If someone runs it through an X-ray as part of the appraisal, they'll know it doesn't match his."

Nikki smiled. "That's perfect. Mia doesn't care if they find out once they try to sell it. It only has to pass muster while hanging in their house." She crawled closer to the canvas. "I say we have some fun. Let's leave a message under the painting for them."

London giggled. "Like a microscopic *screw you*. I like it."

They polished off a bottle of wine while London sketched some ideas to hide a message under another modern painting that used some kind of hybrid pointillism and paint splatter. Nikki didn't care about any of it, but it was a welcome reprieve from the problems in her life.

Her phone buzzed with a call from Audrey. She pushed it to voicemail. She didn't need a babysitter. Then London's phone pinged. Then hers did again with a text. Turn on the news! NOW!

Nikki glanced around the loft. "You got a TV?"

London stood, pressed a button on a remote and a TV rose up from inside a cabinet that Nikki had assumed housed more art supplies. "I keep it hidden. Serious artists don't dirty their brains with mindless pop culture," she said in a pretentious tone. She turned the TV on, and added, "I have no idea what channel Audrey is talking about. Local news?"

"I guess?"

While London scrolled through channels, Nikki went online to find a story. She texted Audrey. What am I looking for?

A moment later, she had a link. She clicked and a newsreel started. The reporter faced the camera, but behind her, Dodger, Donny, and some other guy were being led by FBI agents to a car in handcuffs. Her heart thudded a few beats and then she was sure it stopped. She scanned the footage for any sign of Wade. She rewound the video and then fast forwarded. London stood beside her, looking over her shoulder.

"What's going on?"

Nikki paused the video. The headline scrolling on the bottom of the screen read Forgery Ring Busted— Famed Devereaux Painting Returned to Carlisle Museum. "That's my dad and his bookie Donny. I'm guessing the other guy is Wolf."

"How did this happen?"

"It must've been Wade. That's why he wouldn't tell me anything."

"Whoa. Does that change things?"

Did it? Nikki pocketed her phone. "I don't know. I have to go think. I'll catch you later. Good luck with the Hardison."

She left the loft and walked. Then she hopped a bus and went to the lake. The rocks at Juneway Beach had been her getaway for as long as she could remember. The first time she'd come here she had been eight. Dodger had yelled at her for not being a better actress to con people, so she'd run away. She pickpocketed cash from a couple and hopped the bus. She took it as far as she could, not understanding that she was still in the city. She'd sat on the rocks and considered her options until a young mother offered to help her.

When she'd gotten home that night, she refused to tell Dodger where she'd gone. From that moment on, she'd learned to keep some things for herself.

The park area was desolate because it was late. Technically the park was open until eleven, but no one was around. She glanced at the concrete steps that led close to the water, but she preferred the rough rock piles.

It was dark, and the lake looked black, except where the moon reflected against some waves. She walked along the line of rocks, looking for the best one to sit on.

From behind a tree, a voice said, "I hoped you would come here."

Wade. She spun and rushed to him as he stepped out of the tree's shadow. Relief surged through her entire body, followed quickly by anger. She punched his shoulder. "You asshole."

"I love you, too, Nikki."

SHE LAUNCHED HERSELF at him and wrapped her arms around his neck. "You stupid man."

His arms came around her and held her close. "I'm fine, babe. I told you I had a plan."

"You should've told me."

Nikki's death grip on him didn't loosen, even as he tried to assure her everything was fine. After the arrest, he'd taken a chance that she might come here to think. It had always been her escape.

"How did you know I'd come here?" Her voice was muffled by his shoulder.

"I know you. Although things change, when life gets bad, we return to comfort. Whenever Dodger pissed you off, you came here. After you left, I came here every day to wait for you, but you didn't show. So I didn't know you would be here tonight, but I hoped."

She finally slid her arms down and stepped out of his embrace. "I saw you. Back then."

It hurt even more to know that she'd been there but hadn't talked to him. "Why didn't you say anything?"

"I was pissed off. First because you stayed with Dodger. Then because you were here in my spot. It was like you were taking everything from me."

He reached for her hand. "I wasn't trying to take anything from you. I just wanted you." He interlaced his fingers with hers and pulled her close. "I still do."

She searched his face and he hoped she saw nothing but honesty. He was tired of games.

Tugging her arm, he said, "Let's walk." He pulled her past the old wooden fence toward the concrete steps. He walked on the step below her, so she towered over him. The breeze from the water cooled the night air and blew her long black hair around.

He loved having Nikki with him again and he knew the next words from his mouth would determine everything. "I love you. I never stopped loving you. No matter who I dated or what job I took, you were always there, a voice in my head telling me when I was making a mistake or cheering me on when I doubted myself. You were in my heart, an obstacle preventing me from ever loving someone else wholly. I don't think we were ready for this back then."

"What do you mean?"

"There is something so deep between us. Whether you believe in fate or destiny or soul mates…it doesn't matter. We collided again because we are meant to be. At twenty, neither of us knew what to do with those feelings. You ran, and I let you."

"I wasn't running from you. I needed the chance to grow and learn without Dodger's constant criticism. It was never you I wanted to leave."

He swallowed. "I know. I'm not saying this now because I want to argue about then. I just want you to know that I'm all grown up now, and I can handle this love."

She released his hand and turned away from him to face the water. "I wasn't expecting that."

"What were you expecting?"

"I came here to think. About you. About us. You asked me to trust you this morning and I couldn't. Not after you lied to me again. Then you came through. You said you had a plan to take care of Wolf and you proved it. But you didn't trust me enough to tell me anything about Wolf, my dad, your plans. That isn't any more mature than before."

How was he losing this? He'd tried to do all the right things. "You're right. I should've trusted you. I didn't because you scare me. You're impulsive and you can be reckless. And I knew you wouldn't like me getting the FBI involved. I felt guilty about not telling you, but when I asked you to stay out of the deal with Donny, you went straight to him."

"Because you were acting shady."

"I was afraid for you. I didn't want you anywhere near the drop and the FBI. And I wanted to be sure it worked before telling you."

She turned back, her arms crossed, brows furrowed. "Now you think I'm stupid? That if you told me what was going down, I'd show up anyway? Thanks for the vote of confidence."

He sighed. "You know I don't think you're stupid. Even if you didn't crash the party, I worried that the FBI would screw up. Then you would think I let you down again."

"What if they did botch it? What was your backup plan for Wolf? To give him me?"

"No. Me."

"What?"

"That's how Dodger got Wolf to show to the meeting. He explained that between my grifting skills and the access to people my security company gives me, I could be as valuable as you."

Her arms dropped. "You were going to give your-self to Wolf. Ruin your whole life to go back to being a criminal even though you got out? Why?"

"For you. You might still be a thief, but you got away from Dodger, just like you wanted. Agreeing to be his thief would've been temporary. I have a team behind me. We would've gotten Wolf."

She smiled and bumped her shoulder into his. "I have a team, too. We were already working to figure out where Wolf would keep the painting so we could turn him in."

"Great minds, huh?"

"Things would've been easier if you trusted me." She looked back out over the water. "When I saw the news tonight, I panicked. I saw Dodger in cuffs and I thought for sure you were there."

"I'm sorry I worried you. I would've called, but you were pretty adamant this morning."

"Wait a minute. Did Dodger know your plan?"

"More or less."

"He walked into a trap? Willingly?"

"When I made the call to the FBI friend of Devon's, I used Dodger's name. He went in knowing he'd get a deal."

"A deal, but not walk free?"

"I might've led him to believe that he'd be free once the feds got them all in custody. But some jail time might do him some good. He chose to go. It was his way of proving we matter to him." Wade shrugged. "He loves us in his own way." He reached over and touched the strand of her hair that had whipped across her cheek. She didn't pull away. "He's missed you."

"I don't know what to say to that."

"You don't have to say anything about Dodger. I was just giving you the information."

"Where do we go from here?" she asked.

"I thought I made my case pretty clear."

"Things were working because you came back over to the dark side for a little while. But like you said, we're not the same people anymore." A corner of her mouth kicked up. "We've both learned to trust other people. We have teams. People who have our backs."

"We can still be that for each other."

She wrinkled her nose. "Can we? I'm not so sure. Your team works to stop mine from doing what we do. We're not on the same side anymore."

"We can be. You can join my team whenever you want."

"That's sweet of you. I'm sure your partners were thrilled with that idea. But I don't know that I'm ready to give up my life."

"Please don't walk away again. We can figure something out."

"Well, I came here to think and you've given me plenty to consider." She reached up and stroked his cheek. "Thanks for looking out for me."

"Always."

She kissed his cheek and stepped away.

"Can I call you tomorrow?"

"I'm busy with another job, so I might not answer." She turned and walked toward the street.

"That wasn't a no!" he yelled after her. If that's all he had to hold onto, he would. She needed to think.

He'd already accepted that their relationship was life-changing. He could wait for her to arrive at the same conclusion: they belonged together.

THIRTY-ONE

NIKKI WANTED TO throw herself into planning the next couple of jobs, so she worked through the night. Audrey and London both tried to talk to her, but she had nothing to say yet. She was still trying to sort out her feelings about Wade. She loved him. Probably had never stopped loving him. But they had moved on from each other. How could this possibly work?

Wade had called, and she didn't answer, but then he texted her information about where Dodger was being held. His lawyer had a meeting with him, and Nikki could tag along as an assistant or junior partner. She didn't know how he'd swung it, and she wasn't completely sure it was a good idea, but she needed to see Dodger.

Outside the federal building, she put on the glasses Wade had given her. Hopefully, they would work on the cameras here as well as they had for the museum. She straightened her blazer and looked for the lawyer. When she saw a man in a suit looking around, she called, "Mr. Collins?"

"Yes." He stepped toward her. "I am doing this as a favor to Wade and your father. Say nothing until we are in the interview room. Understood?"

She nodded and followed him into the building. He spoke to the people at the desk for directions and they went up in the elevator in silence. Upstairs, Collins spoke to other people who did not appear thrilled with his presence.

The agents left them waiting for a few minutes. Then a tall, thin woman wearing a crisp white blouse and black pants came up to them. "Mr. Collins, I'm Agent Eden Stokes." She extended her hand. "Your client has been brought up. I'll show you to the room. He was very helpful in giving us information and that will go a long way in making a deal."

Nikki's ears perked up, but she kept her eyes on the carpet in front of her as she followed Agent Stokes. She couldn't afford for this woman to take an interest in her or her identity.

Agent Stokes paused in front of a door and opened it. "Take your time."

Collins strode in and said, "Hey, Dodger. Looks like you really stepped in it this time."

Dodger was on a nickname basis with his lawyer? She could barely believe Dodger even had a lawyer.

"I had a good run, Pete. And this was all part of the plan." Then his eyes met hers and his jaw dropped. "You're here," he whispered.

Gone was the jovial tone. His eyes filled and he rubbed at them quickly. "When I asked Wade to send you, he didn't think you'd show."

Collins nodded at Nikki, took out his phone and stood in the corner of the room doing his own thing.

She sat down across from Dodger at the table. "I didn't know you'd asked for me. He just sent me the information."

"I'm glad you came."

"I can't believe you willingly participated in this."

"I figured it was about time I listened to Wade. He has a better head on his shoulders than I gave him credit for."

"That's debatable. He stayed with you instead of leaving with me."

Dodger shook his head. "I never meant to separate you. You were restless and you were going to leave me. I knew he would follow."

"You were obviously wrong because he didn't."

"I saw the way he looked at you. He would go anywhere you wanted. I know that because I looked at your mother the same way."

Her heart thudded. Dodger never talked about her mom. Nikki had no memories of her because she'd taken off when Nikki was two. But she'd seen pictures of them together. She knew the look he was talking about.

"I figured if I got him to stay, you would, too. I didn't want to lose you. You're all I had." He smiled. "I didn't account for you being more stubborn than me."

"As it turns out, I am more stubborn and I've done what I've wanted all these years. You told me that if I left, I could never come back. Who says stuff like that to—"

Collins coughed to remind her not to reveal their relationship.

"I was angry. It didn't last. I kept my ear to the ground and I knew you were okay. You made me proud with some of the things you accomplished." He reached across the table, but she pulled her hands back.

He sighed and lowered his voice. "And the Devereaux. That'll be hard to beat."

"Why did you want me to come here?"

"I wanted to apologize. Make amends. I'm not in for some whole twelve-step program, but I am making changes. No more gambling. And I'd like you to come around."

"Did Wade put you up to this?" Dodger would never choose a life of legitimate business. He would probably keel over if he found out about what she'd been doing with Jared and Mia.

"Hell no. I do what I want."

"So do I."

Dodger howled a laugh. "That's my girl."

Nikki rose. "See you around."

"Will I?"

"Maybe," she said with a smile. It had been too long. While she would never work with Dodger again, she might not mind having him in her life.

Now she just needed to figure out how Wade fit in. Could she go legit?

Nikki went back to the apartment. So much had changed in a week's time. The more she considered Wade's offer, the more confused she became. She'd never thought about being anything other than a thief. It was what Dodger had raised her for. But Wade had a point— no one could do this forever. *She* had plenty of good years left in her, but did she want to be like her father in thirty years?

Wade was offering her an out. One where she could

continue to do what she loved without the possible repercussions. Would it be enough?

When she arrived at the apartment, everyone was there. It shouldn't have surprised her since they had started planning a job last night and Mia wanted them to get moving on others. What she hadn't expected was for everyone to turn and stare at her.

"What?" she asked.

Audrey wheeled her chair around to the front of the desk. Without getting up, she said, "What do you mean, what? What happened? We saw the arrest last night, but we didn't see Wade."

"He set it up with the help of his team. My father was arrested but will get a deal because Wade used his name to set it up."

"So we're in the clear then?" Mia asked.

"Uh, yeah."

London leaned her elbows on the table. "And what about Wade? Have you talked to him?"

"Yes."

They waited a few seconds and when she didn't elaborate, Audrey said, "Come on. Tell us what happened."

"He still wants to make a go of us. He offered me a spot on their team. Doing security work." As she said the words, she looked across their faces, gauging reactions. London's smile was just shy of giddy. Mia was the polar opposite—icy.

"I suppose that means we'll need a new thief," Mia said.

"I said he offered. I didn't say I've accepted. I don't know if I want to go legit yet. And I already committed to you. I'll see this through."

"But—" Audrey started.

"But nothing. If I wouldn't go back on my word to a loser like Wolf, why would I do it here?"

Audrey leaned forward like she still had more to say, but she pressed her lips together and rolled back behind the desk.

"Let me go change and I'll be back in a minute." She went to the bedroom and changed into a pair of shorts and tank top and stopped in the kitchen for a slightly stale donut and coffee. "Where are we at with the next jobs?" she asked around a mouthful of glazed goodness.

"Unfortunately, Jerome Bauer has nothing on his social calendar within the next week or two. Something about his wife being ill."

From behind her screen, Audrey said, "Code for boob job or face-lift?"

Mia rolled her eyes. "So we're putting him on the back burner and switching focus to Keaton Bishop and Caleb Small."

Looking over Mia's head, Nikki made eye contact with London, who looked immensely relieved that she had more time to get the Hardison painting done.

"How much time do we have to plan these? Two days?" Nikki said with a side of snark.

"Actually…"

Nikki flicked up a hand. "Are you kidding me? I keep telling you I need more time and you give me less?"

Mia shot her a look. "If you would let me finish. The difference here is that both pieces from these men are being sent to the auction house soon for the same auction. We need to make the switch before they're authenticated at the house."

Mia suddenly looked shifty. The woman was holding something back.

"What aren't you telling us?"

"Nothing."

"So this is a twofer but we have to figure out how to make the switch between the pickup and delivery." As irritated as she wanted to be, part of her was thrilled with the additional challenge.

She didn't know if she'd ever be able to walk away from this.

IT TOOK EVERYTHING in Wade's power to not hunt Nikki down. She needed space to digest and process everything that had happened. He knew it. He just didn't like it. He'd wanted her to jump into his arms and come home with him once she realized he didn't betray her after all.

When Dodger reached out and asked him to bring Nikki to see him, he'd made no promises. He was done making way for Dodger. He never thought Nikki would use the information he sent and actually go see her father. But Mr. Collins said she'd gone and it was a pleasant meeting. Of course Collins didn't really know about the bad relationship they had, but Nikki wouldn't hide anything. Maybe it was time to let it all go.

It was enough to give him hope.

Wade spent the day catching up on work at the office, volunteering to go out on estimates and client meetings so he could keep his mind off Nikki. It was dark by the time he got home. He unlocked his front door and immediately knew something was off.

He eased the door open and Flynn waddled up to him, carrying a pink toy. Was that a turtle? He reached across to the light switch and flicked it on. Flynn dropped the toy turtle and rammed his head into Wade's legs for attention. He bent and pet his dog, keeping his ears tuned for other sounds. The house was silent, but something in the air felt different. He rounded the corner, and propped in front of his TV was a wrapped package—one that looked suspiciously like it could be a painting.

He closed and locked the door behind him and moved across the room to the package. Flynn followed, carrying his new toy. A card was taped to the corner so he peeled it off and read the note.

For a security expert, your house is really easy to break into. Happy Birthday! *N

What? It wasn't his birthday and she knew it. He ripped the paper off and stared at what looked like a Banksy painting. The painting he'd used as inspiration for a con with Nikki and Dodger. Dodger had come up with some grift that required him to become the next Banksy. Nikki had ridiculed him. He wasn't an artist.

He grabbed his phone and called, because she'd opened the line of communication with this stunt.

"Hello."

"Why am I looking at a painting that appears to be a Banksy?"

"I got it years ago, when I thought you'd come after me. I saw it in a newspaper and thought of you. It reminded me of your awful attempt at street art. I wanted you to have something professional to look at so the next time you considered putting your artistic talent to the test, you wouldn't."

Guilt still pinged in his chest because he hadn't gone after her. "You saved it all these years?"

"We both know how hard it is to offload a famous painting."

"So why are you giving it to me now?" He took the fact that she'd come to his house as a sign of hope.

"It's something to remind you of me."

That was not the message he wanted to take from this exchange. He sat up straighter. "Why would I need a painting?"

"Because I won't be around for a while."

Strong emotions warred in him. Fear that she was taking off, but more hope because she implied she'd be back. "Where are you going?"

He was met with silence for so long that he thought she wouldn't answer. "Nikki?"

"Open your door."

He jumped up and raced to open the door. She stood on his porch, dressed in black, hair up in a messy ponytail.

"Hey," she said, as if he'd been expecting her to be there.

"Why didn't you just stay inside?"

"Because I wasn't going to stay at all."

He grabbed her hand and pulled her into the house. "What's going on?" he asked as he closed the door behind them.

She looked over his shoulder to where Flynn was back to gnawing on the plastic turtle she'd given him. "I planned to just leave the painting and wait to see if you'd call."

"Of course I was going to call. How could you think I wouldn't? I told you where I stand with us."

She tilted her head. "I also thought you were coming with me before. Things change. But after I left, I figured I was taking the coward's way out. You deserve answers in person."

They sat on the couch with him still holding her hand. "Tell me," he prompted.

"I'm considering how much I can tell you without betraying other people." She blew out a deep breath. "I want to give us a try. I want to be with you. These last few weeks, with the exception of Donny and Wolf, have been the best I've had in years. I don't think I even realized how much I missed us."

He reined in the surge of joy. "But?"

"I have some jobs that I've already committed to. I can't walk away from them."

"I make enough money. Plus, we can offer you a legit job."

"It's not about the money. While these jobs do pay really well, it's not about the payday. There's more at play that I can't talk about because I'm not in this alone."

"But it's still dangerous." He wasn't asking. Nikki had no fears. She would do whatever she thought she could get away with.

"No more than any other job I do."

"The last job you did before the museum had deadly booby traps. Or have you forgotten that?" His worry had shifted to anger because he'd just gotten her back and she would take risks that could take her away from him.

She stabbed a finger at him. "*That* is why I was going to leave the painting and be on my way. I'm a big girl. I decide what jobs I do. And if you recall, I didn't go into that job blind. I took the precautions that were in my control."

She rose and he took her hand again. "Stop. Don't leave. I worry about you. I always have. That will never change. But I do trust you to do what you do." Standing beside her, he cradled her jaw. "Stay with me."

"Tonight?"

"For good."

"I can't."

"Where are you living? At the apartment I tracked you to?"

"Sort of."

"That isn't an answer. I thought you wanted honesty between us." He stroked her jaw. He wanted this so much. He'd take her any way he could get her.

"Let me talk to my team. I can't expose them any more than you wanted to expose yours."

He pulled her close, his lips a breath away from hers. "Tell me what you're into."

"I can't," she whispered. Then she surged forward, kissing him with her entire being.

This was his Nikki. Secretive. Loving. High energy. All in.

"When will you come back to me?" he asked against her lips.

"I'll call you tomorrow."

"Stay the night."

"Promise to make it worth my time?"

He felt her mouth kick up in the corner as he kissed her again. "It'll be so worth it, you might not want to leave."

"We'll see."

THIRTY-TWO

AFTER A FULL day of talking with Jared, Mia, and Audrey, Nikki convinced them that since Wade was going to continue to be in her life, it was in their best interest to let him in on their heists. Not that he would actively participate, but he had access and knowledge that could make things easier for them. They talked and argued and almost yelled. It was like having a big family meeting, which was a novel concept for her.

Ultimately, they agreed with her. She could be very persuasive when she wanted to be. They didn't want to lose her as their thief, because come on, who were they gonna get who was better? She didn't want to leave either. But she needed to consider her future, which was something else that was a new thing.

Wade was her past, but he was also the future. She wanted to trust him with all parts of her life, and since this team had become important to her, she wanted them to know him. Especially since their first exposure to Wade was him being their competition. For the first time in forever, she was nervous. She paced the living room while Audrey continued to do her hacking thing, looking for ways past systems for upcoming jobs.

Mia and Jared had left, but they would return later. Nikki wanted to have him come to the apartment and explain what she was doing and if all went well, she would introduce him to Mia and Jared. She had no doubts about Wade's ability to keep a secret, but Mia and Jared weren't as sure, which made no sense. Wade could've ruined their plan to get the Devereaux at any time but he hadn't.

The bell rang and Nikki buzzed him up.

"You didn't ask who it was," Audrey noted without looking up from her screen.

"Who else would it be? You're here and everyone else has a key." She opened the door and waited in the hall for him to get off the elevator. At the ding, her heart jumped. She didn't even know why her body was reacting this way.

He stepped off the elevator, looked at her and smiled. "Hi. I get to see your hideaway?"

"Not really mine. I told you. I'm here till the jobs are done."

He came close, kissed her cheek and whispered, "Will you take me to your place? I want to see where you live."

She snorted. If he only knew that the closest thing she had to *her place* was the storage unit where she kept her stuff. "Sure. But you won't be impressed."

"We'll see. So why am I here if this isn't your apartment?"

She took his hand and led him inside. "That is Audrey. She's my hacker. You've already met London, the forger. What you don't know is that we are part of a team who is stealing art from rich losers to pay back people who got screwed over."

Wade glanced around the room, taking it all in, and

Nikki paused, holding her breath, knowing he might look at her differently.

"And because you're helping people, you don't want to walk away from these jobs." He nodded without waiting for her confirmation. "Okay."

"I'm still a thief." She wasn't sure if she was saying it for his benefit or hers.

"Oh, I know. I doubt that'll ever change."

Audrey pushed away from her computer and crossed the room. She extended a hand. "Nice to finally meet you. I've heard a lot about you."

Wade took her hand. "Knowing Nikki, it was probably all true." He winked at Audrey and gave her that special con man smile, the one that charmed strangers into giving him whatever he wanted.

Nikki smacked his arm. "Turn off the charm. She's taken."

He turned that smile on her. "So am I."

Damn, he was good.

"Do you live here, too, Audrey?"

"I crash on occasion, but Nikki only lives here so she'll stay out of trouble."

Nikki laughed. "Kind of like my own personal halfway house."

"Why am I here?" he asked. "You could've told me that in bed this morning."

"First, I needed to talk to the team. The second reason is because while the masterminds behind this plan are very secretive—for good reason—part of how I convinced them to let me tell you was to point out that you could be useful."

At that comment, his eyebrows rose.

"Not that we're recruiting you."

"Just using me?"

Nikki snorted. "You'd love for me to use you. But when you meet the rest of the team and see who our targets are, it'll make sense. You're not only gonna like this. You'll be impressed."

"I'm not easily impressed. You're bringing me into a den of thieves. Been there, done that." He looked over his shoulder to where Audrey was back at her computer. "No offense."

"None taken. We own who we are." Audrey picked up her phone, presumably to text Jared and Mia to make sure they were on their way.

"Coffee?" Nikki offered.

"Sure."

He followed her to the kitchen. "All joking aside, I'm glad you invited me here today. I was afraid you wouldn't let me into your life fully."

"Were you thinking you'd just be my late-night booty call?" She poured two cups of coffee and handed him one.

"Not that I could blame you. I do offer high—quality booty."

She leaned over and kissed him. This had been the right move. Letting people close was feeling a little trippy after years of superficial contact.

The front door opened and she said, "Get ready to be impressed."

WADE HAD NO idea how Nikki thought meeting a couple con men or thieves was supposed to impress him, but he'd play along to keep her happy. He followed her back to the living room with their coffee. A man and a woman both entered the room and made eye contact with him. Something about them looked familiar, but he couldn't quite place them.

Nikki climbed over the back of the couch and sank into the cushions. "Wade, meet Mia Benson and Jared Towers."

"Benson and Towers?" As he said the names aloud, the recognition clicked into place. He slid a glance to Nikki. "I thought you said you were doing good here."

"We are," Mia responded. "Mr....?"

"Palmer."

"Our mission here is to right as many of our fathers' wrongs as we can and hopefully help bring them to justice."

He paused and blinked while that processed. "Okay. Nikki was right. I am duly impressed. How is stealing going to bring justice?"

"Have a seat and we'll walk you through it." Mia strode over to the TV and Jared went over to Audrey at the computer.

"As you know, our fathers scammed people out of money. They were not the only ones to profit. They have friends who made money off that venture. What's worse, we know that they purchased artwork as a safety net for our fathers. We're stealing it, selling it, and paying restitution to their victims."

Wade smiled. "And also taking away their safety net." It was rather brilliant.

The TV lit up behind her and they scrolled through names and photos of twelve men, many of whom Wade was familiar with. Then a big red X landed on some pictures.

"I like the new addition," Nikki called across the room to Audrey. Then she elbowed Wade. "Those are the guys we already stole from."

"You've been busy."

"Better than bored."

Jared came forward. "Nikki has told us you might have some connections that could be of use. We also understand that doing so puts you and your business at risk, so if you want no part, no problem. She has assured us of your discretion."

He didn't have to think about it or look at pros and cons. This was where Nikki was, so he was onboard. "I'm not totally sure how I can help, but I'm in."

"Shouldn't you check with your partners?" Mia asked.

"They'll be fine with this. And if they're not, I'll take a leave." The faster Nikki was done with these jobs, the faster they could get on with their life together. He rose. "I assume that since you have your team, I'll work in more of a consultant capacity, and you'll let me know when you need something."

Mia and Jared nodded.

"One thing before I leave. I don't think Nikki needs to live here anymore."

"As long as she stays out of trouble," Jared said.

"Good luck with that," he said jokingly. "But I'm willing to keep an eye on her."

"Hey," Nikki yelled. "I'm right here. And I've stayed out of trouble for weeks. Still don't need a baby-sitter."

"That's debatable," Wade said. "If we're done here, I think Nikki and I have plans."

Mia and Jared both turned to her. All she did was shrug in response. Out on the street, he asked, "Where to?"

"Trust me to drive?" She held out her hand without waiting for an answer.

"I trust you completely." He handed over the keys.

She took the keys and danced her way over to the driver's side.

"I want you to move in with me."

She didn't even pause. "Okay."

Just like Nikki—jump right in.

"Do you need to give your landlord notice?" Then he remembered that it was unlikely that she'd signed a lease—at least Nikki Russo never signed a lease. Nikki Smith, Nikki Taylor, Nikki Jones. Whatever name she used was never her own.

"Nope. This landlord isn't going to care." She winked and sped down the street to the expressway. Thirty minutes later, they were pulling into a storage facility. She drove around and parked.

"Please tell me that you don't live in one of these units." No way could her life be this bad. She was a successful thief. She always had money.

She unlocked the door and rolled it up. Inside was a lifetime of belongings. "No, I don't live here, but this has been my holding place. Everything I want or need is kept here." She picked up a gym bag and opened a drawer on a small dresser. She began shoving clothes into the bag.

He touched her shoulder to make her turn around.

"Where do you actually live? Sleep? Hang out and watch action movies?"

"For the last month or so, at the apartment we just left. Prior to that, whatever hotel I booked."

"You don't have a home?"

"Well, it's not like I'm homeless."

"That's exactly what not having a permanent address means."

Her eyes softened and she stroked his jaw. "Don't give me that sad look. I chose not to have a regular apartment. Moving around kept me flexible to accept whatever job or score I wanted. I've traveled a lot over the years."

She'd always talked about them running away and getting their own place, a house, something permanent that would be *theirs*. Up on the roof of their crappy apartment building they'd lived in with Dodger. After a heist, they'd met on the roof to drink cheap champagne to celebrate.

Sitting side by side in rickety lawn chairs, he'd held out his hand and she'd taken it, interlocking her fingers with his. "You sure you want to leave?"

"Don't you?"

He'd lifted a shoulder. "I know Dodger's bad, but we have a place to live and food to eat."

"Until he uses the rent money to bet on horses and loses it all." She'd sighed. "I'm tired of doing all this work to see him piss it away. We could do so much more. Together. We can plan our own jobs and not have someone tell us how stupid it is. We can buy a house. Or at least an apartment that isn't a dump. Wouldn't it be nice to have real dishes instead of paper plates?"

Looking at her now, in a storage unit surrounded by all of her belongings, he said, "But you always talked about getting a place."

"When I left, you were no longer in the picture. I didn't see much use in having a place just for me."

"What about now?"

"I guess it's a good thing I've waited. It was always supposed to be you." She wrapped an arm around his neck and kissed his cheek. "Take me home."

"I love you, and I want you to move in, but just so you know, I'm not getting rid of my dog."

"That's okay. Flynn and I have come to terms with each other. I buy him toys, and he stays away from me."

Wade pulled her flush against him, his whole body bursting with happiness to have Nikki in his life again. "And when these jobs are over?"

"We'll figure out what comes next. Together."

It was the best word that could've come from her mouth. It didn't matter what the future brought them as long as they were together.

"Even if I stay legit?" he asked.

"Everyone has their faults. Who knows? You might be able to sway me." She wrapped her arms around his neck and kissed him.

Yeah, there wasn't much in life that was better than Nikki in his arms.

THIRTY-THREE

Mia

Mia couldn't remember a time when the art world was as abuzz as it had been for the last few weeks. First the disappearance of the Devereaux and its arrival at the Carlisle, only to have it reappear during some kind of FBI raid. Nikki and Audrey expressed some concern about the attention. And they were waiting to see if Darren Turner made any headway with the police. Right now, they didn't know if the forgery—or the pen Nikki stole—had been noticed. If these men were smart, they would increase the security on their homes, especially their art.

However, none of them were as smart as she was. They all believed themselves to be invincible. Untouchable. Like her father.

She was going to make sure they found out just how wrong they were.

Some might be running scared. Like Caleb and Keaton, both selling at the same auction house at the same time. The one wrinkle in this master plan was that she hadn't considered checking who insured the art. After meeting Logan Freemont, she had decided to do just that. And the same company insured all of them. What was the likelihood?

So Logan was either in her father's pocket, or he was a legitimate agent who would see these coincidences and investigate deeper. But as long as she and her team were clear, it didn't really matter.

Sitting in her living room, she sipped on a glass of red and studied the newly printed spreadsheet that Audrey had created. The cost of these jobs had made quite the dent in her inheritance, but now they were leveling out. The spreadsheet used Mia's predicted income from each piece of art and then another column listed what they hoped to accomplish.

Of course, their fathers had stolen more than Mia planned to steal, so she might not be able to make amends to everyone, but based on the numbers in front of her, they would make a difference in the lives of many.

For the first time in years, Mia felt a weight lifted from her body. Her chest, her shoulders, everything was looser. She could breathe.

Even with all the lies and deceit she still had in her life, because she had people in her corner, she felt free. As much as she loathed to admit it, Jared had been right about building this team. Of course, none of them had predicted falling in love.

Lord knew she hadn't seen it coming. She thought at most, Jared would take Audrey to bed like he did any other woman who caught his fancy. But over the past few weeks, she'd watched their relationship develop into something more. Their emotions ran deep. And they shared a level of trust she could only imagine.

Seeing Nikki skip happily off with her con man boyfriend was in some ways more disturbing. Nikki was a lone wolf who rarely cared about others. She and the thief had that in common. Or so Mia had thought.

She refocused on the numbers in front of her and began to question the possibility of there being more art with more of her father's friends.

When her phone rang, she answered without even a glance at the screen. The only people who called her these days were Mama and Jared. Everything else was done online. "Hello?"

The line was staticky and crackling and she pulled it away from her ear to identify the caller. Number unavailable.

She was about to hang up when she heard the faint "Mia?"

"Hello?" she asked again, pulling the phone close again.

"Kitten, sweetheart, it's me."

Even with the crackling, she'd know that voice. Her blood iced and her muscles tensed. "Daddy?"

"Yes, I'm so glad you still kept this number and answered." He chuckled. "It's rather unlike you to answer an unknown number."

Regret warred with curiosity. Why was he calling her? Why now?

"I need your help, baby."

And then she knew. The thefts were working. Their friends were panicking.

"Come home and I'll do what I can."

She had to strain to hear him, but his sigh sounded, long and suffering. *The gall of this man.*

"You know I can't do that. Men like me aren't made for prison."

She rose from the couch, needing to move, to think.

She wanted to rail at him and tell him that coming back was his only recourse because she was going to take everything from him, but tipping their hand now would only give him a chance to develop a new plan. No, she allowed the curiosity to squash her rage.

"What can I possibly do?"

"You received your inheritance, right?"

"No. Mama changed the parameters. She feared I would seek you out and give you money. I won't have access for another five years."

He let loose an uncharacteristic stream of cursing. She smirked.

"Then I need access to some of your connections in the art world."

"For what? You've never cared much for art." While he'd indulged her love, he'd never paid much attention to anything but cold, hard cash.

"I know some people who need to sell some art. I'll be in touch on this number." Then the line went dead.

She didn't know if he'd hung up or if the connection had finally quit, but she didn't care. Her plan was working. Now that her father had made contact, she would have definite insight into what art was being sold to fund his lifestyle. She'd make sure they all disappeared before he saw a dime.

She and her team were going to take them down.

ABOUT THE AUTHOR

SLOANE STEELE IS the pen name for Shannyn Schroeder. Shannyn is a part-time English teacher, part-time curriculum editor, and full-time mom, even though her kids are pretty self-sufficient teens. In her downtime, she bakes cookies, reads romance, and watches far too much TV.

If you want to connect with Sloane (and Shannyn), visit her website: www.sloanesteele.com.

Sign up for her newsletter here:
www.subscribepage.com/sloanesteele
www.Twitter.com/SSchroeder_
www.Facebook.com/Shannyn.Schroeder/

Visit ReaderService.com Today!

As a valued member of the Harlequin Reader Service, you'll find these benefits and more at ReaderService.com:

- Try 2 free books from any series
- Access risk-free special offers
- View your account history & manage payments
- Browse the latest Bonus Bucks catalog

Don't miss out!

If you want to stay up-to-date on the latest at the Harlequin Reader Service and enjoy more content, make sure you've signed up for our monthly News & Notes email newsletter. Sign up online at ReaderService.com or by calling Customer Service at 1-800-873-8635.